GUIGNOL
& OTHER SARDONIC TALES

"The horror genre is a many-splintered thing. Grey collects those splinters, mixes and matches them, concocting a beast of a collection that is as fun as it is scary, as charming as it is chilling."
—Philip Gelatt, director of *They Remain*

"In his latest collection, Orrin Grey not only pays homage to the classic horror films of yesteryear, he tears down the silver screen to reveal the true horrors that lurk on the other side. Fans of H. P. Lovecraft, Vincent Price, and the Hammer horror films will feel right at home."
—Ian Rogers, author of *Every House Is Haunted*

"Orrin Grey's work specializes in old-school horror iconography—Universal monster movies, Roger Corman Poe adaptations, found footage epistolary narratives—run through a pop-culture blender set on frappé, and *Painted Monsters* (whose title derives from a quote from Peter Bogdanovich's *Targets*, with old Boris Karloff playing a version of himself while commenting on a version of his career) proves no exception to this rule. The result: inventive, assonant, literally dreadful. If you're looking for something between Ray Bradbury's headlong genre-bending fabulist glee and the *Insidious* movie franchise's unapologetic vaudeville creep, then Grey's your man."
—Gemma Files, author of *Experimental Film*

"Orrin Grey's roots (or should I say tentacles?) run deep, squeezing the best from horrors both classic and obscure, twisting them in his own particular way. He's a fine storyteller who'll pull you in, and so will *Painted Monsters*. Don't miss it!"
—Norman Partridge, author of *Dark Harvest*

GUIGNOL
& OTHER SARDONIC TALES

ORRIN GREY

WORD HORDE
PETALUMA, CA

First Edition

ISBN: 978-1-939905-42-0

A Word Horde Book
www.wordhorde.com

TABLE OF CONTENTS

Introduction by Gemma Files 1

Dream House 5

The Lesser Keys 19

Guignol 43

Shadders 53

The Blue Light 65

A Circle That Ever Returneth In 79

Programmed to Receive 97

The Well and the Wheel 105

Haruspicate or Scry 117

Dark and Deep 133

Invaders of Gla'aki 145

Baron von Werewolf Presents:

Frankenstein Against the Phantom Planet 157

The Cult of Headless Men 175

When a Beast Looks Up at the Stars 203

Afterword & Acknowledgments 217

For Clive Barker, Richard Matheson,
Ray Russell, and Roger Corman.

In spite of Virtue and the Muse,
Nemesis will have her dues,
And all our struggles and our toils
Tighter wind the giant coils.
                    —Ralph Waldo Emerson

INTRODUCTION

GEMMA FILES

I often say of other writers whose work I particularly enjoy that I long to eat their brains (just a slice! A tiny, energizing piece!), and I think this impulse to consume what I love has a lot to do with the fact that all writing—especially horror writing—seems to find its origin in a tangled mixture of obsession, imitation and covetousness. And Orrin Grey ranks especially high on that list, possibly because we're so similar in our interests and patterns, except for the fact that he makes it all look so damn *easy*, the monster-loving skeleton bastard.

Of course, it helps that as fellow self-taught film historians/ genre geeks, Grey and I share a set of references so encyclopedic that we've had whole conversations consisting entirely of the primal fan(atic)s' back-and-forth: "Have you seen [X]? Well, but how about *[X]?*" Both of us have garburator imaginations, our engines apparently fuelled alike by digesting a span of wildly competing influences, letting them ferment, then spitting them back out onto the page. But while my own interests tend to exit me Cronenberg-style, in a lumpy mess of filth and blood, Grey's come out polished and complex, as interlocking puzzles hiding sudden existentially dreadful surprises, like little Lament Configurations.

And now here's his latest, named not only after its titular tale but the legendary Théâtre de Grand Guignol (1897-1962), that infamous Parisian stage show specializing in amoral, grotesquely realistic horror plays—one of the first cultural influxes of splatter/torture porn, in a lot of ways, though its creators took equal inspiration from Grimm fairytales and the black paintings of Goya, the yellow rags, Sensation literature and Penny Dreadfuls of the Victorian era and the much-decried excesses of Elizabethan and Jacobean revenge tragedies, from *Titus Andronicus* to *The Duchess of Malfi*. Hypersexual as well as gruesome (shows were often attended as a sort of foreplay), the Grand Guignol rode that still-undeniable line where horror gets so over the top it becomes humor for all it was worth, routinely finding the happily shocked guffaw hiding inside every scream. They also pioneered the use of special effects onstage, using putty, fake knives and bladders to test the limits of the allowable—audience members in the front rows could pretty much expect to get splashed, especially since the troupe kept a fresh-mixed vat of fake blood simmering behind the scenes every night.

Can readers expect to stumble out the back of this book soaked in gore and horny as hell, then? Maybe not, but they *can* expect to receive a download straight from Grey's ever-boiling brain along with each weird narrative, a meta-tastic mixture of supposedly tired old tropes enthusiastically Frankensteined together to make something far more fresh, its DNA soaked with jokes so in- they turn outwards once more. You absolutely don't have to get all the shout-outs to enjoy these stories, either, though Grey's notes may well send you spiralling down an endless click-hole of research, decoding each shadow on the wall until you feel at least semi-satisfied you might have finally found (most of) Waldo: Roger Corman, H. P. Lovecraft, Robert E. Howard, Universal monster movies, pre-Hayes Code film history/rumour run wild; Hammer horror and Amicus from Cushing and Lee to *Legend of the Seven Golden Vampires;* Toho-inflected J-horror from yurei to kaiju; *Doctor Who* and Nigel Kneale, Choose Your Own Adventures and D & D; pulpy Noir served hot, with a heaping side of cheese. A constantly sparkling film of artifice, only thinly applied over a shit-ton of existential truths.

At all points along the creative curve, Grey remains both a gentleman and a scholar of our own much-decried genre...he never stops learning, which means his fans never do, either. So enter this freakishly inventive cabinet of curiosities if you will, every story providing a redly drippy skull-window straight into the id-vortex of a modern horror master—gape in awe, laugh out loud, feel your mental mouth start to water.

Or, to put it another way: *God damn*, you may very well exclaim, as you finally emerge; *Gemma, you were right. Those really are some tasty, tasty brains.*

DREAM HOUSE

I t was the last night of the Festival, and we were all sitting around one of the long tables out behind the Moon and Sixpence. It was cold enough that my feet were freezing and my hands were shoved into the pockets of my jacket when not gesturing or picking up a drink. Above us, a suitably gibbous moon dipped in-and-out behind clouds that would've otherwise been invisible.

There were still a couple of movies playing, so the back patio wasn't too crowded yet, but I'd talked Simon out of watching *Curse of the Crimson Altar* on account of it being five minutes of awesome and an hour-and-change of people walking around in dark houses, so we were staking out the table 'til the Festival ended and the last movies let out. Simon was telling me about some French movie he'd seen this year that came off as a poor man's John Carpenter, one that seemed to get worse every time he mentioned it.

As the table gradually filled up, the conversation twisted and turned—as conversations like that, in places like those, always do—and somehow or other we got on the subject of Lovecraft in old TV shows. Maybe there was a panel on it, or someone was suggesting one for next year. They'd showed the Stuart Gordon "Dreams in the Witch House" that year, and Nick mentioned that "Pickman's Model" episode of *Night Gallery*, which I'd always

5

loved. I told him it was my favorite adaptation of the story, and someone else—probably Ross—agreed. Sooner or later, of course, somebody brought up *Dream House*.

There wasn't anyone at the table who hadn't seen at least a few episodes—some back when it was still on the air, most of us on reruns on Saturday afternoon when we were kids, or on those two-episode VHS packs that floated around video stores for a while—and nobody had much that was nice to say about it, beyond that it had "potential," the faint praise with which we damn things that we want to like but can't quite. Mostly, we all agreed that it barely counted as Lovecraftian, for all its swinging and missing in that direction, but then a voice brought up the lost episodes.

I didn't recognize the woman doing the talking, but by then that was true of about half the people around the table. She was sitting on the other side of Jesse, and I thought I remembered her coming back with him from one of his trips to the bar for drinks. The corner she was sitting in was the darkest on the patio, her back against the bulbous tree that broke up the back fence line. Her features were mostly lost to shadow, but she was smoking a ciga-rette, and when she took a pull the glow from the cherry would flare up enough to illuminate the edges of her face, which seemed a little worn and creased, not that any of us were looking our best in the dim patio lights at the dregs of the Festival. I asked around afterward, but nobody seemed to know her name, or remember seeing her anyplace else during the weekend.

When she mentioned the lost episodes, someone at the other end of the table laughed and said something like, "Yeah, they're probably great, since nobody's ever seen them." She let out a sigh, the cherry on her cigarette bobbing like the bouncing ball in an old sing-along. "They're around," she said. "They were on YouTube for a while, but they got pulled down."

"The story goes," Cody said, because of course, if anybody knew the story, it was going to be Cody, "that they used to circulate them on recorded tapes, back in the pre-Internet days. Some kid supposedly watched them and then cut up his family and asphyxiated himself with a garbage bag taped around his head. That got more press than the show ever did, even if it's probably not true."

"Early days Marilyn-Manson-made-me-do-it stuff," someone else said, nodding, remembering the legend now. "Wonder if anyone ever got sued over that."

The initial speaker shook her head, ground out her cigarette on the tabletop so that the shadows swallowed her face again. "Naw," she said, "nobody ever got sued, because there wasn't anybody left."

The next morning, most everybody besides the locals flew out, and I drove up with Simon to spend a couple of days in Seattle before heading home. We stayed up late watching *The Lurking Fear* and *Virgin Witch* in his apartment, but I couldn't get the conversation about *Dream House* out of my head. I'd seen maybe seven or eight episodes over the years—it used to play late at night on one of the channels that we got when I was growing up, after *Renegade* and *Kung Fu* but before *Beauty and the Beast* with Ron Perlman, so I usually didn't stay up late enough to catch it.

Now, though, my curiosity was piqued, so I looked it up on Wikipedia, skimmed through episode synopses and cast lists until I came to a headline that simply said "Tragedy" in big black letters.

It seemed that a fire had broken out on set during principal photography. All told, ten people died as a result of the blaze. Investigators expected arson, but according to Wikipedia no arrests were ever made in connection with the disaster, which was partially responsible for the show folding after shooting less than a season's worth of episodes. A couple of the main actors died in the fire, or at the hospital later as a result of smoke inhalation, including Judy Becker, the woman who played Jennifer Cristain/Lady Jenny, the show's main star.

Digging a little deeper, I found that our nameless *Dream House* fan hadn't been wrong. Nobody involved in the show was still alive. A few people who had played bit parts in individual episodes

were still around, some of them had even gone on to have real acting careers, and the actress who played a little girl in the third episode was going to be in a movie opposite Ryan Gosling next year.
But anyone who had played a recurring character or been involved
in writing, directing, or shooting the show was dead. Not one had
survived the show's cancellation by more than five years.

The reasons for those that I could find reasons for spanned the
range of typical Hollywood causes of death—from cancers to car
accidents, drug overdoses and suicides, and at least one disquiet-
ing mass-homicide about which I could find almost no detailed
information online. I was reminded of the rumors about the various fates of the people involved in making *Manos*—famously the
"worst" movie ever shown on *MST3k*, though for that particular plum my pick might have to go to *Hobgoblins*. This, though,
seemed a little more real, the tragedies and mysteries a little easier
to verify.

Before I closed my laptop and turned in for the night, I sent an
email to Shawn, asking him about the so-called "lost episodes."
He'd helped me track down hard-to-find flicks for my Vault of Secrets column before, so I figured if I knew anyone who could find
the *Dream House* episodes, it'd be him.

I didn't hear back from Shawn until after I'd gotten back to Kansas,
but the email he finally sent me had links to two of the "lost episodes" in it. "The most innocuous ones, I'm told," he said. "There's
supposed to be one more, the really bad one, but I couldn't find
hide nor hair of it. Not even a plot synopsis. Seems like it disappeared into the wild blue yonder."

It took a few days of post-trip recovery and catching up on work
before I managed to queue up the episodes. I watched them down-
stairs in my office, on my laptop, with all the lights out and my
headphones on. They looked like shit and sounded worse, and
had obviously been recorded by hooking two VCRs together. The
picture swam and shifted, like when we used to try to pirate pay

channels on my friend's cable when we were kids. One minute the dialogue was so muted that I couldn't make it out, the next I was snatching my headphones off to keep from being deafened.

The first episode seemed like a pretty standard series entry. It focused on the Jennifer/Lady Jenny character, one actress playing both the young woman who came to open Dream House back up and turn it into a bed and breakfast, and the young wife of the slave owner who ran it back when it was still a plantation. It was the main thing I remembered from late nights watching the series as a kid, lots of flashing back and forth between the past and the present. It got a lot of mileage out of that portrait-in-the-entry-way-looks-exactly-like-me trope that Gothic movies love so much.

In this episode, Jennifer was having nightmares about Lady Jenny's life, and when she woke in the mornings, the sheets all mussed alluringly, her bare feet and the hem of her nightdress were dirty. As the episode progressed, she found damp, shapeless footprints on the stairs of the house, and saw bulbous shadows moving along the wall. In my notes I wrote down, "Fungus people?" and circled it. Eventually, the episode culminated in what was maybe supposed to be another dream sequence. A door opened in the corner of Jennifer's bedroom, spilling out a weird greenish light. She rose from the bed and crossed the room, though a close-up shot of her face made it very clear that her eyes were staring, vacant and asleep.

On the other side of the secret door she descended a spiraling hidden staircase until she came to a basement. There, half-glimpsed figures awaited her, surrounding something that I couldn't make out in the murky darkness of the terrible video transfer. A shape that might have been a man knelt on the ground before her, and she was suddenly holding a knife. The scene cut to darkness, like a commercial break, and when it came back up it was daylight, birds were singing in the trees outside, and Jennifer was lying safe in her bed, but with those same tell-tale dirty feet.

The second episode introduced a new character, a reporter named

Wayland whose grandfather had been a slave on the plantation. Wayland was planning to write a book about the strange things that went on at Dream House back in the day, and to that end he convinced modern-day Jennifer to rent him a room, even though the bed and breakfast didn't seem to be technically up and running yet. He snuck around the place a bit, saw some ominous stuff, and found a secret graveyard out behind the main house, but then the episode got really weird.

A door opened into Wayland's room while he was sleeping, spilling that same green light as in the previous episode. A woman came out of the door. It looked like she might have been played by the same actress who played Jennifer/Lady Jenny, but there was something wrong with her face, and the picture was too low-res for me to tell for sure. Whoever she was, she was pale as death, and she had what looked like a man with her, albeit on the end of a leash and walking on all fours. It was either wearing some kind of suit—a bondage suit, on TV in the '60s?—or it was supposed to be an ape or something, because it was so dark that it blended into the shadows.

Wayland got up and followed the woman down the stairs, and in the middle of the same dirt-floored basement that Jennifer had ended up in during the other episode, he found an idol of green stone. It stood roughly the height of a man, and was carved in the shape of a crouching figure, its head spreading out into, well, tentacles, I guess, though their angles were sharper than that word usually calls to mind. There was a noise on the soundtrack like clanking chains, and then Wayland started to scream and the episode cut to black.

That would've probably been the end of it, if I hadn't hit a dry spell. I finished catching up on the work that I'd missed while I was in Portland, and there was nothing waiting on the other side. Just doldrums, and streaming movies on Netflix. I knew that I should take advantage of the slow days to chip into my to-read pile or work on some of my own projects, but I just found myself feeling listless, rewatching old episodes of *The Simpsons* and drifting.

I don't know what would have happened if I hadn't gotten the second email from Shawn. I guess he hadn't been able to leave well enough alone either, and sometime in the midst of my fallow period I got a message from him saying that he'd tracked down the place where they shot the exteriors for *Dream House* on one of those websites that show you the shooting locations of movies and TV shows.

The website showed a screen grab from the show, and below it, a photograph of the actual house from the same angle. It said that some fans of the show had bought the house back in the late '90s and actually turned it into a bed and breakfast for real. They even kept the sign from the show: DREAM HOUSE, Est. 18--. Which, of course, those of us who had seen even a few episodes knew that while the house itself may have been built in 18--, the basement was much older. Hewn from the earth, not by the hands of white settlers, nor by the native tribes who once lived on the land, but by some older race. Knowing Lovecraft, probably serpent men or something.

At the bottom was the address, and a link to the website of the bed and breakfast. Before the end of the day, I had called and booked a room.

I told Grace it was a research trip, that I figured I could get something substantial out of this whole "lost episodes," visit-to-the-actual-house thing. Something I could maybe sell to *Rue Morgue* or some website that paid more than $50 an article. Maybe I even believed it at the time, or maybe I knew better, even then. "If nothing else," Grace said, "it'll be a tax deduction."

She almost went with me, but then her work signed on a big new client and that meant long weeks that she couldn't skip, so I ended up going alone. That's maybe the only good thing that came out of any of this, that she wasn't able to come with me. That she, at least, was spared.

Driving to the place took a couple of days, and I spent the night in a nice suite at a Holiday Inn watching old episodes of *Night Gallery* and *Alfred Hitchcock Presents*. In a story, there would have been a rerun of *Dream House* on, or at least the "Pickman's Model" episode of *Night Gallery*, but in real life nobody shows *Dream House* anymore, and the *Night Gallery* episode maybe had something to do with a lady vampire on a house boat, I was mostly asleep already by the time it came on.

That night I had a dream where I stood outside the front of the bed and breakfast. Someone had spraypainted over the sign, adding the letters "s in the witch" between the words "dream" and "house." My eye was a camera lens taking a time-lapse photo, and I watched the clouds scud across the sky too quickly, the light changing in jerky, stop-motion switches.

In the dream there was a blink, and I was looking at the house from behind and above. It looked strangely innocuous, like a dollhouse, and between me and it there was a field where cars were parked, car after car, from different ages. Old Packards and '50s convertibles with big fins. Nature was gradually erasing their distinguishing features, sun and time scouring the paint from their hoods as kudzu grew up around them, devouring them as it would one day devour everything else.

I woke up feeling unrested, and almost turned the car around then and there, but the website for Dream House had said there was a fee for last-minute cancellations, and I was already so close.

By the time I pulled up in front of the house it was the middle of the afternoon. The sunlight was golden and soft, and everything looked almost exactly like the opening titles of the show. The golden light, the old plantation house with its white paint and columns. I could almost hear that tinkling theme song playing somewhere off in the distance.

When I walked in through the front doors, I expected to find a big painting of Lady Jenny looking down at me, but of course, that had been filmed on a set, and instead I walked in to find the front desk with a painting hanging above it showing some kind of hunting scene, something brought over from the Old World.

The woman behind the counter looked like the mother from a TV show about a pioneer family, her black hair just beginning to go iron-gray at the roots. She wore a blue dress with white flowers—magnolias, perhaps, which would seem appropriate.

She introduced herself as Irene and had me sign in, and I asked her a few questions about the inn, and about the show. It turned out that she and her husband had bought it from the fans who'd originally converted it after they'd gone under, and she wasn't a fan of the show, though she knew a little. "Some of it was shot right here," she told me, "at least that's what they say. I can give you her room, if you want."

I didn't have to ask to which "her" she was referring, and said that yes, I'd love to have Lady Jenny's room, if it was available. She asked if I needed any help with my bags, but I declined. Years of attending conventions had taught me how to pack light.

My room was, in fact, Lady Jenny's, down to most of the furniture, though the knick-knacks on the shelf were different. There was the dressing mirror where Lady Jenny combed her long brown hair. Irene told me that some of the scenes of the bedroom were shot at the house, while others were shot on a sound stage somewhere else. I had the disorienting feeling that comes with walking into a place you know intimately but have never visited; a feeling, I imagine, that is unique to the generations who have grown up with TV and movies.

The room had a window that faced the back of the house, and when Irene left I peered out beyond the lacy curtains, holding my breath in case I was presented with a field of rusting cars. Instead, I saw only picturesque trees strung with Spanish moss. I resolved to go exploring tomorrow, and spent the night setting up my laptop, typing up notes from the road, and responding to emails and Facebook messages. I called Grace and told her goodnight before falling asleep to black-and-white *Dragnet* episodes on the little TV that they'd archaically stuck in the corner of the room.

In my dream it was like I was a camera again, mounted on a tripod in the corner, watching myself sleep. I saw a door open in the wall, the wainscoting and Victorian wallpaper sliding apart to reveal a gap, first of darkness, then filling with a familiar green light. I watched as I rose from my bed and followed the light through the door and down the stairs, my dream-camera coming unmoored and drifting over my shoulder.

The basement was clearer in the dream than it had ever been in the show, the shadows sharp and in high definition, the blackness crisp and hard-edged. Shapes waited for me in those shadows, figures hooded and cowled, shambling things and squirming things that made me think of the rubber-suited ghoul from that *Night Gallery* episode, or the Toho mushroom people in *Matango*. I wanted to look closer, to peer into the shadows and pick out the comforting fakeness of their suits, the seams and zippers, but I was a camera, and I had no free will, so I saw them only peripherally, my gaze fixed ahead.

What I *could* see were the manacles and chains affixed to the stone columns that held up the ceiling. Generations of blood had seeped into the earthen floor and changed its color forever, and I thought of Jennifer's dirty feet in the lost episode, the rusty red that hadn't translated well to the color palette of '60s TV.

In the center of the basement was a statue that I had seen before, its bulk almost human but hunched like a toad up on its haunches, its face a mass of angular tentacles. It was limned in the same sickly green illumination that engulfed me, a light that seemed to sweat from the statue's surface. Next to it stood a figure draped in a black robe, a figure that I recognized as Lady Jenny, though her features were askew, like a mask poorly fitted over some shifting form beneath. Beside her crouched a darker shape which she held on the end of a chain, and when she spoke it wasn't with the voice of Judy Becker. It was the voice of an old drunk, dying from tuberculosis. The voice of a thousand worms, suddenly given the power of speech.

I woke with her words on my tongue, though I couldn't fit them to human vocalization, couldn't make any sense of them, even to write them down. I'll spare you any Lovecraftian attempt at approximating the sounds, which began to die in my memory even as I scrambled for pen and paper.

Irene confirmed my suspicions that many of the rooms in Dream House—my own included—had once had servant's entrances that let onto back stairways winding down to the kitchens and, of course, even the larder in the basement. The doors themselves had been lost to one of the building's renovations, but some of the stairs remained buried behind the walls, and she confirmed, when I pointed to the spot where my dream door had been, that it was about where the servant's entrance appeared in old photographs of the room.

I asked her about the basement, but she said that most of it had been filled up and bricked over since before her time there. "If there's any way into it," she smiled, "I've never seen it."

So here's the lightning round bonus question: When you're dealing with things that exist outside of our normal conception of either space or time, is a dream sequence really any less real than anything else? I think we both know the answer to that one.

That morning, I went out to walk the grounds. I picked my way along a trampled-down path that led around the side of the house, past the trees with their almost staged moss, and across a footbridge that spanned a small stream. The sun was shining, but there was no birdsong, and the farther I walked the more I began to notice kudzu creeping up the trunks of the trees, crowding in on the sides of the path.

I was almost unsurprised when I rounded the corner and saw the rusted shell of the first car. It wasn't a field, like it had been in my dream. Trees grew up among them, hiding them from view from the air or the windows of the house, but here they were, car after car, when you could find them among the foliage run riot. What's more, I'd paid attention on the walk, and I knew that I'd taken more or less the same path that Wayland had in the lost episode, when he'd stumbled upon the secret cemetery.

I didn't get immediately back into my car and drive away, leaving all my stuff up in the room, like I would have encouraged a character to do had I been watching a movie. It wasn't stupidity that drove me back inside—remember that, the next time you're watching a scary movie and someone goes down into the basement—it was curiosity, maybe the only emotion in our repertoire that's capable of overpowering our fear.

Inside the house, I scrutinized the painting on the wall behind the front desk, looking for subtle changes. I asked Irene, casually, about her husband, and she said that he was around there someplace, that he usually tended the grounds while she kept up the house itself. She looked straight at me as she spoke, her eyes brown and deep as wells, and I thought of the scene in *In the Mouth of Madness*, the kindly old lady behind the counter with her husband shackled to her leg, the bloody ax waiting out in the greenhouse.

I went upstairs, packed my bags, and checked out of my room a day early. I drove home without stopping except to fuel up and buy sodas, deleted the lost *Dream House* episodes from my computer, kissed my wife, and lived happily ever after. But of course you and I both know, dear reader, that's not how these stories end. I called yesterday to make my second reservation at Dream House. Irene didn't sound at all surprised to hear from me.

I'll kiss Grace goodbye one last time—I wonder if she'll know, if she'll try to stop me, but I'm beyond stopping now. I'll return to the Dream House, and when I get there I'll drive around the side, along the road I've never taken, to the parking lot that I shouldn't know about, and pull my rental car up alongside the other rusting hulks that lie beneath the kudzu. I'll collect my key from the front desk, and I'll go up to my room—the same room as before—and I'll lie down on the bed and go to sleep, perchance to dream.

Author's Notes: My wife, Grace, is my first reader on every story that I write, and one of the proudest accomplishments in my career so far is that, when she finished reading this story, even *she* had to ask me how much of it was true. To that end, I'm not going to spoil it all for you, dear reader.

The story begins at the H. P. Lovecraft Film Festival in Portland, and, like most of the time I've spent at the H. P. Lovecraft Film Festival over the years, we're sitting and talking out behind the Moon and Sixpence. From there, everything becomes a hodge-podge of truth and make-believe. No names have been changed, because no one is innocent.

THE LESSER KEYS

Opening Bars

Jasper deWitt arrived in Kansas City at half-past-three on a Friday. He stepped off the train in Union Station and tried not to gawk around like an out-of-town rube at all the marble and chandeliers. It wasn't that they didn't have buildings like this in Chicago, they had plenty, but in spite of knowing better Jasper had still been expecting a cowtown, not the Paris of the Plains, as they were calling it.

A taxi took him from Union Station to the boarding house just off Vine where he'd be staying. He didn't have much with him, just one suitcase and a few hundred dollars in folding money secreted in various places about his person; a little in his left shoe, a little pinned to the inside of his cuff, a little tucked into the lining of his bowler hat.

The boarding house was big and white, and the front was full of windows. It had the kind of porch that you sit out on in the summer and complain about the heat and the bugs. His room, when the lady showed it to him, backed right up against the railroad tracks, but that was okay, it just reminded him of home. And from the street out front he could see the lights of the jazz district, so he figured he'd have at least a few good nights.

Really, everything looked pretty good. Deceptively good. Standing out in front of the house after dropping off his suitcase and making sure that he looked presentable in the dressing mirror, he had to remind himself of the Sword of Damocles dangling over his head.

It wasn't like the memory was stale. Just a couple of days ago he'd been back in Chicago, standing in Gerald Tyson's big office above the club, shuffling his feet on Gerald Tyson's expensive rug and drinking Gerald Tyson's expensive Scotch, and being told by that very man in no uncertain terms just what his fate would be if he failed in the job he was being assigned. "I want that band for my club," Tyson was saying in his thick, phlegmy voice. "But I can't get any traction by way of the usual channels, you understand? That town's a goddamn quagmire, they don't know how to play ball proper. So what you're gonna do for me is, you're gonna go down there and you're gonna find those boys and you're gonna explain to 'em that I'm givin' 'em a real good offer. I'll double whatever they're getting now, but I don't want any entanglements, is that clear? They're mine, exclusive. You make 'em understand that's best for everyone, and you bring 'em back with you. And Jasper? Don't make me send anyone else."

Of course he was talking about the Lesser Keys. It seemed like they were all anybody was talking about. Just another jazz ensemble in a sea of jazz ensembles? Maybe, but the word was they were setting Kansas City on fire, and that in spite of the fact that they'd only play at one place, a roadhouse on the outskirts called Solomon King's Mine. They were supposed to be good, damn good, but privately Jasper didn't think that's what Gerald Tyson wanted them for. Privately, though he'd never say it to the big man's face, nor to anyone else who might ever breathe a word of it in that direction, Jasper thought that Gerald Tyson just couldn't handle the thought of anyone having something nice that he couldn't have. He was going to take the Lesser Keys away from Solomon King just to prove that he could.

Before leaving Chicago, Jasper had asked around to learn what he could about Solomon King and the Lesser Keys. It hadn't been a lot. Solomon King ran his roadhouse and was supposed to have some sway in the politics of the city, though no one could say how much or what kind. Jasper figured he was looking at another Gerald Tyson, more or less. But he also learned that Tyson wasn't wrong about the city being a quagmire, something altogether different from Chicago. While the gangsters there owned the politicians, in Kansas City the line between the two seemed even more blurred. The way Jasper heard it, the whole place was in the pocket of this "Boss Tom" character, who made men like Tyson seem petty tyrants by comparison. Jasper wasn't sure how much stock to put into those rumors, but he planned to keep a low profile in the city as best he could, just to be safe. He'd already had enough of powerful white men to last him a lifetime.

Tyson hadn't given him a concrete deadline, but he'd also made no bones about the fact that there *was* a time limit on this job. Still, Jasper was, if nothing else, a man who knew his work, and he knew in his gut that this wasn't going to be as simple a matter as Tyson made it out. Whatever the secrets of the Lesser Keys were, prying them away was going to take more finesse than marching in with a better payday, and that finesse would require that he know his footing a little better. So that Friday night he didn't go to Solomon King's Mine at all. He struck out walking from the front of the boarding house with the intention of sampling the finest night life that Kansas City had to offer. In his experience, that was how you took the measure of a city, and learned what was up from what was down. And Jasper had a feeling that he was going to need to know up from down pretty thoroughly before this job was over.

Caroline Bloom's driver deposited her at the front doors of the Muehlbach Hotel at seven o'clock. The hotel was supposed to be the finest in Kansas City, though that wasn't really what had drawn her there. She was told that it already had its very own ghost, a lady in blue who had maybe once been a singer at the Gayety Theatre across the street. No one seemed to know what her fate had been, but the word went that most of the staff had seen her wandering the halls at one time or another.

Caroline had always been fascinated by spook stories, places where murders had been committed, anything that made her blood run a little cold. "Morbid," is what her mother had called it when she was still alive, as well as "unladylike" and, at times, even less flattering things. Which made it doubly unfair that Jonathon was the one who had gotten into this trouble. Running off halfway across the country with some movie starlet, joining a secret society. These were the kinds of things Caroline longed to do. But because she'd had the misfortune to be born a lady, she had to play at responsibility while Jonathon's rakish proclivities—while frowned upon—were at least tolerated. It's just what indolent young men did, she was told again and again. Once his wild oats were sown, he'd settle down.

She supposed she owed him a little, though, for finally doing something shocking enough that Mr. Benedict, who handled their finances, had sent her west to come and track him down, bring him home. Mr. Benedict had wanted to hire a private detective to do the job, but Caroline had eventually won out. "I know Jonathon better than anyone," she'd told him, more than once before he finally got it through his white-haired old head, "and I'm the only one who's going to convince him to come home without being dragged."

Now she was here, on the not-quite-completely-tamed-yet frontier, embarking on at least a little bit of an adventure. While it wasn't exactly running off with a starlet and joining a cult, it was better than nothing. When she finally tracked Jonathon down, she'd have to thank him for that, right after she socked him in the jaw for running off without telling her. While she thought of Jonathon, she watched the porters unloading her bags from the car and carrying them into the hotel's sparkling lobby. Chandeliers drenched the surroundings in golden light and glinted off the checkered tiles of the lobby floor. Outside, night was falling,

draping the tall buildings in shadowy cloaks, and the lights were
coming on up and down the street as the clubs and dancehalls
came to life. She had some leads on how to find Jonathon, con-
tacts in the city that had known her father, places to start looking.
But she hoped he proved more elusive than he had in the past,
when he'd disappeared on smaller indiscretions closer to home.
She hoped it took her some time to crack him down. It wasn't as
if she'd never been to the big city, or that Kansas City was anywhere near the size of the places she'd gone back home, but it felt
somehow different. Less tame, like the city was just a veneer laid
over a sleeping beast to make it look domestic. She knew that the
night sky out here would be vast and dark and empty in a way that
she'd never seen before, she could feel it in her gut, even though
the sun wasn't yet quite gone. In the spaces between the buildings
the blue of the sky was deepening, the way the ocean did as the
land dropped away, and when the last light was gone it would be
like being in a cave that went on forever. She hoped she would be
here long enough to make that feeling last, at least a little while.

And if she was very lucky, maybe she would even see a ghost.

Solomon King stood at the top of the stairs with his arms clasped
behind his back. He rocked forward onto his toes, enjoying the
feeling that he was about to overbalance, to plunge down into the
darkness below. Then he rocked back onto his heels.

Behind him, he could hear the music coming from the main
room. Not the Lesser Keys playing, not yet. Just some other band,
some boys he paid to entertain the customers. Not bad musicians,
full of the passion that only comes when you're playing to live,
when playing's all you've got to live for. But still just men making
noises that could only aspire to be music, and nothing more. He
tuned them out.

He closed his eyes, as he always did at the top of the stairs, and he
visualized the room below him. The basement of the house, what
he had actually bought the building for. The vast dark catacomb

there, cut into solid rock, connected into a natural cave system that ran out into the surrounding hills. The wooden struts and braces, erected to help support the cavern, to keep the weight of the house above, with all its many revelers and guests, from crashing down into the caves below. The pentagrams, triangles, and Solomonic seals cut carefully into the floor of the chamber, ready to be poured full of sand or salt or blood, as needed. The sigils, painstakingly painted onto the walls, each stroke potentially a literal matter of life or death. The black pool at the back of the cavern, darker and deeper than water could ever be.

The room was perfect, and in it he had already perfected, already set into motion his great machine, the one that would finally do what no one in the debased and cowardly Golden Dawn had achieved, in spite of their grand claims, nor the Rosy Cross who had left them behind, nor the Order of Kings, here in this city, who were taking votes even now as to whether or not to cast him out. He knew of their machinations, knew that they moved against him in their offices and chambers, in their meeting halls in the city proper. His daemons advised him so, and he knew the truth of their words. He had peered into the hearts of these men who thought themselves his betters because their skin was whiter, their money greener. The fools believed that enough corporeal power, fine enough suits, large enough offices, enough land and money could make them great men. There was more power in the silver ring on his finger than in all of their boardrooms and bank accounts combined, and they knew it, in their weak, fearful hearts. They knew it at night, when they lay down to sleep next to their wives or mistresses. They knew real power when they saw it, and it made them afraid, and so they plotted against him now. They believed they had used him, and that now they could cast him aside. At least, that's what they wanted to believe.

His father had believed it as well, and it had cost him dearly. Solomon King smiled, turning the silver ring on his finger. There was a stain on the inside of the band, old and dark as a shadow on a tintype.

In the past, the machinations of the Order of Kings would have enraged him, but he found that now he barely cared. Their schemes were already too late, though they didn't yet realize it. His own machine was now in operation, one much greater than the so-called "Pendergast Machine" that ran this frontier Babylon. They had used his knowledge to strike deals with devils for mortal gain, but he would show them yet the pettiness of their greed. He would show them what a real devil was capable of.

Behind him the sound of horns and pianos slowly died away, to be replaced by the ocean roar of applause, the susurrus of voices from distant rooms. He kept his eyes closed as that sound died away, replaced with a waiting hush, and then the first silver notes of Magda's song. He always had her sing before the Lesser Keys, the warmup, the oil that would lubricate the machine. As her words rang in the air like clear bells, Solomon King smiled a private smile in the dark at the thought of the music that his creation was about to make.

Progression

For his first few nights in town, Jasper deWitt went to what seemed like every speakeasy, dancehall, ballroom, and night club in Kansas City that would let in colored patrons, *except* Solomon King's. He walked down 14th Street, where the whores tapped nickels against their windows at patrons as they passed. If Gerald Tyson could see him, Jasper knew that the big man would be fuming so hot that steam would be coming out of his ears, but there was a reason Tyson had sent him, and this was a job that Jasper knew how to do. Before he could get any good leads on talking that outfit out from under King's thumb, he was going to have to get the lay of the land, and that meant spending time—and more than a little of his folding money—reconnoitering. Not his fault if the majority of that time and money had to be spent in establishments of loose moral virtue.

On Monday night, he finally hired a car to drive him out to

Solomon King's, but he didn't go in. Even on a Monday, the lot was full of cars, and they were parked along the road to either side. Seemed like it was a pretty happening place, which supported what Jasper had already heard. Solomon King's, in spite of its relatively out-of-the-way location, was the most popular night spot in Kansas City, and it had everything to do with the Lesser Keys.

Nobody who had heard them could say what was so special about them. He'd met with an old horn player who could hold forth about every kind of music a man could blow, and the old musician had just gotten a faraway look in his eyes when he tried to talk about the Lesser Keys. "When they play," he said, "it ain't like music at all. I cain't rightly say what it is, but I ain't heard nothin' like it in all my born days."

Whatever it was that the Lesser Keys had, the word was that it brought in everyone who was anyone and a lot of people who weren't. Though King's was always packed, he didn't seem like he was too exclusive. The richest and whitest folks in town rubbed elbows there with petty crooks and street musicians. King seemed to believe in a policy of inclusiveness, and anybody who was on his good list could get in the door of his club. If there was any rhyme or reason to who he let in and who he turned away, Jasper couldn't see it, and nobody else could illuminate it for him.

That Monday night, Jasper watched the windows spill their embers of light out through the cracks in the shutters, he listened to the hum of the music that he could feel as much as hear, and he looked to try to figure out what it was he was looking for.

When the last song that had been thrumming through the night died out, a crystal birdsong that was only audible to Jasper as an echo, like a memory, he turned to the driver to tell him to take them back but then he stopped. Something had changed out there in the dark. The air was suddenly alive, charged like with a summer storm. Jasper realized that his knuckles had whitened on the dash, his fingernails digging into the upholstery. And then the music started back up.

He still couldn't really hear it, not at this distance, but he could feel the difference, just as he had felt the charge in the air that preceded them, and he knew that it was the Lesser Keys. Jasper deWitt wasn't an educated man, and he'd never done anything with his life besides the kind of work he was doing now, but when he was a boy his mother had been deeply religious, and she had taken him to church every Sunday morning. Nothing that the preacher had ever said had gotten through to Jasper, but the music did. The hymns, at their best, could do something more than reach inside a man, he knew that even as a boy. They carried something in them that was more powerful than words and notes, something that could change you, could put you in touch with things that were bigger than you, things that could maybe change everything, at least for a few seconds. His mother called it Jesus, but he wasn't so sure. All he was sure about was that the music was special, powerful, and he felt something in it that he never felt anywhere else.

All his life, he knew music. He spent as much time around it as he could, and the darkest and most disappointing hours of his life were when he realized that he had no talent for it himself. But he understood it, in his gut, and he knew when it was good, when it could move a person. He knew what band playing what song would get them out on the dance floor, and which one would make them drink, and which would make them tell their friends the next day. It's how he'd ended up working for Gerald Tyson, and it was the only thing in a long and mostly wasted life that he'd ever been particularly good at. But in all those years, he'd never heard another song that did what the best of those hymns of his youth had done.

Never, 'til now. Even the few straggling notes, dying out in the night air, even the thrum that he could feel running through the car, even that was enough for him to know that what he was listening to was something *more* than music. If the hymns of his youth had been a peek through the keyhole into another room, this was the door thrown wide open. No wonder Solomon King kept them under his thumb.

When Jasper finally told the driver to take him home, he had to say it three times before the other man snapped out of his reverie and obeyed.

Caroline Bloom stood in Herbert Powell's office, being told for the third time that the Order of Kings was a *fraternal* order, and one that he couldn't get her even a visit with, not under any circumstances. "It's not as if I have any sway with them anyway, Miss Bloom," he said, his bushy eyebrows and mustache making his face seem almost comically expressive. He looked like he would have been at home curating a museum or lecturing a university class, not standing in an office full of dark wood and leather-bound books, with a map of the city on the wall behind him. "I've never been a member, and I've only been to a few meetings as a guest."

"Uncle Herb," Caroline replied, "if you don't start calling me Carol, or at least Caroline, I'm going to come pull your mustache like I did when I was a girl."

The old man smiled, his small eyes twinkling. "I'm sure you would, too. You've never done what you were told, ever since you *were* a little girl."

The office was on the top floor of Powell, Wilfred & Lome. The view over downtown from the big window was commanding, and in spite of the urgency of her need, Caroline had trouble keeping her eyes off it to focus on Uncle Herb's words.

"What I can't understand," he was saying, "is why you wouldn't let Mr. Benedict hire someone to take care of this? Or even if you had to come out, why you can't get a local man? I have people in the city who handle these sorts of things for me, I'd be happy to put them at your disposal."

"As I told Mr. Benedict," Caroline replied, "it's not just a matter of finding him. You know Jonathon, he's as stubborn as a mule when someone tells him he can't have his way, and technically there's not much that could be done about him. I've got to be the one to find him, so that I can convince him to come home under his own steam. Or at least not give all of both our inheritances to some cockamamie cult."

"The Order of Kings is a lot more than just a cult," Powell said, shaking his head sadly, "at least here. Many of the most prominent men in town are members in good standing."

"So what do they do?"

"The usual stuff, for the most part, I imagine. Ritual trappings wrapped around business dealings and excuses for drunken parties, just as with every society I've ever known of, secret or otherwise. There's some inner circle, of course, and lots of talk about magic and hocus-pocus, but I'm sure they're just jumped-up Masons when you strip all that away. And you're certain that Jonathon got initiated?"

"That's what he said in his letter." Caroline passed the folded papers over to the old attorney. "I haven't actually spoken to him."

"Hm," Powell muttered into his mustache, reading over the three typed pages that Jonathon had sent from Kansas City back to Boston a month ago. "This does sound serious. He talks as if he's thinking of marrying this girl."

"From what I can find out, she doesn't sound like the marrying type," Caroline replied. "What do you know about her?"

"I saw one of her films, I think. Beyond that, just that she sings down at Solomon King's sometimes. It's a roadhouse, outside of town. A little rough, but very popular, even with some of the gentry. Now that you mention it, most of the members of the Order have been there at one time or another. It might not be the worst place to start looking for your brother. But," he added hastily, "I wouldn't want you going out there unescorted!"

"Don't worry about me, Uncle Herb." Caroline gave him a peck on the cheek. "I'm sure I can find some gentleman to chaperone my trip."

Solomon King dreamed of darkness and fire and blood. He was told that most men couldn't remember their own births, but he did, which only went to reaffirm what he had always known, that he was different than other men.

Though he looked to all outward eyes like a fit man in his early fifties, he estimated his own age at nearer a century. He had been born on a plantation, a slave, the bastard son of his master and one of the house slaves. After his birth, one of his earliest memories was of watching his father flay his mother alive, and hang her skin on an altar. It was his introduction to magic, and he never looked back.

His father's wife was barren, and the man needed a son. "My own blood," he said, "will make the rituals stronger." He hadn't been wrong.

He'd given Solomon his name, raised him, taught him everything that he knew. Together, they'd opened up black abysses and called forth things that would blast a man's sanity, leave him gibbering and white-haired in a corner. Together they had done unspeakable things, but always he treated Solomon as a slave, never an equal, and so he underestimated his offspring. When Solomon finally grew strong enough to overpower him, to cut the silver ring from his finger and feed his heart to the very devils they had called to do his bidding, he swore to his dying bastard of a father that he would never kneel before another man as long as he lived.

Even as he said those words, though, he had still been young, foolish. He hadn't yet understood the depths of the powers that existed in the world and beyond it, in the spaces between the stars. When he first came to Kansas City, the Order of Kings had sought to deny him his initiation into their number, but his powers had been too great to be denied, even then. As one of them, he had learned new arts, and his powers had grown, but they had never ceased to think of him as something less than they were, just a tool to be used, as his father had, and he knew it was only a matter of time before they demanded that he kneel.

But he saw farther than the other members of the Order. They sought to call up daemons to provision their earthly lives, to grant them material power and material pleasures. They were men of small appetites, small ambitions. The devils they called upon existed on the fringes of things, on the edges of awareness, in the corner of the mind's eye. But there were things that dwelt in the gulfs beyond these, things so titanic in power that they could only exist in small parts at a time, could only brush up against the spheres which marked the outer limits of man's knowledge. And Solomon King knew that these things, too, could be conjured, summoned, and bound. It simply required a larger circle than any that had ever been drawn before, forged of sterner stuff than chalk and salt and blood.

Bridge

Lying in his bed in the boarding house that night, listening to the background hum of the trains and the music from the dancehalls a few blocks away, Jasper deWitt could still hear the music of the Lesser Keys resonating in his skull. And more than that, he could still see the images that the music had conjured for him when he closed his eyes. Not the comforting glow of the hymns he remembered from his childhood, but a flickering darkness against the backs of his eyelids. He felt like fireworks were going off in his brain, and he saw shapes etched in green flame, figures, things that were not men nor beasts but something in between. While his mother had taken him to church, his grandmother had told him stories that she had brought with her from Africa, about things left over from some other, older belief system, and these visions he saw behind his eyes seemed more like something from those stories than anything from his mother's Bible. If he was back in his mother's church, she'd tell him they were devils, and that he had to turn his back on them, tell them to get behind, but he didn't want to turn his back, not just yet.

In the dark places behind his eyes, which seemed darker now, he saw men with the heads of beasts and beasts with the heads of men. A raven wielding a sword of fire rode on a lion, a horse with human hands walked on its hind legs, an old man bearing a staff topped with serpents rode a crocodile. The things moved in the flickering light like marionettes, like the images he'd seen in the moving picture theatres. Somewhere in the back a figure watched him with round golden eyes from beneath a golden crown, and he felt those eyes peering into his soul before he opened his own eyes and stared once again at the ceiling of the boarding house.

He knew in that moment that his job in Kansas City had changed. He wouldn't be bringing these boys back to Gerald Tyson. He'd never been anything more than a jumped-up errand boy his whole life, and he'd never once aspired to much of anything else, but hearing the Lesser Keys play had reminded him that he'd had dreams when he was a boy, and that he'd loved music more than he loved breathing.

Jasper didn't know what kind of music he'd heard that night. He could hardly remember the tune, even as it continued to throb in his bones and in his blood. It wasn't like any music that he'd ever heard before, and he didn't know if it was the music of God or the devil or something in between, but whatever they were doing and however they did it, he knew that it was a miracle, and he'd be damned if he was going to turn that over to a man like Gerald Tyson. He was still going to learn their secret, if it was the last thing he ever did, but now he was doing it for himself alone.

Caroline Bloom had no intention of finding an escort to take her to Solomon King's. She had no doubt that there would be plenty of men there willing to take a few lumps for a decently pretty, unattached girl if the need arose, and she knew how to take care of herself. The Colt in her purse was the only chaperone she needed. Her daddy had made a fortune manufacturing guns, and he'd taught her how to shoot a pistol as soon as she was big enough to hold one. She didn't stop practicing after he died, and by now she could out-shoot any man she'd ever met.

The place itself just looked like a big wood-frame house. It leaned a little bit, like it was worn out, and she was sure that if she saw it in the daytime the paint would be peeling. It sat back from the road, screened mostly by scraggly trees. There was a hand-painted sign and a mailbox on the dirt road. The sign just said "Solomon King's," not the full name of the place. She guessed people just knew that part. Also painted on the sign was a symbol, almost like a signature or a scrawl, but sort of circular. She didn't know what it was.

In front of the house was a graveled-in drive, big and filled with cars. Cars were parked alongside the road, too, for maybe half-a-mile in both directions, and she could hear the music coming out of the building before she even got out of the car.

She got out and sent her driver back to the hotel. She could call him if she needed to, but she figured she'd have no trouble getting a ride home. She said for him to come back at dawn, if he hadn't heard from her.

Inside, Solomon King's Mine didn't look a whole lot more impressive than it had from without. The lights were turned down low, and the main room housed a bar along one wall, and a bunch of tables fitted out with checkered tablecloths and candles that made it look like one of the Italian diners down near the river. Saloon-style swinging doors let into a back kitchen from which the sounds of pots and pans could be heard on the rare occasion when the music and the noise of the patrons died down enough. There was a stage on the far side of the big room, near the stairs that led up to the second story, and a sign above it done in lights that said "The Lesser Keys," though it wasn't illuminated when she came in. An outfit consisting of a pianist, a few horn players, and a fellow on the banjo were playing when she entered, and a space in front of the stage had been cleared of tables and people were dancing.

Segregation obviously wasn't in force here, though the tables still tended to be split up by color. Nobody seemed to get preferential treatment. The men at the best tables were as likely to be black jazz musicians as they were mustachioed white men in double-breasted suits. A few brief chats with men who came up to buy her a drink confirmed what she suspected, that what mattered most in Solomon King's was who had that man's favor, black or white, rich or poor. How exactly that favor was won or lost seemed to be a mystery to most.

Unfortunately, she didn't see Jonathon in the crowd, nor anyone who looked like the actress he'd run off with, Magda Whatsername. She took a seat at the bar, and ordered a drink, content for the time being to wait. She was just raising her glass to her lips when she heard the sound of sirens cutting dully through the din.

Solomon King knew that the police were coming. His enemies in the Order had finally pried the ponderous political machine of Kansas City into action against him. Even now the distant sirens were approaching. He knew that in the club above there would be chaos soon, he didn't need the daemons to show it to him. He could see it if he closed his eyes. The place would explode, the boards would come tumbling down around his patrons. Blood would spill on warped floorboards. He saw men and women trampled in a rush to the exits, he saw the police cars pulling up. There was plenty in the roadhouse that he could be arrested for, now that the protections of Boss Tom's minions were no longer with him. Plenty of legal indiscretions even if they didn't venture down into the caverns and see what he had wrought there. But he didn't panic. In the dim, flickering light of the basement, he even smiled, because he knew that they were too late. They had waited too long to act and now their time was past.

Without rush, savoring each moment, he walked up the basement stairs and into the room where the Lesser Keys waited. The daemons had warned him not to send Magda out first, not this time, and he knew that he didn't need to, that the time for reliance on her was past. He walked around, to each one in turn, and he whispered their instructions in their ears. From their cases they drew their instruments, smooth and sure. In the main room, the last band's final number drew to a close, and in the relative quiet that followed the applause the sound of sirens could be heard, a faint baying from afar. Heads cocked, ears pricked, but before anyone could make a move, Solomon King pushed open the door, and the Lesser Keys took the stage one last time.

Turnaround

There was a growing edge of panic in the air of Solomon King's Mine as the sound of the sirens drew gradually nearer, but all of it ceased when the lights above the stage burst into life. The growing roar of voices hushed, and an eerie silence settled on the whole house. Everyone in the place strained to listen, and the silence seemed to spread outward from the still figures on the little stage until it filled the room, blotting out the distant wailing from outside.

Caroline Bloom sat forward on her barstool, her hand straying unconsciously to the handle of the pistol in her purse. Jasper deWitt stopped leaning against the wall near the exit and turned his eyes to the stage, the matchstick that he'd been absently chewing dropping from his lips. Solomon King stood in the shadowy doorway behind the stage and watched as the ripple spread out across the club's patrons. As one, like puppets all being drawn up by a single cord, the Lesser Keys raised their instruments to their lips, readied their strings for plucking, laid their fingers on the keys of the piano. Solomon King drew a line through the air with his hand, and the first note was played. After that, everything changed.

No official police report was ever filed about the raid on Solomon King's, and of those officers who survived the night, few ever spoke of it except when they had indulged in too much drink, or when they were confessing their sins to their priests, but none of them ever forgot it. How when their cars pulled up to the front doors there was a flash of green light from behind every window, and when they kicked the doors down it was like the shadows inside the roadhouse had come to life. Unnatural things, figures with the heads of beasts, naked men astride crocodiles, things with too many limbs, all dragging the club's patrons into the darkness in the corners. And everyone standing, staring, unable to move, hardly struggling as the terrible things laid hand or claw or hoof on them. And on the stage the band playing on, limned in a green corposant.

The officers were part of the Pendergast machine, and they came knowing that the raid wasn't normal police business. The first ones through the door were armed with Tommy guns, and when they saw what waited for them on the other side, most of them hesitated only a moment before opening fire. There wasn't time for the music to enter them, to stop them and still them, before their bullets started ripping into the crowd.

Darnell Kent was one of the first officers to step into Solomon King's that night. The next morning he was dragged out of the charred wreckage of the roadhouse, badly burnt but still alive. What hair was left on his head had gone from red to completely white. He never spoke again, not about what he saw that night, nor about anything else. And even if he had, he wouldn't have had the words to describe it. Somehow, the press and chaos of the interior of the roadhouse brought him closer to the stage than any other officer, and amid the hail of bullets and the roaring of flames from knocked-over oil lamps, he found himself staring up at the Lesser Keys, who still played in the midst of the chaos. Who played on, even though he had seen bullets tear into them, even though bullets punched through them even as he watched.

He heard their music then, over the roar and the clatter, and the world seemed to freeze, to slow down. He looked up past them, past the green fire that surrounded them, past the ceiling and the rooms on the second floor and past the roof of the house and the clouds overhead and past the night sky and the stars and into something deeper and darker and older than any cave. In the flashes of the muzzle blasts, in the flicker of the flames, he saw something moving there in that darkness, and every thought he had ever had, every word he had ever known, fled his mind forever.

When the Lesser Keys began playing, it was like a switch was flipped. For most of the patrons of Solomon King's Mine, time stopped. They could see individual motes of dust caught in the air, wisps of flame rising up from the lamps. They felt like they could see the notes of the music rising up around the players, and each of them was touched by the music in a way that they had never been touched before. They turned their eyes to the stage, mesmerized.

For Caroline Bloom and Jasper deWitt, the effect was different. A switch still flipped, but the result wasn't a light going out, but one coming on. In that moment, Jasper saw his entire life captured in a prism, a hundred tiny moments in which he had been afraid, stayed his hand, done as he was told. Caroline Bloom saw a hundred paths unwalked, a hundred lives set aside, a hundred desires unpursued. Each one of them remembered suddenly why they had really come to Solomon King's that night, not the reasons they would have given if they had been asked, but the real reason that had driven them. The eye that longed to be pressed to the keyhole of the universe, to hear forbidden sounds and see forbidden sights. Each one of them turned eyes to the stage, not blind, but newly opened, and they saw through the darkness and the smoke, and they learned the secret of the Lesser Keys.

Jonathon Bloom stood on that stage, in white tuxedo and black bowtie. He had always been an indifferent trumpet player, but now he played with a sound that was beyond any human sound, and Caroline saw that it was because he was beyond anything human. His eyes were glassy, his features gray. He was dead, though he walked and stood and played on. Stone dead, as was every man on that stage. Their fingers plucked the strings, danced across the keys. Their lungs worked like bellows to push air through the brass pipes. But they weren't people anymore, they were themselves an instrument, being played by unseen hands.

When the officers burst through the door, when the chatter of the Tommy guns began, Caroline and Jasper were already moving, already pushing past the frozen patrons toward the shadowy doorway behind the stage. They heard the doors come down, heard the gunfire start, heard the crackle of flames. They saw out of the corners of their eyes the hands reaching out of the shadows, the devils come finally to drag the sinners down, but they both knew without having the words that something worse was waiting, and so they didn't turn back.

When the music started, Solomon King turned away from the stage and headed back to the basement stairs. His work up here was done, but there was still more to do. In the cavernous basement all the noise from above was drowned, muffled, and there was only a kind of echoing silence, the sound, he believed, of outer space, or something even further away. The music of the spheres. A humming that filled his bones, that reverberated through the rock itself, that reverberated through this whole miserable world and far beyond it into the dark. A hum that kept him from hearing the footsteps of the two figures that pursued him.

Jasper and Caroline met at the top of the basement stairs, and they didn't say a word to each other. One glance told them both that the other knew enough. Neither of them could really say why they walked down those stairs side-by-side. It was the end result of a lifetime of turning around, for one reason or another. Because they were afraid, because it was expected. At the head of those stairs each one of them realized that they had a choice to make, and that whatever lay at the bottom would change them forever, and they each chose to walk down.

If Solomon King had consulted the daemons that he had at his beck and call, they could have told him the names and the histories of the man and woman who faced him when he turned around. They could have looked into their hearts, and told him what it was that brought them there that night. They could have shown him Jasper, sitting in the church and hearing something more than God in the music. They could have shown him Caroline, huddled around a candle reading ghost stories in bed. But Solomon King didn't ask. He knew his enemies, or thought he did, and when he saw the man and woman come down the stairs, the lady with a gun in her hand, he believed that the Order had sent agents to stop him.

"You're too late," he said, raising his arms in welcome. "You were born too late. My father made me the man I am today more than a hundred years ago, and I unmade him. He taught me everything he knew, and I fed his heart to the devil. Do you think I'm afraid of your gun? Your masters are greedy tyrants who seek to insulate themselves with worldly power. I have seen farther than all of them. No bullet can kill me now."

Caroline raised the gun, but she didn't pull the trigger. Somehow she knew that he wasn't wrong. She could feel the heat draining out of the room, in spite of the fire from up above. She could feel the thrum of buried engines, feel the world turning, feel it hurtling through empty space. She knew that something was happening here that was bigger and stronger than bullets and guns, but still she held onto the pistol, because she had learned over the years to put her trust in steel and in her own aim, and because she didn't know what else to do.

"The ring on his finger," a voice said in Jasper's ear. He didn't have to turn his head to look to know that it was no human voice, and in the sound of the words he could see the face of an enormous owl, a crown on its head. "He took it from a man who took it from one of us. Without it, he is vulnerable."

Jasper remembered his mother's stories about the devil, he remembered the preacher's talk of fire and brimstone, but he also knew that there were worse things than devils in this world, and more than one way to damn yourself. "The ring," he said to the woman beside him, and she raised the gun without questioning him. Solomon King laughed, and she pulled the trigger and two of his fingers were suddenly gone from his hand, and a silver ring struck the cave floor with the sound of a bell, bounced once, and rolled into the oily black pool at the back of the room.

There was no more preamble. From every dark line etched in the floor, from every fold of shadow, figures stepped as if from doorways. A winged thing with the head of a deer, a naked woman astride a camel, a hunter surrounded by horns. They enveloped Solomon King like a flock of crows descending on carrion, and then the cave was empty.

Closing Time

Stories don't ever have endings, not really. They never come to-gether in a way that ties everything up, they never resolve. No wedding, no kiss, not even death ever stops things in their tracks completely. There's no iris out, like in the moving picture theatres. Things just go on, and some things never make sense. Some ques-tions are never answered.

Solomon King's Mine burned to the ground that night. Dozens of bodies were found in the wreckage. Some were identified, some never were. Nine police officers died in the blaze, and no one ever knew how many patrons. In the aftermath, a special detachment explored the catacombs that were found beneath the building. There they uncovered all manner of strange things, including a room full of oblong cabinets, in which reposed the preserved bod-ies of various well-known and influential individuals, among them Magda Gilman. The county coroner determined that most of the bodies had been dead for years, in spite of the fact that many of the individuals had been seen in recent months, out and about, and that Magda Gilman had been heard to perform in Solomon King's Mine the night before. If anything else was found in those caves, it was never reported, and anything that was recovered was placed in underground storage deep beneath the city and forgot-ten.

Caroline Bloom and Jasper deWitt wandered out of a cave

entrance nearly three miles away at half-past-four the following afternoon. They were never connected in any official way with the events at Solomon King's Mine, and neither one of them ever spoke of it, not even to one another. They never revealed what they talked about during their walk through the caves, but it was obvious that some kind of deep connection had been forged in a very short time. They left Kansas City together that night, in Caroline Bloom's sedan. When Caroline returned home she waited the requisite amount of time and then had her brother declared dead *in absentia*. She hired Jasper as her personal valet, though it was known among those close to her that he rarely did much in the way of work, and that he often advised her in matters of business. She provided him a house of his own near the Bloom estate, and he lived there for the rest of this life.

At first, he spent a lot of sleepless nights worrying about Gerald Tyson's wrath, but that wrath never came. What Jasper didn't know was that, on the very night that Solomon King's burned down, Gerald Tyson awoke from a dream in a cold sweat. He dismissed his bodyguards, then killed his mistress with a shotgun and slit his own wrists. He left no explanation behind.

Jasper deWitt's life improved in Caroline Bloom's employ, but he never slept well again. He married eventually, had children and grandchildren, and got to watch them all grow up. He lived to be a very old man. But sometimes at night he would dream, and in his dreams he would rise from his bed and look out the window. On the hilltop outside, he would see the figure of a huge owl with legs like a stork, and on its head was perched a crown. It stared at him with familiar golden eyes, and when he walked out to meet it he heard its voice in his ear again. It told him things that he was pretty sure people weren't meant to know, and he profited by them, but at the end of each dream it would always say the same words to him, and though his life was rich and long, those words would never leave him.

"You will never be rid of us now."

Author's Notes: Originally written for *Jazz Age Cthulhu*, a collection of novelettes and novellas set in the 1920s and edited by Silvia Moreno-Garcia, "The Lesser Keys" may be the most heavily-researched story I have ever written. When the invitation came in, I knew that I wanted to do something based in Kansas City, back when it was still the "Paris of the Plains." To do that, though, I had to learn a lot of details about the city's history, including a few that I didn't get to use in the story.

"The Lesser Keys" just always struck me as a good name for a band, and, from there, the idea of using music to perform Goetic demonology and magic was just a short hop.

GUIGNOL

The house was big and dark and old. It had stood in the same place on the same land since Archibald Patton had it built way back in the day, and every child in the Patton family had been born within its walls. Behind it hung the looming gray shape of the old Patton's Leather Shoes factory, like a mountain rising out of mist. Once, it was the only job in Bowden, and everyone in town had worked there, and every son in the Patton line had taken his turn first as floor manager, and then eventually as owner. Now the factory was closed, sold off to some bigger company that had transferred manufacture to facilities in Thailand.

Donald Patton didn't care, or tried not to. As he drove through town, he tried not to see the shuttered storefronts or the little houses sitting empty, tried not to think about the people who had once lived and worked there. He'd hated Bowden growing up, hated the factory, hated the old house. He still hated it, all of it, a bile in his stomach that time and distance hadn't muted. He tried to believe that everyone else must have hated it all just as much; that he was doing them a favor by selling off the business. That he wasn't killing the town, just putting it out of its misery.

The truth was, he didn't really feel like he had a choice. His legacy was destroying him. The town, the house, the business, all of it. Suffocating him like some ancient and overlarge sweater hauled out of some moldering attic, sweltering and stinking of neglect. Selling the business was a matter of self-preservation, not preference. If it didn't die, then he would.

From the day he had first left home to go to school, every trip back had been a slow death. It reminded him of the feeling he got when he walked into nursing homes and certain wards of certain hospitals. A sense of becoming ossified, of being trapped in amber. The feeling that the next time he walked back out those doors it might somehow already be too late.

He hadn't been back to Bowden since his father's funeral. He'd sold the business remotely, relying on email messages and phone calls and the intercession of a team of attorneys. During his three months as owner of Patton's Leather Shoes—Archibald's idea of humor, and these days largely a misnomer, as only a few of the shoes still used any actual leather—he had never once set foot inside the city limits, let alone the factory walls.

He had hoped to never come back, but now here he was, driving his Lexus through the dreary streets and pulling into the weed-clotted drive of the big, dark house. Elaine had made it sound important in her voice message, saying that she'd found things in the house that might be "of interest to the family." She'd told him that she'd feel more comfortable if he could come back to sign off on their disposition.

Donald had almost told her that he was all that was left of the family, and he didn't care, but he thought better of it. The attorneys of Landau & Clark had been representing the Patton family interests since Archibald hired the original Mr. Clark almost a century ago. Elaine had been with the firm for five years, had been handling the sale of the house and all its contents, and something in the way she had said "of interest" made Donald think that maybe she'd found something more delicate than just a valuable old painting in an upstairs storage space. Like any wealthy and powerful family, Donald knew that his forebears had secrets that were better off being kept, even now that he was the last of the line. So here he was.

The house had always looked to him like a prison or an asylum, all flat walls and narrow windows, and his neglect had done nothing to improve the façade. Though Elaine had kept a few people on the payroll to help keep the place up until it sold, the grounds hadn't been well maintained since before his father's last days and they had gone to riot with almost preternatural speed, as though nature, too long held at bay, was eager to reclaim the house and grounds. The plants along the side of the circle drive were as tall as his waist, huge purple thistle heads nodding lazily as he passed, and the fountain he parked beside was choked with weeds.

Elaine's car was sitting by the front steps, but of her there was no sign. Already inside, he guessed, but when he got out and tried the front door he found it locked. The key was still on his key ring— *not for much longer*, he promised himself—and so he let himself in, calling her name as he went.

He'd met her a few times when she drove up to the city with paperwork for him to sign, had talked to her on the phone more often. He remembered her as a petite woman in her young-looking late thirties, blond hair shot through with brown, wearing glasses with a wide enough rim to make her look serious without appearing too studious.

Inside, the house looked even worse than it had from without. The day was overcast and sinking on toward night, and what little light did manage to seep in through the dusty, thick-paned windows just served to lend the dark interior a submarine quality, making him feel as if he was trapped inside a sinking ship. The outside seemed to press in on the walls with oceanic force, doubling the already claustrophobic atmosphere.

He was reminded instantly of why he hated this place, and he called Elaine's name again, louder and more shrilly than he would have liked, anxious to see whatever he needed to see so that he could get back out to his car and get back on the road, get away from this town and this place and this life that was still clinging to him, still sucking him down like thick mud. But he got no answer, save for the muffled echo of his own voice off the dark wood.

Trudging through the house, passing from room to dim, cob-webbed room like a restless ghost, brought back memories that he'd rather have kept buried. Memories of the last time he had been here, for his father's funeral. His recollections of that day were hazy and scattered already, although only a few months had passed. Mostly, he remembered having to school his features into a furrowed look of grief, to make sure the happiness that he felt stayed off his face as strangers came by to offer him their condolences. It wasn't that he was happy his father was dead, exactly. He hadn't really even known his father, and remembered him primarily as a sort of distant figure, more symbolic than real. He'd been raised mostly by his mother and by a succession of nannies and servants, his father always busy in the factory, or in his workshop up in the attic. At best, his father had been a distant figure seated at the far end of the dining room table at special dinners.

His pleasure at his father's demise had nothing to do with the man himself, and everything to do with what it meant for his future. With the old man's passing, he had felt the last of the fetters that bound him to Bowden and the factory and the house and the family dissolving.

The service had been held in a chapel off the funeral home. It had seemed small to him then, dark and claustrophobic, like the house, like everything in his life. He remembered sitting in the front row, pressed in by black-clad mourners. He remembered the way the wood of the coffin had looked cold to him, sitting in the midst of its bed of flowers, not warm, as the undertaker had described it. Though his father had died in his bed, attended by the best physicians money could summon, the lid of the casket had been closed. There had been no viewing of the corpse; Donald hadn't even seen his father, per some odd stipulation in his will. It made it difficult for the reality of things to sink in. It wasn't until after the burial, when Donald came back to the big house and watched the people covering the furniture in sheets, that he truly felt like his father was gone.

Caught up in the past, it wasn't until he'd already traversed most of the ground floor with no sign of Elaine that he thought to try calling her cell phone. He pulled his own phone out of the pocket of his coat and hit the button to return her call. No one had ever gotten very good reception inside the house, for whatever reason. Something about the pipes, maybe, or was it the wiring? Regardless, all he heard when he held the phone up to his ear was a distant ringing that broke off abruptly with a silly tone and a message of "no signal."

He went upstairs, continuing to occasionally call out Elaine's name, though he felt more and more foolish each time he did so. She was nowhere to be found. He tried her phone a few more times, but none of the calls ever went through. More than once, he considered turning around and leaving, but he remembered her car in the drive, so she must be here, somewhere. He thought about going out to his car to wait, but he knew that he'd feel even more foolish sitting out there, especially as night had fallen beyond the trees. At least he'd kept the electricity to the house turned on, so he didn't have to search in the dark.

By the time the sun was completely gone, he had searched the entire house, except for the attic. He stood at the bottom of the narrow stairs and stared up, delaying his trip. The rest of the house was familiar to him, but the attic was a place he'd virtually never gone. When his father had still been alive it had been off limits, and the couple of times he'd been caught sneaking up the punishments had been severe enough to discourage further attempts.

The attic had been his father's workshop, and where he kept his collection, just as it had been for *his* father and his father's father before him. It seemed that each of the patriarchs of the Patton family had sported an unusual hobby, and the attic had always been the private museum of their obsessions. Each new owner added his own wing to the black museum, and left his predecessor's contributions intact.

There was no light at the top of the stairs, only a small door of dark wood, almost invisible in the gloom; and locked, though the key to it now hung on his key ring as well. He turned it, heard the lock click, and felt a shiver run down his back. Less of what he might find on the other side of the door—he *had* been in the room a couple of times, he knew more-or-less what to expect—and more the childish frisson that came with doing something that he knew was forbidden.

He pushed the door open and groped in the darkness for a light switch. His hand brushed fabric and what felt like bundles of sticks, and then he found the switch and the bulbs in the ceiling fluttered to life, and he had to stifle a gasp.

He'd thought that he had known what to expect, but he'd imagined his father's interest in his peculiar hobby trailing off in his later years, while it looked as if the opposite were true. The room into which he stared was filled with puppets. A forest of puppets, dozens and dozens, hanging from the ceiling and walls in such profusion that he had to push them aside to cross the room. An old king in a fur-lined cloak. A blank-eyed nun in her habit. A skeleton in black armor and a red-painted devil. A magician, his robes embroidered with moons and stars.

Donald's father had collected them since he was a boy, most of them shipped over from Prague and other far-off places. He'd also built them himself, and a few still sat, half-completed, on his workbench on the far side of the room, next to the door. The ones he had collected came in all shapes and sizes, but the ones he built were inevitably marionettes, crudely carved and painted by hand. The tools and supplies for crafting and painting the puppets still lay out on the bench, as if his father had stopped in the midst of work and planned to come back one day, which maybe he had. One jar of paint—deep red, Donald saw—had the lid off and a brush still lying in it, a pool nearby where it had dripped on the table.

Beyond the workbench was another door, and beyond it another room in darkness. Even as he opened the door, Donald knew that Elaine must not be up here, or the door would have been unlocked, the lights turned on. He moved ahead anyway, as if sleepwalking, driven forward by something, maybe just by the lingering remnants of a childhood curiosity to examine the contents of the attic at his leisure. His hand found the switch, and the long, low room flooded with illumination.

His father's hobby had been strange, but his grandfather's and great-grandfather's had been stranger still. When Archibald Patton had the house built, he had already owned a rather significant collection of implements of torture, many of them dating back several hundred years, and his son Reginald had continued the collection and expanded it during his lifetime. Now, the room was filled with racks and stocks, iron maidens and strappados and witch's chairs, some of which had seen use by no less august a company of torturers than the Spanish Inquisition itself.

Donald stood, staring down the long room, his heart thudding heavily in his chest, just as it had when he had come here as a child, though now there was no one left who could punish him for his trespasses. This macabre museum was his now, to use or dispose of as he saw fit. He'd already given orders for all of it to be sold off at auction to collectors or museums or whoever might want it. Just as he hadn't inherited his family's feelings of duty toward the business or the house, he hadn't inherited their attractions to torture dungeons and dolls.

He walked down the length of the room, letting his fingers run over the cold, rough iron of the implements, and only then did he notice that the two collections had begun to develop an odd sort of overlap. Several of his father's puppets were in this room now, placed to mime undergoing the rigors of one device or another. Here the arms and legs of a puppet in jester's attire were wrenched out of place by chains, there a wooden head was slowly crushed to splinters in a vise.

Obviously, his father had gotten a little unstable in his old age. Was this what Elaine had called him about? It seemed sinister, certainly, but nothing that she couldn't have handled on her own.

Thinking of her, Donald reached into his pocket to try calling once more. Maybe the attic would get better reception than the rest of the house. If she didn't answer this time, he resolved to just go back down to his car and drive away. He'd leave her a voice mail saying that he didn't care *what* she'd found, she should just dispose of it according to her best judgment and not trouble him any further. He should never have let her talk him into coming back to this house, and he was just composing his angry retort to her in his mind as he pressed the button to make the call and heard a tinny song start up at the far side of the long room.

His stomach dropped, sudden and heavy. He stood frozen as his mind scrabbled for some logical explanation, but he could find none. The room had been dark when he came up, the attic door locked. If she'd been here already and departed, why would she have left her phone?

Slowly, ever so slowly, he walked down the aisle between the infernal devices. He imagined a hundred dreadful scenarios waiting for him at the other end of the room. Elaine's body broken on one of the machines, dissected into bloody bits straight out of some horror film. Elaine waiting for him in the shadows with a rag of ether and him awakening in one of the devices himself, the culmination of some unknown vendetta against his family; her brother put out of work, her father humiliated, something.

The bright ceiling lights were clustered mainly near the door, and the far end of the gallery was lost to murky shadow. Through a tiny, round window set high in the wall he could see just a corner of the night sky, the undersides of the clouds painted with what little light the town still produced. Below the window, shoved away from the rest of the collection into a place of either pride or distaste, sat a final implement of torture, one for which he didn't know the name. A thing almost akin to an electric chair in size and shape, but differentiated from that more merciful cousin by the terrible array that sprouted from it. A do-it-yourself dentist kit, he might have called the dizzying assembly of blood-stained blades and hooks and screws, had he been in a more jocular frame of mind.

Elaine's phone lay on the floor next to the chair, glowing and buzzing across the floorboards, still emitting its feeble song. And in the chair itself: a manikin, a tiny, perfect puppet. Letting the phone fall from his ear, he used its light to inspect the puppet, his growing unease temporarily pushed aside by his confusion. It had been more than a month since he last saw Elaine in person, but he remembered her features well enough, and he recognized them now in the face that stared back at him with a frozen expression of unmistakable horror.

He ran. There was a bad moment when he pushed into his father's workshop and the dummies seemed to crowd suddenly round him, their wooden hands pulling at his clothes, their eyes accusing. Then he broke through the attic door and stumbled down the steps and away from the gallery of horrors.

His phone was no longer in his hand. He must have dropped it somewhere upstairs, but that didn't matter, because he was too terrified to dial it now anyway. Too afraid that, instead of the police dispatcher, some other voice might speak to him from the other end of the line.

The dash through the house was a blur of dark rooms and sheeted furniture. He didn't stop until he was standing in the living room just off the main entryway. The front door was only a few paces distant, and beyond it his car and the highway and freedom, but he stood frozen in his tracks, alerted by an animal's instinct that something in the room was *wrong*. His eyes traveled slowly across the sheeted forms that dotted the room—any one of which, he suddenly realized, could be anything, a corpse or a murderer or worse—and finally came to rest on the fireplace.

His family crest—which Archibald Patton had brought with

him when he came over from the old country—was inlaid into the stone above the hearth. Standing on the mantel before it were two puppets, like the ones in his father's workshop. They hadn't been there when he passed through before, he was sure of it. One of them looked exactly like his father, the other exactly like his grandfather. They turned their wooden heads toward him, their painted eyes burned into him. Upstairs, the chair waited, with its bloody hooks and screws, and he knew exactly who it waited for.

Author's Notes: I guess I've developed something of a reputation for writing stories that are inspired by unlikely sources, and this one definitely counts. The genesis of "Guignol" comes from one particular scene in Stuart Gordon's delightful (and delightfully out-of-its-time) old dark house flick *Dolls*. In it, one of the film's very British punk rocker girls is being transformed into a doll via a process that is gruesome in ways that the rest of the movie never quite matches. Combine that with my affection for marionettes and, especially, Mike Mignola's drawings of same, and you pretty much arrive at "Guignol," which found its title when I learned that the phrase "Grand Guignol," the name of an early French theatre known for its grisly and horrific plays, roughly translated to "giant puppet."

This is actually one of the oldest stories in this collection, in spite of not seeing print until December of 2015, when it appeared in *The Burning Maiden 2* edited by Greg Kishbaugh.

SHADDERS

T he life of a chimneysweep is hard and dirty and often terrifying and brutally short. One boy I knew surprised a flock of bats in a chimney. Bats like chimneys, for what is a chimney but a cave turned up on its side? I imagine it must have seemed to him as if the darkness suddenly came to life, all beating wings and needle teeth. He fell three stories, and when they pulled him out his bones were all broken and his limbs were like India rubber and he was stone dead.

So it may seem odd that any would choose this life, but for some of us there is no better work to be had, and not all of us have the same choices as others do. My elder brother chose to run off and join the fighting in the desert and never come back, leaving my Gram and me to fend for ourselves. But my Gram didn't choose to develop the cough that more and more often kept her abed and stained her kerchiefs with blood. So my choices were limited accordingly, and one day I cut my hair short and dressed myself in the clothes my brother had left behind so I could pass as a boy, and I apprenticed myself to a chimneysweep. There were worse ways to pay for the food we ate and the laudanum for Gram's cough, and I had never been afraid of the dark, or of small spaces.

These are the traits you need to excel as a chimneysweep: Strong arms and legs. Small stature. Good lungs. No fear of darkness or closeness or great heights. All these things I had, and I found a master in the form of Mr. Stefan.

Mr. Stefan had been a chimneysweep when he was a boy, before he went off to fight in the war in the desert. A different war from the one my brother was fighting, but the same desert. Mr. Stefan had lost his left leg to a cannon, and in its place was a wood and metal contraption that let you always hear him coming: CLANK-step, CLANK-step. And so the boys who stopped to smoke coffin nails instead of sweeping knew to stub them out in time to get back to work.

Mr. Stefan's leg also prevented him from going in the chimneys himself, even the biggest ones. The leg was fine enough to get around on, or so he proclaimed proudly, thumping it with his fist, but it was no good for maneuvering inside a chimney. Still, Mr. Stefan knew his old trade backward and front, and he passed his knowledge on to those of us who served under him.

He was a gruff and hardened man with leathery skin and a big bulbous nose and whiskers as thick and stiff as any chimney brush. A terse master, though sometimes when the work was done he would take pulls from a bottle of watery liquor which he shared with the oldest of the boys and tell us wild stories about the war that were probably only half true. I can't say whether he was better or worse than most masters, for he was the only one I ever served under, but I can say that on those rare occasions when he clapped you on the shoulder and said simply, "Good work," it meant more than a commendation from the Queen herself.

Of the boys who worked under Mr. Stefan, Conner was the biggest, though he was younger than at least two of the others. He liked to push the big boys around, but he was always kind to the smallest ones, and he once gave me a toffee candy rather than eating it himself, so I liked him.

Conner died in one of the chimneys of the old munitions plant, the one we all called the "Cannon Factory." With the war gearing back up, we all had to chip in to what the politicians called the "war effort," which included getting the Cannon Factory back up and running, though it was a task none of us were keen on. The Cannon Factory was what Mr. Stefan called a "bad 'un."

Bad 'uns were places where—for no good reason that you could think of—everything always went wrong. You misplaced your brushes, you lost your footing. Ropes frayed. The chimneys in bad 'uns were always tight, always filled with the hardest soot. After a while, you developed a sixth sense for them, and when you walked into one, you could just tell, a feeling, like someone had walked over your grave, as my Gram would say.

Of all the bad 'uns we ever worked, the Cannon Factory was the worst. Not only was it big and dark and lonesome, but the chimneys were particularly tall and strangely narrow, and they bent at odd angles inside. Toby said that they must have been designed by sadists who hated chimneysweeps. And the soot that collected in them was of the worst kind; enameled black, as hard and shiny and slick as ice.

Devon said that it was because the factory made implements of war. He said it was the sins of war and killing that polluted the air and made the soot so maleficent. Devon was a religiously minded lad, with a silver cross that he wore around his neck and worried at constantly with his thumb, and he talked a lot about things like sin and maleficence.

Conner had another theory. He said that the reason the factory had closed down was because the owner's own son had been killed in the war when one of the cannons made in his father's factory blew up in his face. The father, distraught, hanged himself right there on the factory floor—and Conner would point up at the rafters, as if he knew just which one the man had chosen for the deed. "That's not the worst part, though," Conner would say. "The worst part is, when the workers came the next day, they found his body with its jaw broken, dislocated, his mouth frozen open in a silent scream directed up at Heaven."

As much as Devon liked to talk about sin, Conner liked to tell stories like that—stories about ghosts and murder and bloody bones—but when I asked Mr. Stefan if it was true that a man had killed himself in the Cannon Factory, he just replied, "Best not to think on it."

We all knew that the Cannon Factory had been a bad 'un even before it closed down this most recent time, for whatever reason. Home to an unusual number of accidents and injuries. Young workmen losing fingers, hands, sometimes even their lives to the machines.

My Gram liked ghost stories, too, though she didn't take Conner's macabre glee in them. She was a believer, thought that the dead could come back to right wrongs that had been done to them in life, contact loved ones, avenge murders. She had gone to séances and heard table-rappings, listened to the dead speak through someone else's mouth. I remember when I was very little I asked her what a ghost *was*. I'd learned about the soul by then, from the sermons that Gram took me to on Sunday, but I didn't really understand it.

She had pointed to the fireplace and said, "When a log burns, what becomes of it? It goes away, but where has it gone? Does the fire eat it, or does it *become* the fire? You want to know what a ghost is? A ghost is to a body what the fire is to a log."

I'll admit that it didn't clear the matter up much when I was little, but I had cause to think back on it later.

Conner died on our first day in the Cannon Factory. Normally we worked in pairs, but Conner was a confident boy, and the Cannon Factory had a lot of chimneys. They bristled up out of it like artillery pointed Heavenward, and to make the job go quicker he volunteered to tackle one of the chimneys on his own. When the other boys finished, they banged on the metal door of the furnace. When Conner didn't bang back they assumed that he'd simply finished up early and nipped out.

When he didn't show up for work the next day, Mr. Stefan was visibly concerned, but everyone knew Conner's father was a mean drunk, and we thought maybe Conner was simply lying low someplace. There was a brewery that needed urgent attention that morning, so no one returned to resume work on the Cannon Factory until the next day, when they found Conner's body wedged into one of the turns in the chimney. He must have screamed and screamed to no avail. By the time they dragged his body into the light, his jaw was broken, his mouth stretched open in an unending wail of mute horror.

Though it wasn't the first time one of us had died on the job, it made the Cannon Factory an object of even greater loathsomeness, so that we all trudged back to work even more subdued than we had been previously. I even saw Devon cross himself as he passed into the shadow of the place. We worked through the morning hours uneventfully, and after our first break Nicolas headed up to finish the chimney where Conner had died. Unlucky or not, it had to be cleaned, and as Mr. Stefan always said, "Bad 'uns pay just as good as good 'uns do."

I don't know how long Nicolas was in there before we heard the shout, followed by a dry thump and a resounding clang. We found Nicolas huddled in a corner of the factory floor, as far as he could crawl from the door to the furnace, which he had first shut and latched behind him, though his hands were scraped bloody. His leg was broken and already swelling purple, and Mr. Stefan, who had stayed to oversee the work that day, sent Toby running to fetch a doctor.

"What happened?" Mr. Stefan asked him. "What was it?"

"Shadders," Nicolas said, his way of pronouncing 'shadows,' and "shadders" is all he would say until the doctor arrived and carried him off and, as far as I know, all he has ever said since.

After that, work stopped for a time, and we apprentices sat in the bright sunshine outside the factory and watched while Mr. Stefan had harsh words with a man in a fancy suit who Toby figured must have been the owner of the factory. In the end, Mr. Stefan returned shaking his head. "A job's a job," is all he said, "and we still have ours to do." He told us that no one would be punished for not continuing the work, but that it had to be done, and any of us who stayed on would be paid triple our usual wage.

Most of the boys stayed, though they went to far corners of the factory to work, as far as they could from the chimney where Conner had died. Devon, myself, and a quiet boy named Samuel all volunteered to tackle that chimney together, and we drew matchsticks for who would have to go up inside. Samuel pulled the shortest one, and so he and I climbed up to the roof of the factory while Devon waited at the bottom in case anything went wrong. Samuel tied the rope around his waist and strapped his brushes to his back, and I stood on the ladder leaned against the side of the chimney and let the rope play out as he lowered himself in.

He hadn't gotten far when I heard a strangled noise from inside the chimney, something between a cough and a shout, and the rope pulled tight in my hands. I looked down into the dark mouth of the chimney and called out Samuel's name. In response, the tightness of the rope went slack for a moment, and then it was jerked out of my grip so quickly that it burned my palms.

I nearly fell as the ladder tumbled out from under me, but I was able to save myself by hooking my elbows onto the rim of the chimney. From below I heard sounds like a scuffle, and then I saw something rising up out of the darkness toward me.

The thing was black, blacker than soot, blacker than the inside of the chimney. I thought it was covered in some sort of rough fur, but it was hard to say, since it was just a darker shape in the darkness below. Its head seemed hollow, like a skull, and the only light which let me see it at all spilled out from the round saucers of its eyes and its gaping mouth, which glowed like a carved turnip on All Hallow's, but bright blue. I'd once seen weird sea creatures that glowed in the dark at an exhibition that Gram had taken me to when I was little. They had been a similar color. I couldn't make out the shape of the thing, but it had wings that ended in long fingers with sucking pads that helped it to grip the soot-slicked walls.

It stopped at the edge of the sliver of light which the late afternoon sun cast on the rim of the chimney, and then it turned somehow, its body boneless and rubbery, and it disappeared into the depths of the chimney. Hanging there, I looked around, but couldn't see anybody else up on the parts of the roof that were within my view. I started to shout, when below me, echoing up from somewhere far away, I heard Devon calling out, first Samuel's name, then mine. Then I heard a scream that choked off in a gurgling sound, and I knew I didn't have time to wait for someone to come rescue me. I was too high on the chimney to drop down to the roof safely. I'd turn an ankle or break my legs, then go tumbling off the side into a fall I'd never survive. So instead, I pulled myself up and over, and dropped down into the chimney itself.

Under Mr. Stefan's tutelage, we were told never to go into a chimney without a rope to hold us up. Going in like that was asking to fall, to plunge through the darkness and die or be crippled. But sometimes, when we were in a hurry, we'd forego the rope so we could do the job faster, so that no one had to stand at the top of the chimney and pay it out. Creeping down into the darkness, I was keenly aware of the rope's absence around my waist. I dug my elbows and knees into the sides of the chimney, and worked my way down slowly, pausing every few feet to listen. I heard only ghostly echoes from the factory floor, sounds divorced from words or sense.

When I had crawled down for what felt like forever, my foot touched something in the darkness below me, something that gave softly under my weight. I froze, holding my breath until it ached in my chest, expecting at any moment to feel those long, sucking fingers wrap around my ankle. But nothing happened. After an interminable span, I let out my breath in one huge gust, sucked in another greedy lungful, held it, exhaled more gently, and finally lowered myself down.

In the darkness, I felt what I had touched, and found that it was what must have been Samuel's body. My fingertips touched his face, and found that his mouth was open, his bottom jaw hanging slack, dislocated. I shuddered and considered going back up, but the only thing harder than climbing the rest of the way down through the darkness would be going back up the chimney, and even if I did, I'd be trapped on the rim, waiting for someone to come find me. And what happened if night fell before they did? I had the sense that the sunlight had been all that kept the creature at bay.

So I continued down, squeezing myself past Samuel's body, even though the touch of his skin sent shivers through every part of me. In the distance, I heard a sound that might have been thunder. I prayed that it wasn't, because when I got out of the chimney I desperately needed the sun to still be shining and not obscured by clouds. I crept through the darkness, expecting at every turn to see that blue glow seeping up, but instead it was a different light I saw, the filtered light of the factory floor that came in through the door of the furnace. My feet touched the bottom, sunk deep into piled soot, and I dropped to my hands and knees to crawl out and into the open air again.

The factory floor was not light enough to truly call it light, and the huge machines cast vast pools of shadow. Even so, I saw enough to see that something terrible had happened. As I stepped out of the furnace, I slipped in blood that had pooled there, next to where Devon's body lay ravaged, his mouth formed into a broken scream. In the dim light, the blood looked like a shadow on the floor.

The sounds I had heard as I crept down the chimney were silent now, and I started to move forward, ready to run toward the door of the factory and the sunlight that I saw through the high-set green glass windows. I hadn't taken two steps when the creature came around the edge of the machine and stood in front of me.

It was shaped like a bat, but was as big as me, and it moved like a bat on the ground, though I got the impression that it had never flown and that it never could. Like a malevolent parasol creeping toward me through the gloom. Even here it was so black it was almost invisible, the only light the blue glow that streamed out of its mouth and the sightless sockets of its eyes.

And then there was another one, and then another. From the way they held their heads, I imagined they were scenting for terror or despair. I heard a sound behind me, and for a moment I feared that another creature had rounded the furnace at my back, but then I realized that the sound was familiar. CLANK-step, and then Mr. Stefan was standing beside me. He was carrying a hurricane lantern, which cast a cone of buttery light that seemed woefully dim and small in the gloom of the factory, but was enough to push the creatures back to its edge. In his other hand he held a pistol that he raised and fired, making the sound of thunder I had heard from inside the chimney.

He handed the lantern to me, and motioned me toward the door. As we walked, Mr. Stefan's CLANK-step keeping time behind me, we passed the savaged bodies of the boys, their mouths all bent into yawning circles. The creatures teemed on the edges of the light, but they wouldn't pierce its rim. Then there was a sound from somewhere deeper in the factory, a voice, one of the boys calling out, and Mr. Stefan stopped just one step sooner than I did. A pair of jaws darted out of the darkness and fastened on his wood and metal leg, pulled him down. As he fell his arm flew out and struck the lantern, sent it tumbling from my hands to crash on the floor in a bloom of flame. The fire sent the creatures scuttling back, but the one that had grabbed Mr. Stefan kept its hold, pulled him with it into the shadows. "Go," he barked at me as he vanished. "Run."

And so I ran, without looking back to see the flashes of Mr. Stefan's pistol in the darkness, chased by the sound of thunder until even that sound stopped and I stood, panting in the sunlight while behind me the fire kindled by the lantern continued to grow.

That was my last day as an apprentice chimneysweep, for on that day I gained something which no chimneysweep can possess: a fear of the dark. I walked home as night fell around me, and I found my Gram dead in her chair by the hearth, "carried off," as they say, by her cough. But I also heard a rattling coming from up the chimney, and so I left to fetch the doctor to come round for her body, and it was the last time I ever set foot in our rooms.

The Cannon Factory burned to the ground that night, and I jumped on a steamer ship bound for the Americas, one where oil lamps burned belowdecks at all hours.

I've thought long and hard about all that I saw and heard that day, and I think I know where the creatures came from, what they were: Nicolas' "shadders," Gram's ghosts, whatever was left when the fire claimed the log. Not the spirit, not all of it anyway, but the terror and despair that devoured the spirit in the moment of death. The agony of the worker who died in the cogs, guilt of the father hanging from the beam, the horror of Conner trapped in the darkness alone. Not content with the first spark that gave them life, they reproduced in the darkness by sowing more terror and death.

Were they, as Devon had it, the wages of our own folly and sin? Perhaps, but I think that if it hadn't been the war effort, it would have been something else. There are always people with no other choices, who must labor in the dark places and who sometimes perish there. Progress is an enormous wheel upon which the best and the brightest of us balance, and which is bound to plow the rest of us under. Industry a dazzling light, and those creatures its inevitable shadows.

One day, they tell me we'll have electric lights in every home, on every street. But there will always be places where the light doesn't reach, places where "shadders" can gather, and they will haunt me as long as I live.

Author's Notes: I originally wrote this for a steampunk ghost anthology that ultimately passed on it for not being steampunk enough. They were probably right. It's really more about the nature of ghosts, and the cost of industrialization. I polished it up a few times over the years, but it never found another home. Still, I always rather liked my descriptions of the glowing-eyed, bat-like "shadders," so I kept it around, and I think maybe it finally found the place where it fits.

This is its first time in print.

THE BLUE LIGHT

The Soldier walks toward the City. With every step, his boots kick up little clouds of dust and grit, and sink down past their soles. If a wind were ever to blow here, it would raise a layer of topsoil who-knows-how-deep, but the wind hasn't blown here in a long time. The dust settles on everything, coating it layer-upon-layer. The people have taken to sleeping covered in a thin sheet, and when they wake they shake off a measure of dust before they rise. Those who forget, or throw their sheet aside in the night, wake with the dust thick in their mouths.

It has been this way for as long as the Soldier can remember, but it is getting worse. When he left the City, the dust was a nuisance. He remembers his mother sweeping it from tables and counters, from the mantel, out the front door; and he remembers when she gave it up.

When he walked out of the City—marched, really, alongside countless other men dressed in the same uniforms, carrying the same weapons—the walls were surrounded by graves. There was no room left for burial within the City, and so the boneyards had spilled out into the surrounding countryside. He remembers tall, narrow stones carved with names and dates; now only their rounded tops jut up from the dusty soil, which has risen nearly a pace while he was away.

The City looks shorter than he remembers, not because the towers haven't grown, or because he has, but because the walls are silted in, the dust collected in drifts against the rusting metal. High above him, fans turn slowly, ever-so-slowly, so as not to disturb too much of the dust, pulling in just enough air to ventilate the City and prevent its inhabitants from choking to death.

At the gates, a man in a hat like a stovepipe stares down at him through filmed goggles. With one thumb, the guard reaches up and smudges the dirt around on each of his blue-tinted lenses. "Who goes?" he asks, and the Soldier replies with a name taken from a fallen comrade, on the off chance that his own name has arrived here ahead of him. "Don't mean nothing to me," the gatekeeper replies. "You look like a soldier, though. Did we win?"

The Soldier considers this for a moment, and then shouts back up, "Do we ever?" The guard laughs, but this seems adequate to placate him, and he steps to the side and laboriously turns a crank. Within the wall there is the sound of gears slipping and grinding, slowly turning in some dark, close space. Bits of metal break loose and come tinkling down within the wall, and the Soldier wonders how long it will be before the mechanisms are gone completely, and if the gates will be open or closed when they go.

Finally, at the end of a cacophonous series of mechanical noises, a symphony for stripped gears and rusted chains, a tiny aperture opens in the foot of the wall, allowing a small avalanche of dust to come tumbling inside. It's an underwhelming result, after so much noise, and as the Soldier steps beyond the threshold, he hears the guard shout from above, "Kick the dirt aside, so the door'll go shut!"

The Soldier stands in the shadow of the City and looks down at his boots. The dust behind him is higher than in front, and so he kicks the dust from the doorway into the City, and he walks on as he hears the rumbling, grinding sound of the gate closing behind him.

Inside the City, it is dark everywhere. Lanterns burn in darkened corners, powered by thin filaments that were bright once but are now the orange of banked embers. The people he passes walk hunched forward, even the young, and wear masks of paper and fabric over their mouths. Most were white, but have turned to gray over time. The Soldier pulls up his own bandana to cover the bottom of his face, for while the dust outside the City lay dead on the ground, here it drifts everywhere in the air, stirred by even the ghosts of breezes conjured by the City's enormous fans.

Where people step, the dust rises and swirls, forms miniature clouds before settling once more to the earth. The streets here are all dirt, and they have risen while he was gone, deeper yet than the dust outside the City walls. The lowest level of shops and houses lie buried completely, the tops of their windows and doorways barely showing above the road, creating small sinkholes of dust that seep slowly into their vacant innards. Now and then he sees glittering eyes peering at him from the darkened apertures, and he shivers, partly with revulsion, and partly with memory.

The house that he once shared with his mother sits higher than the others. The last time he was here, he walked down ten steps from the front door to the street. Now he climbs only three. He finds the metal door ajar, and inside the house the dust has gathered in thick hills and hummocks on tables and chairs. His mother sits by the fireplace, which is long extinguished, a mound of dirt lying where the coals would once have burned. Dust has gathered in her lap, in her eyes, in her mouth.

The Soldier turns away. His pockets are heavy, but there is nothing in them that will do him any good here. Still, he reaches into one, and pulls out the Blue Light. He holds it in his hand, his thumb poised upon its switch. He stands there long enough that the dust begins to settle on his arm. Then he pushes the button.

War was hell, and when the Soldier had reached his fill of killing and dying, the heat of the filament gun in his hands, the sour sizzle of cooking flesh, he walked away from battle just as he had walked away from the City so long before. One day, he simply found himself alone, the last man near him—either friend or foe—lay dead in the trench, and all he could see in every direction was smoke. So he turned his feet away from the noise of battle, and he walked until he could breathe fresh air again, until he could see the sky.

Not knowing where else to go, he walked home, back to the City. He knew the way, all he had to do was retrace his steps, though he worried, with every step homeward, that perhaps his desertion would be discovered and there would be a gallows waiting for him when he arrived back at the City. Still, he would choose a gallows over another day in the trench, and so on he walked.

He had traveled for three days and nights when he met the Wizard. The Soldier didn't know what else to call the man, who stood by the side of the road wearing a strange conical hat and a pair of goggles so thick they made him look like a frog. On his back was a series of bulbs and tubes that glowed and flickered in an array of colors, some of which the Soldier had never seen before. Attached to this strange array with a coiled length of wire was a long metal wand, which the Wizard was waving in the air above a hole in the ground as the Soldier approached.

"What's in the hole?" the Soldier asked, and the Wizard glanced up from his arcane calculations, blinking at him from behind lenses as thick and green as the bottles in the apothecary shop.

"Treasure," he said, his voice high and thin. "Treasure the like of which, I'd wager, a poor soldier like yourself has never seen. Treasure enough to make you a king."

"Why would it make *me* a king?" the Soldier asked. "Looks to me like you're the one staking the claim."

The Wizard shook his head. "I'm an old man," he said, reaching down one bony hand to knock on his own knee, as if to illustrate the point. "Far too old for treasures and thrones. No, there's only one thing down there I want, the missing piece that I need to complete my invention. Once that's done, I can die in peace."

"So why don't you go down there and get it?" the Soldier asked.

"I'm an old man," the Wizard repeated. "It's a long climb down, and I fear that I would never make it. What if I were to slip and fall? Then what? I'd lie down there at the bottom of the ladder, just a stone's throw from the completion of my life's ambitions, and starve. No, better to wait up here, wait until some strong young man like yourself comes by. A man who could benefit by what lies beyond, and help me out as well."

The Soldier paced around the hole in the ground. It was as round as a lens, ringed in metal, and the Soldier could just see the top few rungs of a metal ladder reaching down. Alongside it was a metal cover that had been painstakingly pulled aside, bit by bit, and a place where the dust—not as thick here as nearer the City, but thick enough—had been brushed aside. The cover bore writing on it, but not anything that the Soldier could read.

"So what you're proposing," he said, "is that I go down into that hole and bring you back whatever it is you're looking for, and in exchange…"

"You can keep anything else you find," the Wizard said. "Just bring me back the Blue Light."

The Soldier, in his short stint in the army, had grown wise enough to know when he was being taken for a ride, but he was intrigued by the hole, and the Wizard's claims as to its contents, and besides it was better than what he had left behind, and so he agreed. Leaving the old man standing above, he turned on the dim bulbs on the shoulders of his uniform and climbed down into the darkness.

The ladder seemed to extend down forever, and he found himself thinking that the Wizard had probably been wise not to attempt the descent himself. Deeper into the hole, the rungs grew clammy and damp, dampness not being a condition that the Soldier had very frequently encountered in his life. Water was a precious resource in the City, pumped up from wells that burrowed deep beneath the earth, and the moisture that gathered on the rungs of the ladder made the Soldier wonder how far down he had come. The circle of light through which he had entered was just a pinprick above his head when his boot finally stepped off the bottom rung and onto a solid floor.

Looking around, the Soldier saw that he was in a long tunnel made of rough-hewn stone, not metal. At one end, the tunnel had been sealed up, but at the other it branched into three separate chambers. Everything here was damp, and the stones of the floor shone slickly in the feeble light from his shoulder lamps.

Above, the Wizard had warned him of what to expect, at least somewhat. "There are three chambers, each filled with treasure. They are yours for the taking. But at the bottom of the ladder, you will find the Blue Light. So long as it is burning, you will be safe from harm below. Take all that you wish, but bring the Light to me."

The Soldier looked around, and found the Blue Light in a metal niche set in the wall. It looked like it had once been protected by a barrier of glass, though now only jagged shards hung like fangs in a maw. Words were printed on the metal that surrounded the opening, but as on the metal lid above, they were nothing the Soldier could read. Breaking off the remaining bits of glass and stacking them carefully in the palm of his left hand—something told him that he wanted to make as little sound as possible until the Blue Light was burning—he picked up the Wizard's prize in his right glove.

It was small, and not much to look at. Like the pocket lanterns people sometimes carried in the City. Just a short metal tube, closed at both ends, with a blue lens on the top and a button on the side. The Soldier pushed the button, and the Blue Light came to life.

The illumination it created, while brighter than his shoulder lanterns, was ghostly and unpleasant. It made the damp walls of the tunnel seem to slither with invisible life. But the Soldier kept it on, because the Wizard had said it would keep him safe, and while he didn't believe for one moment that the Wizard had his best interests at heart, it would do the old man no good if the Soldier died in this hole without bringing up his prize.

By the unsettling blue glow, the Soldier walked to the arched door of the first chamber. It was so wide that he could not have touched both sides at once, even with his arms extended all the way, and within the chamber he saw the ghost light glitter off of a pile of gems as big as his bed. The gems were the kind that he had seen polished and used to make lenses for the more powerful filament weapons, and he knew that each one of them was worth more than he or his mother had ever earned.

As he stepped into the chamber to fill his pockets, he saw a sudden flicker of movement in the shadows. For a breathless moment, he thought that it was another trick of the Blue Light, but then it resolved itself, a darker shape moving out of the darkness. Its hide seemed polished, like the beetles that he had sometimes seen in his travels, and it glittered with all the colors of the gems that lay piled in its lair. It was as big as a man, but it moved on all fours, claws clicking on the stone floor as it slithered along the wall, a long tail sliding sinuously behind.

Its head was unusually large compared to the rest of its body, and as the Soldier stood frozen it opened its eyes. They were round as saucers and bright as lamps, brighter than any light the Soldier had ever seen, brighter than the lanterns back in the city, or those on his uniform. Brighter than the faded disk of the sun that hung in the dusty sky. They washed the room with white illumination, chasing away the strange shadows conjured by the Blue Light. And the Soldier's blood froze as answering lights appeared behind him.

Slowly he turned, just craning his neck, to see that two other creatures, twins to the first, but each one bigger than the last, crouched in the tunnel behind him. They barely fit into the space he had just passed through, the one too large for him to touch the sides. The biggest of the two was larger than his mother's living room, its head hanging low, its lantern eyes each the size of a door. As he stared at them and they stared back, he saw small variations between them besides their size, though they were obviously all of the same breed. The largest seemed more heavily armored than its

siblings, the plates of its chitinous body less polished. The middle
one seemed almost to be made of metal, and was so dark that its
skin seemed to drink the light.

The Soldier's heart was pounding, his blood roaring in his veins
so that it was all he could hear. With a movement as slow as the
settling dust, the largest of the creatures reached one of its horned
purple-black claws toward him. Its palm was as large as his torso,
and he knew that it could rend him to pieces with the same ease
with which a cat slays a bird. But instead it placed its claw on the
ground, and lowered its head before him in a bow, its lantern eyes
briefly extinguished. As it did so, the other lights went out as well,
and the Soldier looked around to see three monsters, all kneeling
before him, like hounds trained for the hunt.

Slowly, ever so slowly, the Soldier took first one step, then another, sliding past the enormous beasts and out of the chamber of
gems. As he did so they opened their eyes, but made no move to
stop him, following the Blue Light with their luminous gaze.

In that moment, the Soldier knew—or *thought* he knew—the
Wizard's plan. He would wait at the top of the ladder, and the Soldier would bring up the treasure and the Blue Light. The Wizard
would ask only for the Light, saying that the Soldier could keep
the treasure. But now the Soldier knew the secret, that the Light
controlled these creatures somehow. How, the Soldier couldn't say,
perhaps it was the light itself, perhaps some sound the device emit-
ted that only they could hear, like the whistles that had been used
to call the war dogs back in the army. However it worked, as soon
as the Wizard had it, he would sic the beasts upon the Soldier, and
take both treasure and Light for himself.

In the next chamber, the Soldier found more treasure still. In-
gots of precious metals, stacked higher even than the jewels in the
chamber before. The third and final chamber seemed the most
roughly-hewn, with stalactites and other natural rock formations
dripping onto a pile of gemstones larger and more valuable than
those in the chamber before. So the Soldier filled his pockets, all

the while making sure that the Blue Light stayed burning. He even emptied out his army bag so that he could fill it with treasure, leaving behind his spare uniform, helmet, and replacement bulbs and filaments for his weapon and his shoulder lanterns. Then he turned and climbed back up the ladder, leaving the strange creatures in the darkness below. Only when sunlight once again touched his face did he press the button on the side of the Light and let it go out, dropping it into one of his many pockets.

"Did you find it?" the Wizard demanded, before he had half-pulled himself out of the hole. The Soldier nodded and stretched, listening to the crackle of the bones in his neck. "Give it to me," the Wizard's shrill voice called. "I must have it! We had a deal!"

"We did," the Soldier said, his hand on the grip of his filament weapon. Then he pulled the trigger and watched the Wizard die. He'd seen so many die in battle, after all, what was one more? He would not realize until later, as he was trudging toward the city, that even had the Wizard attempted treachery, only one of the creatures could possibly have fit up through the hole in the ground.

Standing in the dusty emptiness of his mother's house, the Soldier pushes the button on the side of the Blue Light. He expects nothing, for he has left the creatures so far behind, out of the sight of the city, and entombed in their strange underground lair, but he has nothing left to lose. The Blue Light makes the flecks of dust that hang in the air look like strange jewels, or tiny fish swimming in a dark ocean. Where it made the damp tunnel threatening, it makes his mother's empty house beautiful. The Soldier feels like he could stand here forever, but he hears the distant screams of men and the sound of rending metal, and then the creatures are breathing outside his mother's door.

He turns, and the smallest of the three creatures is looking in the doorway at him, the lanterns of its eyes bathing him in light. The shoulder of its brother is barely visible below the top of the doorway, and the flank of the largest one is like a wall outside, pulsing with breath.

There is blood on the dusty road where they crouch and wait, for they have spared no one in their rush to reach the Light. The Soldier can look toward the wall, and he will see an uninterrupted avenue of destruction and death, but he doesn't. Instead, he looks up.

All his life, he has heard stories of those who live in the tallest towers of the City. The ones for whom the rest of the populace labors, for whom they fight and die. He has heard that they live in luxury there, above the ever-hanging cloud of dust. That they see sunsets out their windows, and eat fruits and berries raised on the water that is pulled laboriously up from beneath the ground. He has heard that they are kings and princes, and he remembers the Wizard telling him that he would find treasure enough to make himself a king. Perhaps he has, in the gemstones that he now carries, but that road to kingship is a slow one, and he has spent all that remains of his patience. Instead, he swings up onto the back of the middle creature, and, the Blue Light gripped tight in his hand, orders them up the sides of the towers.

Up and up they go, with the Soldier gripping tightly the beetle-like carapace of his mount. The claws of the creatures sink into the metal sides of the towers as easily as a bayonet sinks into flesh, and they haul themselves up with the gait of a lizard. Up and up, past the highest reaches of the City that the Soldier has ever seen. Up into the choking clouds of dust stirred up by the massive fans, and then above them, into the sunlight.

This high up, only a few towers jut metal fingers above the city, like a gauntleted hand that is slowly closing. The creatures climb them easily, leaping dizzyingly from one tower to the next. They pass windows of thick, tinted glass, and on the other side the Soldier can see wilted plants and luxurious furnishings, free from dust. This high up, a wind blows constantly, causing the metal towers to whistle and keen.

Here, huge machines turn day and night, powered by the wind, to generate the power that feeds into the City below, to pull the water up from the deep, deep wells, growing deeper every day. The enormous turbines make a sound like grinding teeth as the creatures climb past them.

At the topmost point of the tallest tower, they find a skylight, and at the Soldier's command the largest of their number punches through it as easily as if it were made of spun sugar. The creatures drop lithely in and land without a sound, their eyes filling the darkness with light. Slowly, the Soldier dismounts.

All his life, he has heard stories of the luxurious life of those who live in the highest towers. It was all that his mother would ever talk about, all that anyone in the City below aspired to. Now he stands in the highest chamber, and looks around him, and sees only decay.

The plush chairs hold mummified skeletons, still draped in their finery. The plants that once grew fruit and berries are long dead, the books that line the walls have grown brittle with age, so that they would crumble to dust if he were to try and read them. The Soldier walks through chamber after chamber, each one immaculate and empty as a tomb, with the beasts always at his heels, their eyes following the Blue Light. Beyond an ornate doorway he finds a massive throne of precious metals, studded with gems that make the ones in his pockets seem petty bits of colored glass. On the throne is nothing more than a pile of dust and bones.

In his rage, the Soldier sends the largest of the creatures out to bring him the ruler of the enemy city. Perhaps he means to put a stop to the war, or merely to vent his anger, even he doesn't know. But when the creature returns days later, it carries only ancient bones and tattered rags, and the Soldier laughs, alone in his tower, above a City where the people move to and fro like ghosts, in the service of the dead.

Beneath its choking cloud of dust, the City labors on, as bit by bit it falls apart. Gears continue to turn and grind in darkness, water continues to be pulled up from the deepest wells. In some far off field, men fight and die for reasons that they have long forgotten or never knew. The dust buries the city deeper and deeper every day.

But the people who live in its shadows tell different stories than the ones they told before. Stories of a day when monsters tore open the gates of the City and scaled its towers. They say that the monsters carried a new king to the highest throne, and that he rules there now, the three great beasts crouched at his feet. They say that his charges will bring him anything he might desire, and little children are made to behave with warnings that they might one day be carried off by the king's creatures.

What the stories don't tell is that the king rules alone, his only companion a gnawing fear, as he waits with dread for the day when the Blue Light will eventually burn out.

Author's Notes: When I was invited to submit a story for an anthology of retellings of fairy tales through "the language of our own post-industrial mythology," I knew that it would be a stretch outside my usual comfort zone. However, I was told that I could pick my own fairy tale, and my wife Grace suggested "The Tinderbox," by Hans Christian Andersen, which had always been one of my favorites. I read it when I was a kid and the image of the huge dogs with their saucer eyes had always haunted me.

The title and form of this particular story came about as I was researching "The Tinderbox" and learned that it was one of a handful of similar folk legends, categorized in the Aarne-Thompson classification system as "type 562: The Spirit in the Blue Light." I then tracked down the other stories under this classification and pulled in bits from all of them to put this story together.

It was written for an anthology called *Beauty and Ruin*, which, at the time of this writing, still hasn't seen print, but editor Josh Finney was kind enough to release me to include it here, anyway.

A CIRCLE THAT EVER RETURNETH IN

As you sit at your usual table in a dark corner of the Jeweled Remora in Lankhende, greatest metropolis in the West, you spy three unusual figures making their way into the establishment: a Sell-Sword, a Cutpurse, and a Doll Mage, by the look of them. They order their drinks and take a table near the hearth, though it is the Year of the Fly and the night outside is sticky and close. Perhaps they hope to disguise their voices with the crackling of the fire, for they are holding what appears to be an animated conversation, but one that their hunched postures and furtive glances show that they would rather not share with outsiders.

You are not just any outsider, however, and Nathor of the Guild once said that your ears were keen enough to detect a flea breaking wind. You edge closer and cock one of those impressive ears toward their conversation. You are not disappointed.

They speak of a treasure, a jewel. They call it something that sounds like the "Shining Trapezohedron," but you're unsure what kind of stone Trapezohedron is, so it's possible that you may have misheard. Regardless, it sounds quite rare and, as rare things are, quite valuable. It seems that each of the three possesses one portion of a riddle, map, or clue meant to lead them to the jewel, but there is some disagreement as to how these tidbits should be shared. Each one believes their portion to be the most pertinent and therefore of the most value, which in turn should, to their thinking, award them the greatest share of the bounty.

Fortunately, before the conversation can turn violent enough to draw the attention of the entire tavern, the Sell-Sword dashes her drink to the floor, calls her compatriots some choice epithets, and all three of them angrily go their separate ways. Sensing a rare opportunity, you slip out of the Jeweled Remora and into the smoky streets of Lankhende after them.

If you follow the Sell-Sword, refer to passage I.
If you follow the Cutpurse, refer to passage II.
If you follow the Doll Mage, refer to passage III.

I

The Sell-Sword has made her camp in the swampy mangrove forests that surround the walls of Lankhende. Though you keep a safe distance and stay in the shadows, still she must detect you, for she stiffens and places her hand on the sword at her hip as she calls you out. Knowing when you're fairly caught, you step out with your palms held toward her, to show that you're unarmed. "You don't look like much, and you came alone," she says. "You're either very brave, or very foolish."

"Any reason I can't be a bit of both?" you ask.

After digesting that for a moment, she laughs a surprisingly unguarded laugh and tells you to start a fire while you explain why you're following her. Once a couple of lizard-bats are roasting over the embers, you tell her that you know she seeks the Shining Trapezohedron—saying a silent prayer to all the gods of Lankhende that you pronounce it correctly—and that you know of someone who can help her to find it, if she's interested in sharing the wealth.

She is, and she tells you her name is Vlana. You tell her your name, and lead her to the lair of the Seer with Many Faces, in a ruined temple high atop Mount Grond, the strange lone peak that stands to the south of Lankhende.

At first glance, the Seer appears to be a statue of greenish stone that sits atop a raised dais, human in shape but with numerous arms radiating out from the trunk of its body, its head carved with faces on three sides, the one turned toward you as you enter contemplative, serene. Each of its many arms has an upturned palm, and in each hand rests some strange object: a golden carving of the sun, the skull of a bird, a trio of ordinary pebbles.

Seeing that you haven't completely misled her, Vlana places before the Seer a scrap of faded leather or hide onto which someone has drawn—or more likely tattooed, for on closer inspection the scrap appears to be of flayed skin—a portion of a map. For a moment there is silence in the temple, and then there is a sound like the grinding of ancient machinery, a loud clank that is equal parts metal and stone, and the Seer moves, each arm switching positions slightly, and the head atop its trunk rotating so that a façade of terror is suddenly presented to you.

"I know what it is you would seek," the Seer says, its voice an echo coming from somewhere deep in a cave, "and on your life I warn you to turn back."

Neither you nor Vlana can be dissuaded, and the Seer seems to sense it, for there is another grinding clank, another repositioning of arms and head, and now the visage that faces you is a mask of wrath. "Then go, but fairly warned. Your path will take you through the city of ghouls, to the throne of the Yellow King. There you will find your prize, and though you will return to Lankhende time and again, it will not be in your grasp."

The road to Ghulende is a long one, and on the way Vlana teaches you the art of the sword. Her own blade is longer and of finer craftsmanship than the short one which hangs on your belt. She tells you that it is named Heartseeker, and that she forged it herself, as all warriors of her tribe must do before they can truly enter into adulthood.

As you draw nearer to Ghulende, the land becomes dryer, the trees short and dead and twisted. Gravestones line the road on every side, canting off at odd angles. They are memorials from every era of the world's history, and every nation with which you are familiar—and many with which you aren't—and you wonder if they're drawn to Ghulende like iron to a lodestone.

The city itself looks as if some great metropolis like Lankhende was dashed to pieces by a giant hand. Gone are the cyclopean walls, the towering buildings with their many windows for trysts and burglaries. Here the walls lie in rubble, the towers rise a few stories and then terminate abruptly. It is a ruin, and what better place than a ruin for ghouls to dwell.

You have never seen a ghoul, though the old ladies in your village told you tales of them when you were a child. They were said to have skin and organs so translucent as to be virtually invisible, so that they appeared as living skeletons. They were also said to eat only human flesh, and that while they were generally content to feast upon the dead—for dead flesh was considered by ghouls the more succulent—they were more than happy to render living flesh dead, should the opportunity arise.

Before you have a chance to ask Vlana if *she* has ever seen a ghoul, you are suddenly presented, from every rubble-strewn alley and leaning doorway, vivid evidence of the truth of your elders' tales. At a glance, the ghouls that surround you, clutching in their bony fists odd weapons of blackened iron, would look exactly like human skeletons up and wandering about. The only thing to mark them out—besides their ambulation—is that instead of the white ivory shine of human bone, their skeletons are the green of tarnished copper.

One near the front of the pack barks something at you in what you assume must be Ghulese, but to you is simply nonsense. You glance at Vlana, but while she registers no more comprehension of the words than you do, she seems to understand the situation perfectly, for Heartseeker is already in her hand.

If you stand and fight, refer to passage IV.
If you turn tail and run, refer to passage VII.

II

Though you believed that you knew Lankhende like the palm of your hand, no sooner are you out the door of the Jeweled Remora than you've lost the trail of the Cutpurse. You duck into a dark alley to collect your thoughts, when you feel the cold kiss of a dagger pressed to your neck.

"Give me one good reason why I shouldn't slice your throat," the Cutpurse says from behind you.

You tell her enough to convince her that you know what she's looking for and can help her get it, and she agrees to take you with her. She says that her name is Samanda, and that she has in her possession a clue that tells her where to seek the Shining Trapezohedron. There's only one catch: in order to reach her destination, she has to travel to the bottom of the Western Sea.

You lead her to the strange hut of the Seer with Many Faces, built high in a tall tree in the swampy forests that surround Lankhende, accessible only by climbing a series of rickety platforms. As you both scale the trunk, you marvel at Samanda's agility, her sure-footedness never wavering once, even as you ascend the highest and most precarious ledges.

The Seer sits in the dark, where an owl, a bat, and a toad also crouch. Shrouded from head-to-foot in tattered robes that prevent you from seeing what sort of body it might possess, the only defining traits of the Seer are its iron claws and the masks which float in a circle around its hooded face. They pass before it in a slow dance, first one and then another, now the snarling face of a devil, now the leering expression of a lecherous old man, now the innocent visage of a child. When you tell the Seer what you seek, a voice speaks to you from the mouth of the owl. "You should return to Lankhende," the voice says. Then, another voice speaks from the lips of the toad, "No good will come of what you seek."

But neither you nor Samanda can be dissuaded, and the Seer seems to know this immediately, this time speaking from the mouth of the bat, "If you insist upon pursuing your quest, then you will need a way to survive the ocean floor. Take these two stones," and one of the iron claws reaches out, presenting two unremarkable-looking pebbles, "and hold them in your mouth. So long as you have them, you will have no need to breathe at all. But I warn you, lose them for even a moment, and *you* will be lost."

Before you step into the ocean, you each pop one of the pebbles into your mouth and try to hold your breath but realize immediately that, just as the Seer promised, you no longer feel the need to breathe at all. Your lungs no longer inflate and deflate, you no longer feel any tightness or pressure in your chest. You simply *are*.

It also doesn't take you long to realize that you can't speak well with the stones in your mouth, so you go over the plan then and there. Samanda tells you that the Shining Trapezohedron is guarded by an entity known as the Yellow King, "Maybe a man, maybe a monster, possibly a god, but certainly something that we can rob."

As you step into the sea, the water feels cold and briny around you until you are completely submerged and then, suddenly, it is as if the water isn't there at all. The temperature turns normal, your movements no longer sluggish, and you silently thank the Seer with Many Faces for its intervention on your behalf, though past experience has taught you that such intervention seldom comes without a price.

The bottom of the ocean is a remarkably beautiful place, more verdant and strange than any non-aquatic garden. You pass coral reefs as vibrant as any flower, tenanted by fish and eels and squid in every color of the rainbow. As the ocean floor drops away from the land, translucent serpents and fish that glow with their own inner light swim by you in the depths.

Finally, at the bottom of the sea, you come to a sunken city. It is a nameless place, built before men, and its massive carvings show cephalopods and crustaceans and things with the heads of dolphins. The steps you ascend to its shattered columns are larger than any steps humans would ever have carved.

At the top you find yourselves in broad and strangely-angled avenues, now covered over by barnacles and other sea growths. Ahead of you, what looked to be paving stones suddenly rise up and skitter forward on spindly legs. Enormous blue crabs with eyes that glow in the dim sea bottom, their pincers poised for destruction. One of them rises up near Samanda, reaching out toward her with its gargantuan claw, and you have to make a decision.

If you go to her aid, refer to passage V.

If you leave her to her fate, refer to passage VIII.

III

The Doll Mage spends the night in Lankhende before leaving the city alone the next morning, without contracting any mercenaries or bodyguards to assist in her journey.

You trail her for most of the next day, and it is only as night begins to fall that you suddenly feel the strange sensation, the invisible tugging that seems to come from within your muscles. Once, you had a wound stitched up by a barber after a particularly fierce battle, and though pain and booze had numbed your senses, you still had been able to feel the tugging as the thread was pulled tight. This feels like that, and you realize that you can no longer move. Then you *do* move, but not at all in the way that you had intended.

Your motions jerky, you stand up, step out of your hiding place, and walk out to where the Doll Mage has made her camp. She sits, smiling up at you pleasantly. "I know you've been following me since the Jeweled Remora," she says, "but you seemed capable enough at it, and I thought you might prove useful."

You see that she is holding a doll, a tiny effigy of cloth and wax, and you notice with a start that it looks like you. "I'll give you leave to talk," she says, "so that you can tell me whether you'd like to assist me by choice, or if we'll do this the other way."

She pulls out a black stitch from across the doll's mouth, and suddenly you find your voice. You tell her that you'll happily help her of your own volition, especially now that you know the alternative.

She tells you that her name is Ivrian, and that she has the first part of a riddle that is supposed to help guide her to the Shining Trapezohedron: "A destination that few men seek." You take her to cave of the Seer of Many Faces, the only person you know of—if person it can indeed be called—who may know the rest. The cave is long and damp, and at the back of it the Seer waits in a chair that seems to have grown up from the stone of the cave itself. The Seer appears to have been formed from shadow or tar. Only its face is visible, and that is a mirror, in which each supplicant sees only herself.

"A destination that few men seek," the Seer says, "but that all men find. That is your riddle, and the answer is death, for death is what awaits you if you persist in your folly—but only for the lucky among you, for the riddle is itself a lie, and in the lie is the answer you desire. For some unlucky few, death is a destination that is never found, and they persist forever in something worse than death. If you go to where those unfortunate souls languish, you will find your prize, but I warn you against it, for the pursuit will cost you dearly, and success more dearly still."

But neither of you can be dissuaded, and from the Seer's cryptic remarks Ivrian discerns where you must head: The Forbidden Plateau.

The journey is long, and on the way she explains to you the nature of her magic, teaching you how to make the effigies of wax and cloth. "We are all just puppets, really," she tells you, "dancing on something's strings. Our passions, our desires, the burdens that we carry. A doll mage simply learns how to pluck those strings."

The Forbidden Plateau waits at the top of three thousand nine hundred and ninety-nine steps; a place that grows thick with fungus and mushrooms the like of which you have never seen. Huge beds of fungus, in purples and blues and greens, mushrooms that stretch up taller than trees, raining down glittering spores from the gills on their undersides. At first it is beautiful, until you notice the bodies, dozens upon dozens of corpses lying amidst the fungus, with fungus grown up around and through them, mushrooms sprouting from their eyes, their mouths. The bodies of all those who have visited the Plateau before you.

Before you arrived, Ivrian warned you that you must not eat even a bite. "Once you eat of the fungus," she told you, "you do not die, but you also no longer live. The fungus becomes your body, and only your bones remain."

As you pick your way carefully among the fruiting bodies, toward the far end of the Plateau where a distant temple waits, you find your stomach growling. The fungus looks so delicious, and in spite of the evidence of your eyes, you can't quite believe Ivrian's story. One bite, after all, could never do so much harm.

If you eat of the fungus, refer to passage VI.

If you refrain, refer to passage IX.

IV

Over the course of your travels, Vlana has impressed you with her skill with a blade, and you assume that your best chance of survival is at her side. You draw your own shorter sword and stand back-to-back as the ghouls surround you. The one who previously spoke barks something else in Ghulese, and Vlana shouts back at him a choice insult about his parentage. Then, in one quick motion, she steps forward and severs his bony head from his shoulders.

It is an odd sight, to watch the ghoul's head come off. Because the muscles and tendons that connect the bone are invisible, it is like watching the sword part air, and then the skull seems to simply decide that it no longer has any interest in the body, and rolls away. The blood of the ghouls must be as transparent as their flesh, for there is no visible spray. The body simply stumbles, and then falls to the ground.

"They can be killed!" Vlana shouts, and then the battle is joined.

You fight as swiftly and as fiercely as you know how, your sword arm improved by Vlana's schooling over the recent days. But you are nothing compared to her. She carves through the ghouls like a shark through minnows. Heartseeker flashes, and bony limbs and skulls leap free of their bondage and scatter across the ground.

Unfortunately, you haven't the leisure to sit back and admire Vlana's handiwork. Two ghouls approach you at the same time, wielding wickedly hooked blades. You parry each one, but they force you back, until you feel a column against your backside. With nothing else left to do, you duck, and the ghoul's black blade bites into the column above your head while you stick your sword into the invisible guts of your other opponent, snatching up his weapon even as it slips from bony fingers. The metal tingles under your grasp, but still you use it to slice the throat of your other foe, and you feel a spray of cold blood strike your face, though you cannot see it.

Panting, you turn back to Vlana, and you see only a street strewn with the dead, though it is difficult indeed to tell a dead ghoul from a live one, except by the places where they've been hacked to pieces. Casting about, you spot Vlana, lying where she has fallen, pierced through and through with various ghoulish weapons. You walk over to her body, but she is already gone. There is nothing left for you but to heft Heartseeker and continue on through Ghulende to the throne of the Yellow King.

The throne isn't difficult to find. It stands at the far end of the city, alone on a raised platform next to a vast black chasm which splits open the earth. You encounter no other ghoulish interference, and when you reach the throne, you have no doubt at all that you've arrived at the right place.

The Yellow King himself looks at home among the ghouls who

make up his court. He appears as a plague corpse, wrapped head-to-foot in winding sheets, with a crown of candles upon his brow. In his left hand he holds a scepter, topped with an object that can only be the Shining Trapezohedron. The gem is nearly black in color, striated with bands of red, and as you gaze at it the world seems to tilt beneath you for a moment before you pull your eyes away.

With Heartseeker in your hand, you feel braver than you otherwise might, and you advance on the Yellow King with your shoulders back, your head high. It is difficult to make out any expression on the corpse-gaunt face, but it seems to you that he smiles as you approach.

He doesn't speak, but simply holds out the scepter, offering you the stone. You sense a trap, but you have little fear of this gaunt creature after those you have just faced, and Vlana's sword in your hand steels you. You reach out and take the stone from the scepter, and even as you do the Yellow King seems to wither further, his bones turning to dust, his flesh crumpling inward, until only the winding sheet is left, and then even it blows away into the chasm.

You have attained your goal, and the Shining Trapezohedron is now in your grasp, but even as you touch it you feel seized by a compulsion at once to gaze into it and to cast it into the abyss.

If you cast the Shining Trapezohedron away, refer to passage X.

If you gaze into the Shining Trapezohedron, refer to passage XI.

V

You'll need Samanda to retrieve the stone, and as you interpose yourself between her and the crab, she nods to you and slips to the side, making her way down the boulevard and toward the center of the aquatic city. The claw that was meant for her you block with your sword, but there are other crabs rising up all around. Without thinking, you open your mouth to call out for her help, and the ocean rushes in. You snap your jaws closed, tasting the brine of deep sea water.

At the other end of the street, Samanda's ankle is caught in the grip of a gigantic crab. Desperately, you bat at the claws that surround you with your blade, but they are too many. As you fight for your life, you see the magic pebble slip out of Samanda's mouth and drift away through the water, you see her body go limp as she floats instead of falling, the water once more granted its power over her.

As the crabs close around you, you wonder if drowning would perhaps be a more pleasant end than the one that you face, but unfortunately for you, you aren't given the choice.

You have died.

VI

When Ivrian isn't looking, you break off a piece of the fungus and pop it into your mouth. The moment you do so, you wonder why you waited so long. It is the most exquisite flavor you have ever tasted.

By the time Ivrian realizes what you've done and comes to stop you, you hardly notice that she is even there. You try to explain to her, around mouthfuls of fungus, that you have never before known happiness. You hold the fungus out to her, and she strikes it away, and you're only distantly surprised to see part of your hand break off with it. Ivrian is surprised though, or disgusted, or maybe terrified. You find it hard to tell what her expressions mean anymore, but she flees. Still, you are untroubled. You know that she won't get far. You are the Plateau now, the fungal beds that spread across its entire length and breadth, and those like you won't ever let her reach the Yellow King.

You lie back in contentment, as you feel the hyphae begin to grow through you. It will be a long time now before the pain begins, and longer still before it ever stops.

You haven't died, but you'll soon wish that you had.

VII

Deciding that discretion is the better part of valor, you hope that you can make your way to the throne of the Yellow King while the ghouls are busy digesting Vlana. As she rushes into battle, you turn and dart between two verdigris-colored skeletons and into a dark alleyway.

The alley you have chosen for your escape leans perilously, and once you're inside it you find that it is plagued with sudden switchbacks, so that in no time at all you've lost your way. The fog causes the sounds of clashing steel to echo and reecho, sounding at every moment like they are just around the next bend, or over the next wall.

As the sounds of conflict fade, you take a few tentative steps forward, and peer out from a ruined archway. Before you, the fog discloses a grisly scene. Several ghouls lie strewn about the street, looking no different in death than they did in life, but the vast majority of the throng are gathered in the center of the road, tearing pieces from Vlana's fallen body. Apparently, your flight has taken you in a circle and returned you back again to the place from whence you departed.

Heartseeker has fallen from Vlana's grasp and lies outside the ring of feeding ghouls, and you step forward to lift it, but even as you do you feel a clammy hand fasten around your wrist, and the ghouls who were waiting on either side of the archway are suddenly upon you, pressing you to the ground, their cold teeth sinking into your warm flesh.

You have died.

VIII

As more and more of the enormous crabs rise from the city streets, you realize that you didn't sign on for this. You'd apologize to

Samanda if you could, but your mouth is full of magic rock. Even as you dart past her, the claw of the enormous crab fastens around her waist, and the pebble is squeezed from her mouth. You take comfort in the knowledge that she'll probably drown before the crabs can tear her apart.

The crabs are surprisingly quick for such huge beasts, and several times you have to deflect snapping claws with the blade of your sword. At the end of the lane, a creature so massive that it makes its brethren look regular-sized rises up before you, the entire end of the street yawning upward into a gargantuan blue carapace. Your blade licks out and slices off a wavering eye-stalk, and then you're stepping atop the monster even as it levers itself upward, and using its height to boost you onto the avenue above.

You find yourself in a broad thoroughfare lined with cyclopean pillars that must have once reached to the heavens, if this city ever existed above the waves. At its far end, you see the gates of some temple or fane. As you pass through, you discover that the interior is not an interior at all, but that some ancient cataclysm has rent the building, destroying the roof and bringing down most of the walls, so that the temple is now open to the sea and to a massive chasm that splits the sea bed behind it. Here you find the throne of the Yellow King, and the King himself asleep upon it. Samanda was right when she hypothesized that the King might not be a man. What lies upon the throne is an enormous worm, fat as a maggot, its yellow flesh the color of infection.

Next to the throne is a heap of gold and jewels, and atop the heap the treasure that you seek, what can only be the Shining Tra-pezohedron. Black and shot through with red, it seems to call out to you, and you slip noiselessly across the temple floor toward your prize. You had believed that you might need Samanda's skills to steal the stone, but it seems now that you may be stealthy enough after all, and you reach the pile of treasure without the King so much as stirring.

You reach out one shaking hand, close your fist around the

Trapezohedron, and as you do so, you hear a sound behind you, a sound out of place in the soundless depths of the ocean. You turn, and you see that the worm that is the Yellow King terminates in a human face, and that face is directing its mocking laughter at you, and you realize that, while you've gotten what you came for, you've also fallen into a trap.

If you cast the Shining Trapezohedron away, refer to passage X.

If you gaze into the Shining Trapezohedron, refer to passage XI.

IX

You fight the unnatural pull of the mushrooms that surround you, and follow Ivrian through the strange fields of the Plateau. As you near the temple steps, however, you notice that the fungus seems to have shifted slightly. Each time you look away, the topography has changed when you look back. Before you can point the phenomenon out to Ivrian, one of the corpses tears itself free from its fungal bed and lunges at you. Your sword comes up and slices off an arm. The sensation is oddly repellent, not the clean bite of a normal blade cutting normal flesh.

All around you, the bodies within the fungus are rising up. Mushrooms in vivid blues and greens and purples burst from their bodies as they clamber, shamble, or even crawl toward you, and you know, even as you try to fend them off, that the fungus is what controls them, what makes them move, and that gives you an idea.

"Ivrian," you shout, "their bones are still intact!"

And she, to her credit, sees what you mean immediately, plucks a fingerbone from the putrefying mass of the arm you just hacked off, and from it begins fashioning a hasty doll. In moments, one of the fungus people is fighting at your side, and shortly thereafter, another has joined it, and then another.

The creatures are not formidable in combat, too slow and too soft, but they cannot be slain as any living foe can, by cutting off a head or stopping a heart. No matter what you do to them they keep coming, and even with your reinforcements, you know that you won't last long. You turn to Ivrian, to tell her that one of you has to make it to the temple, just in time to see two of the creatures hauling her down. You slash at them, reducing them to quivering masses, but by the time you reach her it's too late, she has already swallowed the fungus they jammed in her mouth.

She presses half-made dolls into your hands and tells you to go to the temple, that she'll hold them off as long as she can. You consider trying to argue, but already her skin is taking on an unhealthy grayish tinge, and so you take the dolls and run.

The temple steps flash under your feet, and you don't stop until you are beyond its golden doors, and those doors shut firmly behind you. You see that the temple is only a façade, that within it is open to the elements, and the back "wall" of the chamber not a wall but a cliff that drops off into a gorge that seems to go down forever. Between you and the cliff there sits a golden throne, and upon it reclines the fattest man you have ever seen. His flesh hangs over itself in massive folds, like an avalanche of a person, a mountain of flesh that cascades ever down and down. Covering his face is a mask of yellow silk, and to each side of him stand guardians in golden masks, holding curved golden swords. In one of his massive hands, he holds what must be the Shining Trapezohedron, a black stone striated with red that seems to pull you toward it.

The Yellow King holds out the stone, as though inviting you to come take it, but as you start to move forward so too do his twin guards. You glance down at the sword in your hand, and then at the dolls that Ivrian gave you. Hastily you begin shaping one of the dolls, pressing into its face a piece of gold prized from the door at your back. You hear the footsteps of the guards coming closer, and you use the doll as Ivrian taught you. When you look up, one of the guards has turned stiffly, and cut the other down.

You smile in triumph as the guard whose strings you now hold turns and advances on his former master, and the Yellow King is silent even as the guard cuts off his hand so that the Trapezohedron rolls free. It is only as you pick it up that you realize why this came to you so easily. The moment you touch the stone, you feel its power, feel it drawing your gaze, gathering up your strings as readily as Ivrian ever did, and you realize that you are the puppet, and that you always were.

If you cast the Shining Trapezohedron away, refer to passage X.
If you gaze into the Shining Trapezohedron, refer to passage XI.

X

Realizing that the Shining Trapezohedron is something more than a jewel, some cursed and terrible artifact that can bring you only doom, you raise your arm to cast it into the chasm behind the Yellow King's throne. At least, you intend to. But while the signal races from your mind, it never seems to reach your hand, which stays where it is, gripping the stone tightly.

You understand that you are no longer in control of yourself. That you are a puppet, being pulled by strings which you cannot see or imagine. Though your will screams against it, you turn your gaze toward the stone in your hand.

Refer to passage XI.

XI

You cannot resist the pull of the stone, and inside the Shining Trapezohedron you see at first only swirling clouds of red and black. Then the clouds part and you are looking into the past and the future. You see yourself entering the Jeweled Remora in Lankhende, taking a table near the hearth in spite of the heat and closeness of the night. There you meet with your companions, and you speak of your quest for the jewel. You keep your voices lowered, but a stranger watches you avidly from the shadows.

From the depths of the stone, you hear a voice at once strange and familiar, reciting a rhyme that stirs dim memories that seem to come from another life: "... and much of Madness, and more of Sin, and Horror the soul of the plot."

Author's Notes: Even before I received the invitation from Jesse Bullington and Molly Tanzer to contribute a story to *Swords v Cthulhu*, I was already embroiled in an online discussion about how difficult it was to do anything new with the meeting place between Lovecraftian mythos and sword-and-sorcery, given that the two have been cross-pollinating since at least the days of Robert E. Howard. I had previously written a very brief little confection on the theme for *Sword & Mythos*, edited by Silvia Moreno-Garcia and Paula R. Stiles, but for this I wanted to try my hand at something robust.

I knew that I wanted my primary inspirations to be Fritz Leiber's Fafhrd and the Gray Mouser tales, which remain probably my favorite sword-and-sorcery stories, but I wasn't sure how to avoid producing just another flat pastiche until I finally landed on the idea of doing a choose-your-own-adventure-type story. But a proper choose-your-own-adventure tale, complete with good endings and bad ones, didn't feel quite right for a Lovecraft anthology. So I took a few pages from Poe, and the result was a choose-your-own-adventure where even the best paths didn't lead anywhere very pleasant—or maybe much of anywhere at all.

PROGRAMMED TO RECEIVE

1. The Tower

When Kelly is a little girl, the Tower is right next to her bedroom window. With the purple curtains open, it becomes her nightlight, and she lies in bed staring up at it and the stars beyond.

Her dad was one of the men who helped build it, and now he watches over it. That's what he says, the words he uses. He likes to tell her about the Tower, to point up at it and explain that it's one of the most powerful broadcast towers this side of the Mississippi. When she asks him what it broadcasts, he just says, "Honey, this thing could send a signal all the way to outer space!"

Kelly has an imaginary friend who lives at the top of the tower. At least, that's what her mother says, "imaginary." Her mother says that when *she* was a little girl, she had imaginary friends, too, but they were always other little girls like her, girls she could have tea parties with. Kelly's imaginary friend isn't a girl like her. He's kind of like a bug and kind of like a flower, and he glows with his own light. He lives at the top of the Tower, but sometimes he comes down, and Kelly can always hear him, his voice a drone, like the TV on in the other room.

Kelly calls him Lenny, but she doesn't know why. On the wide-lined paper that they give her in school to practice penmanship, she writes: *Sumday I'll clime up the Tower an get on Lennys back an he'll take me to see his frends. He says the signul isn't strong enough yet. He wants me to help make the Tower bigger, but I don't know how.*

2. The Moon

When Kelly is twelve, she and her dad move away from the Tower. Her mother has already left by then. Kelly remembers her parents standing in the front door, the sound of the trucks passing on the highway outside, punctuating their conversation. She remembers her mother saying to her dad, "This is your fault. You did this."

Kelly and her dad move to a lake where Kelly's dad is building a dam. The lake is big and flat, the color of the slate tiles that Kelly sees in Home Depot. They live in a trailer park near the dam site. It's a lot smaller than their old house, and the Tower is too far away to see. The sky here is always gray, like the lake, and Kelly never remembers seeing the sun. It's cold and her breath comes out as steam in the air as she gathers with the other kids to wait for a bus that takes them to school in a cinderblock building surrounded by evergreens. The bus isn't yellow, like her old one was, but gray, like everything else here, with green letters.

With the Tower so far away, Kelly doesn't hear Lenny anymore. She doesn't have any friends now. There are kids in the trailer park, but they feel temporary. She knows that soon enough she'll be moving on. That her dad doesn't watch over the dam, like he did the Tower. Kelly feels different from the other kids, but she also knows enough to know that all kids feel that way, so maybe it's nothing.

She spends a lot of time down by the side of the lake, looking out across the water. There's something that lives at the bottom of the lake, something that glows like the moon. She thinks that maybe it's like Lenny, but she never sees it, never hears it. She just knows that it's there.

3. The Magician

When Kelly is old enough, she moves away from her dad and goes to the University of Kansas. She cuts her hair boy-short and dyes it bright pink and wears a faded black T-shirt with the letters T.S.O.L. stenciled on it in purple. By now the headaches have started, stabbing pain across the inside of her skull, along the back of her forehead. Like a railroad spike, working its way out between her eyes. Her dad took her to the doctor the first time it happened, and they called them migraines, gave her yellow-and-red pills which she dutifully takes whenever she feels a headache building.

She majors in art history with a minor in chemistry, which is where she learns how to make the bombs that blow up part of the KLMB television studio. She watches on the little TV in her dorm room as the police drag away the members of the campus protest group who set the bombs, their faces blurred out in a storm of pixels. They shout about television, calling it the "brainwashing tool of the oligarchy."

Kelly recognizes one of them as the boy who sat next to her in ethics, the one she slept with a few times before he finally got up the nerve to ask her about the movement, about bombs. He's wearing a T-shirt with a picture of one of the aliens from *They Live*, posed to look like Uncle Sam.

She expects the police to knock on her door, to show up in one of her classes. Every day for weeks she waits, but they never come. She claimed no affiliation with the group, and she was nowhere near the blast, and she guesses that the boy didn't rat her out, that the police, having found their culprits, didn't probe too deep. In a way, she's disappointed.

The boy never asked her why she was willing to help. He just assumed that she had the same goals he did. She never tells anyone about the bombs, never has anyone to talk to about why she made them. She doesn't keep a diary or a journal of her thoughts, but that night she draws a picture of the Tower on the inside cover of her notebook, surrounded by flames.

4. The Hanged Man

When Kelly's dad hangs himself, men from his work come and take the papers out of the big four-drawer filing cabinet that has always stood in his office, wherever they lived. But they don't know what Kelly knows, about the papers that her dad keeps in an old boot box at the top of his closet, next to the pistol that Kelly was never allowed to touch.

By then Kelly is out of school, and doing nothing to help her alma mater's reputation by working as a custodian. She remembers the custodians at her various schools, pushing brooms and running floor buffers, seemingly lost in their own solitary orbits. That feels right to her, safe. She stays away from people when she can, and stays isolated from them when she can't. She knows by now that she sees things other people don't, and she's beginning to learn why.

When the funeral is over and everyone is gone, Kelly takes down the boot box and looks through it, sitting cross-legged—what they used to call "Indian-style" in her elementary school—on her dad's bed. That's where she learns about the machine.

They found it at a crime scene back in the '30s, half-destroyed by a bullet from a revolver. They put it back together, bit by bit over the years, shuttling it from secret bunker to secret bunker, making it the provenance of first one bureau and then another through the Cold War, until it ended up in a repurposed missile silo in Kansas, where they built a Tower over it and attached it to a transmitter, just to see what would happen.

When she's done reading, she burns most of her father's papers in the fireplace, and the others she takes back to her room, placing them in a pile atop books on Jungian archetypes and the pineal gland, schizophrenia and the Tarot.

5. The Hierophant

When Kelly is ready, she takes two weeks off work, gets in her car and drives south and west. She leaves her dad's house burning behind her, all her books and papers inside. In the car she listens to the radio, the irony not lost on her. Franz Ferdinand admonishes her to "Turn It On," though she intends to do just the opposite.

A mile from their old house she hits the first roadblock. Night has fallen outside, and she can already see the Tower's lights in the distance, blinking to warn off planes. Blue and red lights pulse in the darkness at the roadblock, the SUVs stopped at forty-five degree angles, sawhorses up across the road. She coasts to a stop, turns off the radio, rolls her window down.

The guy in the sheriff's department jacket walks up to the car, his gun unsnapped in its holster. His hair is cropped military-short, and there's a hole in his forehead the size of a nickel, a single black line of blood running down his face, along the right side of his nose, around his lip. The hole looks just like the one a bullet would make in a movie, like a trephination wound. Kelly figures that's not far off. The deputy looks at her. His eyes are that blue they call "cornflower," but they don't focus on her, they're looking past her. Something else is looking at her through him, and it's not using his eyes. She looks at the hole, at the darkness on the other side of it. He nods and moves aside, and others like him move the sawhorses, pull one of the SUVs to the side of the road so she can drive past.

She leaves her window rolled down, the radio off. She can hear it now, the static in the air, the sound, musical and familiar, like a TV on in the next room. The air outside is too cold, and there's a breeze that comes from nowhere and goes nowhere. What her dad used to call "wind from Pluto."

There are cars parked everywhere at her old house. More police cars and an ambulance, their lights strobing the darkness, a station wagon, pickup trucks. News and television vans are clustered at the base of the Tower, their own satellite dishes and broadcast arrays extended. Everywhere, people are milling around, and Kelly doesn't have to look to see the holes in their foreheads, all of them identical.

All the lights are on in her old house, and the wall nearest the Tower has been torn down. There's the room that was her bedroom, stripped now of anything that could identify it except geography. Everywhere she sees piles of equipment. Car stereos, TVs, speakers, those small satellite dishes that go on the sides of houses. The zombies are carrying it from the cars to the house, where it's sorted into piles, and then from the house to the Tower.

The top of the Tower isn't where Lenny lives. Kelly knows that now. She had it wrong as a little girl.

The door of the maintenance hatch at the base of the Tower— the one that her dad used to go down once every few months— stands open now, so that the zombies can carry in their supplies of old transistors and copper wire. She waits for a gap in the procession, and then she follows it down.

6. Judgment

When Kelly gets to the bottom, she finds a massive room, like an airplane hangar made of vaulted concrete. Left over from the missile silo days, or something else. Now, it houses a jumble of electronic equipment. Amps and old radios and TV tubes, all cobbled together with a jungle of cables that run everywhere like spilled intestines. And in the center of the chaos, what her dad's papers called the Resonator, a machine like a tuning fork that emits—or maybe inhabits—a purple glow that Kelly knows she doesn't see with her eyes.

Coiled around the Resonator, through it, a part of it, is Lenny. He no longer looks much like a bug or a flower, though still a bit of both. He's partially transparent, like a special effect in an old movie super-imposed on the film of reality. His tendrils or roots or hyphae extend out, reach through the walls of the chamber into the earth and the Tower above. Claws like the pincers of an enormous crayfish manipulate wires and knobs. Everywhere, luminous eyes turn on truncated stalks. His mouth—if that's what it is—opens and closes, emitting a light that sets Kelly's brain on fire.

No, not her whole brain. The pineal gland, the third eye. She can feel it growing, pressing against her skull, threatening to break through. And she knows that when it does she won't be Kelly anymore—whatever that means. A transmission is no good without a receiver, after all. But she won't just be a receiver, either. That's what the zombies are. She'll be something else, like a cellphone tower, something for the signal to ping off of and go further. That's what she's always been, and she can remember her mother standing in the doorway, telling her dad, "You did this," and her dad hanging from the beam in his workshop, an extension cord coiled tight round his neck.

Lenny's eyes turn toward her, his mouth is open, she remembers his voice, which she knows now she never heard with anything that could be called hearing. She remembers his promises to her when she was a girl, that he would show her where his friends lived. She looks up, and she can no longer see the roof of the hangar. She is in the center of a living darkness, shot through with something that is not light, illuminated by stars that are not stars. They are drawing nearer. Her dad is telling her that the Tower is one of the strongest transmitters this side of the Mississippi, that it can send a signal all the way to outer space. She can make out their shapes now, and her throat is making a sound that she can't hear over the music of the spheres.

Lenny reaches out with a pseudopod to embrace her, maybe, lift her up, and she activates the charges that are concealed under her jacket. The moment before the blast stretches out forever, becomes multifaceted, and she can see into the past and the future. A little girl lies in bed and stares up at the Tower, watching as the bomb she'll set in twenty years rips apart its foundation and brings it tumbling down into fire and smoke.

Author's Notes: "From Beyond" has always been one of my favorite H. P. Lovecraft stories, and I'd had this title kicking around in my notebook for years, so when Scott R. Jones put out a call for *Resonator*, an anthology of new stories inspired by "From Beyond," that seemed like the time to use it.

The Tower in the story is inspired by one on the road leading out of one of the towns where I grew up. I think once I started capitalizing Tower, it started to make me think tarot cards, and from there the idea of using tarot imagery to break up the story crept in.

THE WELL AND THE WHEEL

After the divorce, my dad moved into the old house. Mom said that it had been in his family for years, though I'd never seen it, and he'd never talked about it. The first time I laid eyes on the place was a month after the divorce, sitting in Mom's Suburban in the gravel drive with the engine running while she talked to him on the front porch, the collar of her coat turned up against the cold. A weathered, one-story building the color of unfinished wood left out in the elements, it looked more like a shed than a house, though it already had new windows and a little satellite dish bolted onto the roof.

The house was outside of town, on a twenty-acre plot of land that had once been part of a farm, and the corpses of old farm buildings still dotted the edges of the big yard. Not even ruins anymore, just jumbles of sunbleached wood. Out behind the house were what was left of some cattle pens, reduced now to splinters and rust. And on the top of the hill, an old stone well with a single dead tree beside it, denuded of branches, the trunk curling toward the well as if the tree was being sucked inside or trying to crawl in.

While my dad was alive, I never set foot in the house. I only ever saw Mom go in once, but she told me to wait outside, and so that day I explored the yard, poking at the remains of fallen-down buildings with the toe of my boots. It was a few months after the divorce, the weather starting to warm back up, the sky gray and filled with moisture, giving the whole property the air of a Gothic novel. I saw the well then, but I didn't go near it, because at that moment my mom came outside and called my name. Did she look a little shaken on the drive back into town? That I don't remember.

Dad didn't get any custody rights from the divorce; didn't, I think, even ask for them, which hurt my feelings at the time, though I pretended that it didn't, even to myself. Sometimes he would pick me up in his beat-up old truck, the one that smelled of stale dust and seemed to let in as much air as it kept out, so that in the winter months the heater was waging a constant battle against the cold that froze your toes and fingers. He'd take me out to the mall where we'd eat in the food court and look in the shops, or he'd take me to a movie and buy me a giant Icee and a tub of popcorn.

When I was old enough to drive, I'd go visit him instead, but I still didn't go into the house. I was never told that I couldn't, but somehow by then it was just an unspoken rule, something that I accepted without question. I'd pull my Ford Fiesta into the drive and honk the horn, and my dad would come out onto the porch and wave at me, and then we'd go to dinner at Chili's or Olive Garden or shopping at Sam's Club, where he'd buy bottled water in enormous quantities. I assumed that the tap water in the house was no good to drink—probably hard as a rock, maybe pulled up from that old well out back—and I asked him why he didn't get a water filter, but he just shook his head, hefted one of the bottles, and said, "I like this."

Neither he nor my mom ever remarried. She had a regular boyfriend for years, and moved in with him after I went to college. Dad lived alone in that house until the day he died.

The day he died was the week after my twenty-eighth birthday, though he sat in the green metal rocking chair that he kept on the front porch for three days before anyone found his body. A neighbor noticed that she'd seen him sitting out there on her way to and from work every day, and on the third day she stopped, the wheels of her car crunching on the gravel, and got out to see if he was okay. She later told me that it "just looked like he was asleep."

The doctor said that it was a heart attack, "but not the bad kind." I had no idea what that meant. Was there a kind of heart attack worse than the one that kills you?

My dad had a piece of paper crumpled in his left fist when he died, something torn out of a notebook and written in purple ink that had smudged from the elements. It was addressed to me, and all it said was, "Sorry, Emmy." Dad was the only one who ever called me Emmy. To everyone else it was Emma, and Emmanuel no place but on my driver's license. I didn't know then what he was sorry for, or why he was holding that note so tight when he died. Had he known, somehow, that it was coming? Does the not-so-bad kind of heart attack give you a nice warning in advance?

Because my mom and dad had been divorced for more than half my life, and he had no one else left, I inherited everything he had to his name: the house and everything in it, and the land on which it stood. While he was still alive, my dad had hired a lawyer in town, a short, round man named Mr. Beaumont whose office was in a square brick building that looked like a post office.

Mr. Beaumont handled all the paperwork associated with my dad's estate, and handed me the ring of keys that my dad had worn on his belt for as long as I could remember. He hadn't wanted a funeral, and besides, there really wasn't anybody to come besides me and my mom and her new boyfriend. His body was cremated, and they gave me his ashes in a plastic bag inside a cardboard box. I figured that I would dump them somewhere on the property, thinking that he must have liked it there. My eyes stayed dry until I pulled my car into the drive and sat looking down at the ring of keys in my hand, realizing that I didn't have any idea which one unlocked the front door.

I planned to sell the house. Mr. Beaumont had offered to take care of the "disposition of the estate" for me, but I wanted to at least see it all for myself first. Go through my father's things, see if there was anything I recognized, anything I might want to keep. When I pulled into the drive I already had a duffel bag full of clothes and toiletries in the back seat.

My roommate and I had fought about something stupid maybe a week before I got the news, and it had been cold silences and little passive aggressive gestures whenever we had to be in the apartment together. Of course, Amanda forgave and forgot the moment I heard about my dad's death, but I still hadn't yet, and I wasn't ready to be around people, not even ones who meant well. Maybe especially not those.

So I took the opportunity to move into my dad's old house. I told Amanda that it would just be for a few weeks, while I sorted out his things, and at the time that's probably what I had in mind. Work had already told me to take as much time as I needed, and I'd already told my boss that I wouldn't be back for at least two weeks, after which I'd check in. Was cutting myself off from everybody I knew and moving to a new place forty minutes from town a great idea when I'd just lost my dad? Probably not, but it was the only thing that felt right to me then.

It was raining when I stood on the porch and tried keys until I found the one that unlocked the front door. Someone had removed the green metal rocking chair, and I was grateful for that, but nobody had so much as set foot inside my dad's house since he'd passed. That's the pleasant euphemism they always use, right? Passed? Instead of stopped, broke down, died.

If you've never walked into a house where someone once lived but no longer does, then you're lucky. I recommend avoiding it for as long as you can manage. It's a different feeling than walking into a house that happens to be empty, say because everyone is at work or out to a movie, or even a house that's sitting empty because it's for sale. There's a vacancy that houses only get when their occupants have vanished in the middle of things, as if you can feel the vacuum left behind by death. That's what I felt as I stepped through the front door of my dad's house for the first time.

It was dark inside. The walls felt close, the ceiling light in the front hall produced only a dull, amber-colored glow, and the sideboard was stacked with mail and papers. Walking slowly through the house, room by room, I could get some sense of the rhythm of my dad's life. There was a big room near one end of the house—we would have called it a living room in any normal place, though in my dad's house it seemed to be something else. There was a couch and a recliner there, both old and ratty with stuffing showing through, the former covered in a faded blanket. There was a fireplace that was cold now and dark, though wood was stacked beside it. I recognized the wood immediately as old lumber from the tumble-down buildings that dotted the yard.

I could tell just by looking that this was the room where my dad had spent most of his time. An electric blanket was plugged into the same outlet as the floor lamp and piled at the foot of the recliner, and I knew, without any more substantial evidence, that he had slept there more often than in the bed, which I hadn't yet seen. On the floor next to the chair was a stack of books, and there was also a roll-top desk in one corner of the room, and a TV in the other. The desk was locked, and I didn't bother right then to try any of the keys on Dad's key ring.

A trail of clutter led from the living room to the kitchen in an elliptical pattern, as food made its way from the latter to the former, and then dishes, occasionally, made the return trip, though some of them had ended up stacked here and there on the living room floor, or around the brick fireplace. Next to the refrigerator was a stack of bottled water as high as I am tall, the top case opened and several bottles missing. The fridge had also been stocked with dozens of bottles, as well as cans of beer and food in various stages of going bad.

Walking through the rest of the house, signs of habitation dropped off sharply. None of the windows had blinds or curtains, and instead heavy blankets had been draped or nailed over them to block the light. There was a bathroom just off the kitchen, and at the farthest end of the house from the living room were two bedrooms across the hall from each other. One I recognized as my dad's—clothes that I had seen him wear hung in the closet—while the other was locked from the outside with a deadbolt and held nothing but a bed with a heavy wooden frame.

The bed was made, and next to the pillow lay one of my old stuffed animals from when I was a kid, a bunny named Mr. Stuffles who had since turned gray with age and started to pill up. He was the first thing I noticed upon opening the door, and I crossed the room to pick him up before I saw what else was on the bed. Chains attached to the frame at head and foot, ending in thick leather cuffs that looked like they had been homemade from old belts.

Was that my first indication that something was terribly wrong? I can't really say anymore. I try to tell myself that something felt off from the first moment I walked through the front door; that a germ of concern, rather than simply too-late-in-coming pity, had started in my mind when I saw the state of my dad's living room. Maybe I had, after all, seen enough of the titles of the books that lay piled beside his recliner to make me worry. It's possible that I had even suspected something more sinister for months now, years, as long as he had been living his strange life in this strange house.

Whatever the truth of it is, I know that I didn't feel the surprise, the dread or shock or nausea that should have overwhelmed me when I saw those well-worn restraints dangling from the heavy wooden frame of that bed in a room that locked from the outside. Just as I know that I didn't suspect, not for one moment, that what I had stumbled on was nothing more than the secret of my dad's interest in some kind of kinky sexual fetish.

I don't remember making my way from the bedroom back to the cluttered living room, or sinking down onto the couch there. When I did, I was still holding Mr. Stuffles limply in my left hand, just as my dad had, perhaps unconsciously, clutched his apology.

Was this what he was sorry for?

I can't say how long I sat there. Minutes? Hours? The blankets over the windows made time impossible to gauge, even if the wet October day outside had given any indication. All I know is that the room grew subtly darker still, until finally I had to stir to turn on the floor lamp. When I did, I noticed once more the pile of books that lay next to my dad's recliner.

When he had still lived at home, my dad seldom read anything at all, and on the occasion that he did it was mostly Tom Clancy and John Grisham novels. The closest he had ever come to the supernatural was an occasional dalliance with Dean Koontz.

The books in the pile next to his chair were, to a volume, put out by no-name presses, with uninspiring covers featuring blurry photographs or simple line drawings of pentagrams and something that looked sort of like the veins of a leaf. Their titles were filled with words like "occult" and "paranormal" and "Satanic" and "demonology." They were not the sorts of things that the dad I had thought I'd known would even have been aware of, let alone interested in reading about, and yet the broken spines and curling covers showed that his interest hadn't been an idle one. These books had been read again and again, paged through, consulted. Post-it notes flagged pages, corners had been turned down, and notes were written in ball-point pen in the margins. Whole sections were underlined, or angrily scribbled through.

I read enough to make me more confused, rather than less, and tossed books aside one by one, the pile beside my dad's recliner becoming a sort of avalanche of my frustration. Finally, I walked over to the roll-top desk. The drawers were unlocked, and contained the things you might expect to find in a desk drawer, along with a revolver that I had never seen before, but nothing that shed any light on what was going on. I started trying keys until I found the one that unlocked the top of the desk.

I don't know what I expected to find when I rolled it open, but it was tidier inside than I had imagined. There were scraps of paper here and there, covered in my dad's handwriting, but what drew my attention immediately—as, I think, it was meant to—was a binder, like a photo book or a wedding album, with a faux-leather cover. It was unmarked on the outside, but I could see that it was thick with whatever contents it held.

There may have been a moment, while my fingertips rested on the cover of the binder, when I considered walking away. Calling the police, perhaps, or at least Mr. Beaumont. Letting this all become someone else's problem. But I had to know, so I opened the cover.

Ever since I was a little kid, I've had a habit of opening books to the back pages first. I don't know why I developed it, but it has stuck with me most of my life, so when I opened the scrapbook, it was to the last page onto which anything had been pasted. The date was only a few weeks before, on my birthday. It started with the words, "Sorry, Emmy, but I'm beginning to wear thin."

I called the binder a scrapbook, and so it was. Newspaper clippings, photographs, and meticulous notes recorded in purple pen in my dad's handwriting. Not the grim trophies of a serial killer, but the careful records of a man who can't afford to make a mistake. One entry a year, going back twenty-eight years. Each one of them the same. A picture of a girl beside a set of vital statistics: approximate height and weight, eye color, hair color, age. Twenty-eight, then twenty-seven, twenty-six, twenty-five. The first entry in the book was a photograph of a newborn, the kind that they stick up in maternity wards. It was dated twenty-eight years ago, on my birthday.

Never having been in the house before, I nonetheless remembered seeing a back door that opened off the kitchen, and that was where I stumbled then, the shock and nausea that should have overwhelmed me before suddenly welling up inside, as I remembered birthdays that my dad had missed, arrived at late, left early. One girl a year, one girl my age, every year for my entire life.

I thought that I might be sick, that I might vomit up what little food I'd managed to eat in the last twenty-four hours out behind the house, but somehow, once the damp air hit my lungs, I seemed to calm down. Still, I wasn't ready to go back into that house, so I stood in the back yard and looked up the hill, past the old cattle pens, to the well and the bent tree.

It was a cold October day, getting on toward evening, and though it was no longer raining, fog hung thick over everything. The grass of the back yard looked jewel-green, and the fog closed everything in, so that the hill was the most distant thing I could see. It felt as if I had stumbled out of the house and into a different world, for more reasons than one. Without thinking, I started to climb.

By the time I had reached the lip of the old stone well, I knew, with a knowledge that went beyond fact, that this was where he had put them. I pictured them wrapped in canvas, tied with sturdy ropes. A slightly bigger bundle each year. Were they still alive as they went down, struggling and squirming? Did they scream as they fell?

I half expected to be hit with a fetid stench as I reached the mouth of the well, the odor of almost three decades of decay. But the only smell that came from the dark hole was damp stone. What I found instead was a series of metal rungs set into the side of the well, a ladder descending down into darkness. Was it some fatalism, some sense of assumed guilt that drove my actions as I gripped the first of those iron rungs and started down into the pit? What did I think to find down there, without even a light to guide me?

When I was still in high school, I had a boyfriend who abandoned me at the county fair. After he had gone and left me with no ride home, I wandered the midway in my bare feet—maybe my shoes were still in the car; I can't remember why I didn't have them, any more than I can remember why he left—until I came to a tent, far out on the edge of the fairgrounds. The sign above the entrance to the tent didn't have any words on it, just an enormous violet eye painted on a white banner, with lines coming off it that could have been lashes but that I saw then as beams or rays of some kind.

It was a fortune teller's booth. The woman inside looked as old as sand, though there was enough light getting in from outside to let me know that at least some of it was pancake makeup applied to add years. I had been crying, I think, and my own makeup had run down my face, but she didn't make any mention of it, just accepted my crumpled five-dollar bill and proceeded to read my fortune.

The darkness of the tent flickered with light from outside, blinking on and off, first illuminated, then in shadow. The fortune teller laid down a card with a picture of a wheel, marked with symbols I didn't recognize, held up by a red devil and mounted by a blue sphinx. It said, "La Roue." Over it, at a ninety-degree angle, she laid another. A picture of a naked woman surrounded by some kind of wreath, flanked by stylized drawings of a lion, a cow, a bird, and a golden face: "Le Monde."

She must have told me something, to accompany that cryptic action. For it to have been a proper Tarot reading, she should have put down more cards. But I don't remember any of that. I don't remember her saying a single word. Maybe I wouldn't have remembered it, even if she did. What I wanted to know, in that moment, was about the boy who had just ditched me, about how I was going to do in school, about when I was going to get my own car, be able to get away. This fortune had nothing to do with my heartbreak, with my troubles, and so I'm sure that I blanked it out. All I remember are those two cards, the wheel and the world, in the blinking light of the midway. That's what I think about, as I descend the cold rungs of the ladder into the well.

How far down do I go, into that damp darkness? Far enough that what light remains in the gray sky above disappears, and I should be climbing in blackness, but I'm not. Far enough that I begin to think about theories of the hollow earth, of dinosaurs and ancient civilizations and inner suns. Far enough that my arms and legs begin to ache, and I should worry about how I'm going to climb back to the surface, but I don't.

When my foot finally touches the ground, I expect it to crunch among old bones, or to sink into icy water, but the floor of the well isn't even damp or muddy. It feels solid and dry. It should be dark, but I can see the stone wall in front of me, see the last few rungs of the ladder that I've been climbing down. I can feel the light against my back, and I can feel that which makes the light, waiting for me to turn and face it.

What is it that I see, when I turn around? Another world in the heart of this one, spinning clockwise? A nuclear flame, burning fetid green? A congeries of iridescent spheres? A formless mass, as big as the universe, fit inside a globe of finite space? Any of that, or none of it?

I'll tell you what I see. I see a fortune teller, in the blinking darkness of her tent, laying down first one card and then another. The wheel, and then the world. It's tempting to take the easy way out, to say that I hear the voice in my head, but that's a lie. I *feel* its longing inside my brain and my bones, just as I *know* what it wants, what it has always wanted, without the need for words. It wants me. It has wanted me for twenty-eight years.

The wheel knew me on the day that I came into this world, knew who and what I was, knew me better than I have ever known myself, just as my father knew his duty, and his father before him, and his father before him. Was it love of me that made my dad defy this calling? How could such a love kindle so quickly? Whatever drove his decision, he had found another way to do what he must. Year after year, another girl to take my place. Not what the wheel wanted, but enough to keep it spinning, year after year. Until he had grown too old. Until, as his note had said, he had worn thin.

And now, at last, I am here, where I was always meant to be. At the bottom of the darkness, with the wheel that turns the world.

Author's Notes: Tarot imagery makes its triumphant thematic return in "The Well and the Wheel," a story that I originally wrote for *Autumn Cthulhu*, edited by Mike Davis, and one that probably started with the title. Looking back, I imagine that title probably came about because of Fritz Leiber's story "The Hill and the Hole," though I didn't realize it at the time.

HARUSPICATE OR SCRY

D r. Hartledge was my faculty advisor back in college, not to mention the university's only professor of philosophy, tucked away in a tiny office taller than it was wide in the basement of Wolfram Hall. I met him in my philosophy of religion class freshmen year, back when I was still majoring in English, and he convinced me to double-major, which was convenient enough, since Wolfram Hall also housed the English department up on the third floor. He had a quotation from Bertrand Russell taped to his windowless office door, "From a scientific point of view, we can make no distinction between the man who eats little and sees heaven and the man who drinks much and sees snakes."

As one of only four students in the entire school majoring in either philosophy or religion—the sole religion professor, Dr. Mead, occupied a much more spacious office down the hall—I got a lot of individual attention. Mostly, Dr. Hartledge tried to talk me out of majoring in English in favor of focusing exclusively on philosophy. He had an anecdote that he liked to tell, about an English class he'd taken when he was in college, where he had written a story featuring a lengthy description of a pear. While workshopping the story the next day, the professor and the other students had praised highly his imagery, drawing parallels between the pear and the womb. "I didn't mean any of that stuff," Dr. Hartledge told me more than once. "I was just writing about a damn pear."

During gap periods between classes I would clear the piles of books off the narrow wooden chair beside his desk and spend my time debating philosophical points with him, or, if he wasn't in, reading books from his teetering shelves. He gave me a hardcover copy of *Thus Spake Zarathustra* and a battered old paperback of *Four Quartets*. Over time, he gradually came to replace the figure of my father, who had died when I was young and who had, in my memory, become little more than a stern black cloud "that took the form of a demon in my view."

When I married Gavin during my senior year, I cemented Dr. Hartledge's place as my substitute father by asking him to walk me down the aisle, which he consented to do, even though he didn't much approve of weddings, seeing in them, "Little more than sound and fury, signifying nothing."

He dressed much as he did when he was lecturing, though the suit he wore was darker and his bowtie more subdued. I would have asked for nothing different, and Gavin understood my attachment to the old professor, and deflected his family's objections. We got married in the school chapel, though neither of us was very religious; Gavin a lapsed Catholic, myself a skeptic from a young age, gradually being groomed into atheism by Dr. Hartledge's example.

For all his gruff dismissal of the frippery of weddings, when Dr. Hartledge turned me over to Gavin at the altar he was smiling, and his eyes shone. It meant almost as much to me as when Gavin said, "I do."

I spent the remainder of my senior year as Dr. Hartledge's office assistant, which meant that I had a key to his coat closet of an office, and also to the storeroom down the hall where the philosophy and religion department records were kept. Gavin and I moved into an old three-story house that was entirely too big for us, but the down-payment on it was a wedding present from his parents, along with the money he needed to start up a graphic design business, which he ran out of the back half of the first floor, with little parking spaces off the alley for when the occasional client came for a meeting.

Gavin's parents were both still alive and still together after thirty-five years, his father an architect who wore navy blue suits to work at an office that had his name on the outside of the building. He had designed the new city hall in town. When Gavin wasn't doing graphic design work, he sometimes assisted his father, helping to bring the firm into the twentieth century with more green-friendly buildings.

This meant that there was always plenty of money, even if it came tangled in the strings of Gavin's extensive and demanding family. We spent every holiday with them, my mother invited for the first few years, but gradually demurring and fading away, becoming thinner and grayer like a ghost. Intimidated by them, I think, like I was, but better able to slip away unnoticed.

After graduation, I started taking classes at a bigger university in the city, working toward my master's degrees in both English and philosophy, much to Dr. Hartledge's consternation. He lived in the city, too, in a big dark house filled with wood paneling and old books and framed posters from old magic acts. "Do the dead materialize?" the posters demanded to know. "Do the spirits come back?"

He was a widower, his wife having died years ago, long before I ever met him. There were photographs of the two of them together in his house, Dr. Hartledge a young man, impossible to reconcile with the person I knew.

Some nights, when I didn't feel like making the drive back to Barnett, I slept at his place, in the guest bedroom that was decorated in a much more modern style than the rest of the house. We would stay up late drinking decent Scotch and talking about his current crop of students. Looking back, I wonder now how many people thought we were sleeping together, then and when he had been my advisor. I wonder why Gavin never thought so?

I was, after all, a young woman, and while I kept my hair cut "short like a boy's," as my mom said, and dressed in jeans and faded T-shirts emblazoned with the covers of famous books, and still "had a little baby fat," my mom's words again, I wasn't altogether unattractive, and I obviously had a bad case of hero worship where Dr. Hartledge was concerned. Did he ever consider it? Was our entire relationship an elaborate courtship on his part, trying to work up the nerve, waiting for me to instigate a kiss or a touch? If so, it never came.

For my part, I truly did see him as a father, and nothing more. The idea of any romantic relationship didn't even occur to me until years after it would have been too late to do anything about it, long after I probably should have been concerned about my reputation. Did that explain the hostility that Gavin's parents always seemed to have toward me, a blind spot I had never thought to shine a light upon? I guess I may never know.

It is perhaps just as well, as a sexual relationship would have been incredibly awkward, our significant age difference notwithstanding. Though his first name was Roland, I could only ever call him Dr. Hartledge, a habit ingrained in me by my undergraduate days and one I was never able to shake. Not very sexy during the act.

By the time Nathanial—a family name, and not one that I would have chosen—was born, Dr. Hartledge was already in the ground. "Food for the worms," as he would have called it, though perhaps not so much these days, with modern advances in embalming and virtually impregnable caskets. But before that ever happened, he began what would prove to be the last leg of his career.

"My semi-retirement," was his wording. He had tenure at the university, so he didn't quit teaching entirely, but there hadn't been anything like a philosophy department there for years, even during my time, so while he was still on the payroll and still had that tiny office, he reduced his course load to a handful of hours per week.

The rest of the time he embarked upon a project that he had been planning for years, something that he had been interested in since his own undergraduate days. In one room of his house was a library full of books on stage magic, illusion, prestidigitation. He was fascinated by the magicians of the past who had worked as tireless skeptics, debunking fraudulent spiritualists. Some of his favorites were those he called "the three Harrys;" Houdini, Price, and Kellar.

Finally, with the advent of reality TV and the resultant popularity of "ghost hunting" shows, his hour had come 'round at last. There weren't many spiritualists or séances anymore, but now there were plenty of haunted houses for Dr. Hartledge to debunk, and in my spare time I became his assistant once more, traipsing out to abandoned asylums—most of which had actually been schools and not asylums at all—or spending the frigid night in some unheated old pile that had supposedly been the site of one brutal slaying or another.

It was not an enterprise calculated to make him very popular, as the market for paranormal investigators at the time favored a more credulous approach, and had little room for Dr. Hartledge's indefatigable skepticism. Still, he had a weekly radio show debunking paranormal phenomena on the college radio station of the larger university in the city, the one where I was doing my graduate work. He named it after an unfinished manuscript that Houdini had commissioned H. P. Lovecraft and C. M. Eddy to write before his death, The Cancer of Superstition.

It was on an episode of Cancer that he once said, "There is nothing waiting for us on the other side of the grave but ashes and dust, of that I am certain. One need not look far to see that we are not beautiful spirits. We are a collection of chemical and electrical impulses, animating a mannequin of rotting meat. When those impulses cease, then we cease."

Dr. Hartledge was particularly fascinated by the pact that Houdini had made with his widow, that if there were any way to communicate with the living from whatever waited on the other side, then he would reach out to her.

A séance was held every Halloween, and Houdini was supposed to communicate the code "Rosabelle believe" if there truly was any existence from beyond. After the tenth unsuccessful séance, held on the roof of Knickerbocker Hotel, Houdini's wife concluded that there was no way for the dead to contact the living, and put out the candle that she had kept burning beside his picture since his death, saying that "ten years is long enough to wait for any man."

It was Dr. Hartledge's favorite story, and he repeated it time and again, adding that even after Bess Houdini gave up, annual Houdini séances continued to be held by other magicians up to the present day, to no avail. So it should have come as no surprise to me when, called to his hospital bed as he lay dying of leukemia, he asked me to perform one last favor for him, for old time's sake.

When he was gone, he said, his house would sit empty for some time before it was sold. He had stipulated it in his will, and apparently had gone through a number of lawyers to ensure that it was ironclad. During that time, he wanted me to go there once a week, and hold every kind of séance that I could think of, try every form of divination that I could muster, to attempt to reach his wayward spirit. "If I can be reached anywhere, it will be there."

I had nine months in which to complete this procedure. If, at the end of that time, I had received no positive proof of Dr. Hartledge's presence, then I was to take that as positive proof of his absence, and the absence of any sort of life after death. "Beyond that," he said, "you can do what you like. Feel free to make a thesis project of it, write a book, whatever you want. Just do this for me, please?"

He held my hand as he said it, the only time he had ever held my hand, and his skin felt like soft paper, his bones beneath brittle and hollow like a bird's. So of course I said yes.

It was a week after I watched them lower Dr. Hatrledge's casket

into the ground—black and shiny as the carapace of a beetle—
that I found out I was pregnant.

I never had any desire to be a mother. When friends or relations
had children and asked if I wanted to hold the baby, I always de-
murred with some excuse.

Before the wedding, Gavin and I had discussed the possibility
of kids, and how neither of us was ready, and might never be.
I doubt now that I was forceful enough on the subject, because
when you're a woman, it isn't okay to say that you will never want
kids, that you don't believe you have within yourself the capacity
to love a child. And while I was content with being a loner and a
rebel and never any good, I wasn't quite ready to be the abomination such an admission would make me in the eyes of Gavin's
family, and the world.

When I went to Gavin with the news, I hoped that he would
be as horrified by it as I secretly was. That he would say, "It's your
choice, but we have options," and I would be given the out I needed to go to the clinic. Instead he hugged me tight, laughed. I
said, "I know we weren't planning for this," trying to ease into the
admission, but he replied, "We're doing great, what's the harm in
trying?"

And I didn't say, "Because a child isn't something that you *try*.
I can't return it to the store when I find out that I don't want it."
Instead, I attempted to smile, to let him mistake the tears in my
eyes for joy.

Even then, there might have been hope. I might have worked
up the nerve, in time, to say that I wasn't ready, wouldn't ever be
ready, but then Gavin told his parents without asking me, and it
was all over, my choices gone. From that moment I had to have the
baby, or become a monster that they could never forgive.

So began nine months of misery that I pretended was morning
sickness and "first baby jitters," but was actually a crawling terror
of the life that was growing inside of me with each passing day.
My body changed in ways that disgusted and frightened me, and

I found myself doted upon by people who, up to that point, had not ever liked me very much. Gavin's family organized baby showers, and I dutifully unwrapped brightly colored paper concealing strollers and diapers and bottles and all the other countless accoutrements that babies apparently need. But through it all I knew that it was actually the thing growing in my womb that they were showering with affection, and that I was just the vessel.

Gavin was everything that a husband is supposed to be. He bought baby things, he got me anything that I wanted to eat, he scheduled Lamaze classes. He did everything except realize how much I didn't want this.

The only thing he objected to were the séances, the ones that I still went to at Dr. Hartledge's house every Saturday night, no matter how much my stomach swelled, or how sick and terrified I felt. "That atmosphere," he said, on one of the many nights that he tried to "talk sense" into me, "it can't be good for the baby."

And I didn't spit in his face that I didn't give a good goddamn what was good for the baby, what about what was good for me? Instead, I reminded him that I had promised Dr. Hartledge, who had been like a father to me, who had given me away at our wedding, and who was not yet a year in the ground, and after all, we were neither of us believers, what harm could it possibly do?

In Dr. Hartledge's rolodex were the names of dozens of people who practiced every manner of contact with the dead that you could imagine. Automatic writers, physical mediums who claimed to channel ectoplasm from their bodies, psychics and spiritualists and even engineers who argued that what we thought of as spirits were simply energy, operating on another frequency, and that the right radio receiver could pick them up.

One by one I called them up, and we had sittings at the old dark house where Dr. Hartledge had lived, in the room containing his books and his magic posters, the room that he had loved the most in life. We set up a round table in the middle of the chamber, pushing aside his desk and an old steamer trunk. There we would sit holding hands, or with our palms flat on the table, or our fingertips resting on the planchette of some talking board.

Oh, talking boards, we tried so many. A genuine Ouija board, branded by Hasbro that I bought at the local Target. Other variations on the subject, built by their practitioners. Dice with letters printed on the sides, intended to spell out words when they were randomly rolled. Actual Scrabble tiles, with the scores printed on them and everything, pulled from a black satin bag by a young man with horn rim glasses and slicked down black hair, someone I might have dated when I was ten years younger myself. Letters written on a long sheet of paper, with an upside-down glass acting as a planchette.

Around the table were always the same people, more or less. Myself, Dr. Hartledge's attorney Mr. Knowles, Teresa Osborne, a grad student from one of the classes that I was TAing, there to act as an impartial observer, and whatever kook or medium or psychic or weirdo we had called up that week.

Before he died, Dr. Hartledge had given me a code, one that I had never told to anyone, not even Gavin. One he said that only he and I knew. He had asked me to memorize it, but I didn't have to, because I already knew it by heart. A snippet from a poem, one in that battered T.S. Eliot book that Dr. Hartledge had given me so many years ago. "In my end is my beginning."

For nine long months I grew gravid with child, as they would have said in one of the Victorian novels that I had to read in school, and my only solace, the only hours of the day that were truly *mine* came in those séances in Dr. Hartledge's old study. And yet, even they were bittersweet, at best, as time and again fakers delivered incorrect messages, or apparent true believers walked away baffled by their inability to give me what I was looking for.

After a time, I began to *long* to hear those six words, to see them spelled out by the planchette, the tiles, the glass. I considered slipping one of the mediums a note, but what would that accomplish? The whole enterprise was for no one's benefit but mine and Dr.

Hartledge's, and both of us would know the truth, if indeed, he was in a position to know anything.

Nine months, in this case, amounted to forty séances. Forty, I was told, was a mystical number, of great import. That it appeared time and again in the Bible, most famously in the great flood that lasted for forty days and forty nights. We ended the fortieth evening with another crack at a talking board, with no medium or spiritualist or anyone else but the lawyer, Teresa, and me, but all we got were jumbled letters, from which we could make little sense. "Are you there, Roland?" Mr. Knowles asked the dark, silent air as the hands of the clock crept toward midnight. Finally, when they were just one black line, pointing straight up, and the chiming of the clock broke the silence, I pushed the planchette to the word NO.

"The end is where we start from," I said myself, before I blew out the candle.

The next day I went into labor. It would have been more in keeping with my mood had it been a difficult birth, filled with terrible pain and complications, but in fact, Nathanial was born in just a few hours, and the pain and the discomfort and even the embarrassment and grief were not nearly as strong as I had expected. "It was like he was ready to come out," one of the nurses said, and I guessed I had to agree.

Throughout it all, I had held on to one desperate hope. I had read so many accounts online, of women who hadn't thought themselves ready to be mothers, who hadn't expected to feel any affection for their child, who suddenly had a change of heart, felt a swelling of love and protectiveness when they held the minute creature in their arms. I had been told by so many friends and in-laws that "it's different when it's yours." I had hoped that I would be one of those women, that some alchemical transformation would occur, and that Nathanial's tiny body in my arms, his fingers wrapping around mine, his mouth at my breast, would be the philosopher's stone that transmuted the lead of my disdain into the gold of motherhood.

Chemicals, Dr. Hartledge would have dismissed them as. Dumped into our bloodstream to perpetuate our species, nothing more. But I was fine with that, so long as it took some of the sting from my guilt at not caring at all for this *thing* that had been growing inside me for most of a year.

Gavin was there, pushing the sweat-damp hair from my forehead, beaming at me over his beard, so happy, so proud of me. I tried to be happy too, I really did, but when they handed my baby to me, my hopes were dashed. He was red and wet, a few strands of black hair plastered to the top of his squishy-looking head. His features seemed smooshed, his eyes mostly closed, his lips a puckered circle like the suction cup on the bottom of a tentacle. I felt nothing but disgust, and as I took him in my arms I began to cry, and Gavin put his arms around me and the nurses cooed, and I supposed they must have thought it was joy, or relief, or anything at all except despair, bottomless and cold.

"Postpartum depression," is what they called the weeks and months that followed. I took a semester off from school, and Gavin was once more solicitous and kind and I could find nothing to complain about, though I was sullen and withdrawn, stared out the windows or read fitfully or simply curled up in the dark and wept. Did anything, really, but look after my baby, when I could avoid it.

Gavin's mother came to stay with us in a guest room, and spent hours with Nathanial, much more time than I ever did. I kept hoping that I would grow to feel something for him, that he would ever seem like anything but a squat homunculus. Even a tiny stranger would have been preferable to the inscrutable creature I saw staring out of his beady, dark eyes, the ones that his family said came from his grandfather, for whom he was named.

A baby is supposed to be a symbol of the love that you feel for each other, isn't it? Part of someone you love, and part of yourself. Formed by "the fusion of two mysteries, or rather two sets of a trillion mysteries each; formed by a fusion which is, at the same time, a matter of choice and a matter of chance and a matter of pure enchantment," as Nabokov would have it. But when I looked at Nathanial I could see nothing to love. Nothing of Gavin, and nothing of myself, and worse, I felt his presence diminishing my love for Gavin, for myself, for anything at all.

When my "postpartum depression" stretched on far beyond what anyone considered "normal," the doctor gave me pills that made me feel numb and distant almost all the time, which I readily accepted, because I found that dull and drifting state preferable to the alternative.

Even with the pills, though, I could only go so long without seeing my son, and as the days became weeks and the weeks became months and the months stretched on into years, I gradually got to know him, even as he gradually became more and more like a human being. A tiny stranger, shrunken and wizened, living in my house.

It should have helped that Nathanial was a precociously well-behaved child, the kind that you see in horror movies that never turn out well. As with Gavin, there was nothing that I had to complain about. In almost every instance, Nathanial was quiet, reserved, quick to develop, or so I was told, and generally happy to play by himself. And yet the one time that he *did* begin to cry, loudly and inconsolably and, to my mind at least, without adequate reason, in a restaurant, I immediately wanted to strike him. I felt the itch in my arm, a physical sensation. Instead, I just got up from the table and walked away, let Gavin and his mother deal with it.

I wanted them to shout at me, to scold me for leaving. I wanted their anger to push me away, to give me the excuse that I needed to run. But they never even brought it up.

One of the favorite pastimes at Gavin's family gatherings became debating which family member Nathanial had inherited which features from. No one there knew what my ancestors looked like, but every now and then they would toss me a bone, saying that he had my cheeks or nose. I couldn't see it, though. Not the resemblance to me—besides maybe his hair, which was black as a slick of oil—nor to any of the laundry list of relatives that Gavin's family trotted out. Instead, I began to see something else. Someone else. Dr. Hartledge.

I told myself that it was wishful thinking, projection. That I missed the man who had been my substitute father, that I was still grieving his death, and so I was personifying his presence in Nathanial. Maybe, I reasoned, it was a way for my brain to try to trick me into loving this small person who had come out of me, who was literally made out of my flesh, and yet to whom I felt no attachment whatsoever.

Morbidly I imagined, at times, an exchange that was far more literal. That if we were to dig up Dr. Hartledge's grave, we would find in his coffin a shrunken doll, like a ventriloquist dummy. His physical essence somehow siphoned into my growing son.

Nathanial was fascinated with magicians from a very young age, but he always wanted to know how the tricks were performed. He was never content with wonder. Gavin said that he took after me, but I wasn't so sure.

When Nathanial was only three years old, a gray streak appeared in his hair that would never go away. The doctors said that it was nothing to worry about, that sometimes it happened, but I saw in it the gray hair that Dr. Hartledge had sported throughout the years I knew him, and I remembered the pictures that I had seen in his house, of him and his wife when he was a young man, when his hair had still been black as pitch.

I became obsessed with the idea of Dr. Hartledge's corpse slowly shrinking away, his flesh vanishing, his bones reducing, as my son's grew.

Was this paranoia? Schizophrenia? I had read about women who drowned their children, poisoned them, locked them in freezers. Were these the kinds of thoughts they had, before committing such an act?

Perversely, while my delusions made me afraid of my infant son, they also made me more fond of him. They gave me something to connect him with, some way to see him as more than just a tottering golem, a creature. In his dark eyes, so dark they were almost black, I could imagine Dr. Hartledge looking out, and I could remember that glitter in his eyes on my wedding day. It wasn't the love of a mother for her son, but for a while it was enough, and gradually I stopped taking the pills that the doctor had given me, started paying a little more attention to Nathanial.

I found that I could bear the touch of his clammy hand without flinching, that I could care for him as a mother should, if not with genuine affection, then at least with tenderness. It was enough to placate everyone around me, to let Gavin feel freed up to treat me like a person again, and not like an invalid. It was enough, I supposed, to make a life.

Gavin and I started going on dates again. One night a month we'd leave Nathanial with Gavin's parents and we would go out to dinner and then catch an old classic at the revival theater in town. *Laura* or *Vertigo* or *Forbidden Planet*. Or we would go to a concert at the university. Gavin had been in a jazz band in college, and though he never played anymore, he still liked to go and sit in the dark and listen to the horns.

One night, when Nathanial was five years old, Gavin and I were playing a game of Scrabble in the living room, with candles and glasses of wine, while Nathanial played with his toys on the floor next to us. When we were done, Gavin went up to shower, and I lay on the couch with my eyes closed until I felt Nathanial tugging on the sleeve of my robe. "Can I play with the tiles, Mommy?" he asked, and I said of course, as long as he stayed where I could watch him.

He dumped the tiles out of the satin bag onto the hardwood floor, and turned them all over, until the letters were facing up. He pushed aside the two blank tiles, and then began to rearrange the others, his brow furrowed in concentration. He would push a few letters together, as if trying to form a word, and I smiled, both at his acumen, and at his struggle.

As he worked, I drifted, my fingertip faintly circling the rim of my wineglass, making it sing. I thought, for some reason, about school, about the way that the light had filtered into Dr. Hartledge's office through those high, high windows. About the motes of dust caught in the air. A snippet from *Four Quartets* came into my mind, thinking of those dust motes. "At the still point, there the dance is."

I was startled from my reverie when Nathanial proudly announced, "Done!" I leaned out from the couch to look over his shoulder, to see what word—perhaps real, perhaps nonsensical— he had managed to spell out from the Scrabble tiles. Instead I saw a string of tiles, broken up into small groups with one long stretch near the end. Not one word, but six. "In my end is my beginning."

Nathanial beamed up at me from his message, his eyes looking nothing like his grandfather's, and my wineglass fell from my hand.

for Dr. Hatcher,
sorry I kind of made you the monster in this one.

Author's Notes: Written for Ross Lockhart's *Tales from a Talking Board*, this is emphatically *not* the "talking board" story that I would have expected myself to write, but it's the one that came out when I sat down at the keyboard.

I dedicated this story to Dr. Hatcher, who was one of my philosophy professors and really *was* my faculty advisor in college. A lot of the elements of Dr. Hartledge are lifted directly from my real memories of Dr. Hatcher and his office, but the real Dr. Hatcher was into fly fishing, not stage magicians or ghost debunking. I'm sure that he would have happily debunked a ghost or two if the opportunity had presented itself, however.

DARK AND DEEP

The place was right where Sophie had said it would be: the middle of the desert, in a low-slung yellow building under a sign that asked, demanded, "What is IT?" in eight-foot letters that dripped black paint. All around in every direction the ground was baked hard and crumbly, like a cake left too long in the oven. The closest thing to water was the heat haze that hung everywhere in the air, and the sweat that gathered at her temples, her armpits, and between her breasts.

Next to the building was an old gas station, with a broken neon sign in the shape of a nautilus shell and a hand-painted slogan in the window—maybe intended to be ironic—that said "live bait." The shell on the sign was a reminder that this had all been an ocean once; that archaeologists and even just kids with shovels and pails still dug up trilobites and crinoid stems on the regular. Reminders were important, because without them it would be impossible to ever believe it.

Besides the two buildings and a pile of red boulders off in the distance, there was nothing anywhere but her car and the heat haze and the flat black snake of the road. For hours now she had been driving through this—through kilned earth and heat so intense that the air conditioner in her station wagon couldn't keep up. Driving away from her cramped apartment, from the nursing home where her mom now languished, from everything but her memories. Now she sat still and leaned forward, shielding her eyes with her hand and feeling the heat of the sun through the windshield tightening the skin on the back of her arm.

Reluctantly, she shut off the engine, and immediately the temperature inside began to climb. She rolled down her window, then reached across and rolled the passenger side down too, even though no breeze stirred the scorched air.

She got out, started to shut the door, then reconsidered, left it hanging open. Not like there was anything in her car worth stealing anyway. Cans of off-brand lemon-lime soda floating in a cooler full of dirty water, empty wrappers from candy bars and beef jerky, a book of burned CDs and a Discman with one of those cassette tape converter thingies that let her play it through the car's ancient stereo.

She wore a stretched black Clash T-shirt—Paul Simonon smashing his bass on the stage of the Palladium—over cutoff denim shorts, sunglasses that she'd bought at a truck stop in the Texas panhandle and not enough sunscreen. Her left arm was already turning red.

The heat that bounced back from the ground warmed the bottoms of her feet even through her sneakers as she walked around to the back of the car, opened it up. Inside, next to the army blanket and jumper cables, were a ball-peen hammer and a pair of bolt cutters with orange handles. She tucked the hammer through her belt loop, grabbed the bolt cutters, and left the back door ajar behind her. If she found what she'd come for she'd have to move everything around anyway. She would need the space.

The place looked deserted, but she didn't want surprises. She walked around the old gas station first—its pumps had been removed years ago, but the awning remained, casting a feeble shadow—then the low yellow building itself, knocking on every door she could find. She got no answer. No sound from inside, no flicker of movement glimpsed through the filmed-over windows. No one and nothing.

The only windows in the low yellow building were thick horizontal slits set high in the walls, to keep the curious from peering inside without paying their nickel. The door in the back was unpainted metal, the one in front the same color as the rest of the building. It was held shut with a rusting chain, but she had expected that. It's what the bolt cutters were for.

Once the chain had slithered to the dirt in a puff of dust that seemed to just hang in the still air, she stepped into the dimness of the building. She had brought a small Maglight, but the grimy windows let in enough illumination that she didn't need it, not right away. The ceilings inside were low, claustrophobic, and there was a layer of dust as thick as a coat of paint over every surface. She had to wipe it away to read the hand-painted sign that rattled off prices for admission and for sodas and snacks.

Beyond the entryway was a beaded curtain that made the welcome sound of rain as she passed through it, and, on the other side, long glass cases like the kind watches and rings were kept in at the jewelry store. When she wiped away the layers of dust she could see that the cases held taxidermied animals and broken fossils. Some were normal—snakes and scorpions, frozen in threatening poses—while others had been subjected to postmortem vivisection to transform them into *lusus naturae*; a Jackalope, a trout covered in fine black fur.

Past these cabinets of curiosities was another doorway, this one arched and covered in a black sheet turned gray by dust and years. Above it was written the same legend she had seen outside, in letters more reasonably sized this time. On the other side, she knew, there wouldn't be any more windows. This was the main attraction. She fished the tiny Maglight out of her pocket and thumbed the black rubber button. The beam of silvery illumination seemed thin even in the dusty dimness of the outer room, but it was what she had.

She took a deep breath before pushing past the curtain, like a diver getting ready to jump from the board. Partly to steel her nerves, partly so that she wouldn't breathe in the cloud of dust that she knew she was about to dislodge. Then she stepped through the doorway, and saw IT.

Abby can't remember when she first met Sophie. In her mind, Sophie has always been the nice old lady up the street, the one who tells her stories and sends her home with jars of bread and butter pickles and apricot preserves.

Sophie's husband is dead—she has a picture on her nightstand, of the two of them on their wedding day, that looks to Abby like a picture from an old movie—and her daughter is grown and lives in Seattle. Since Abby is little, she doesn't think of Sophie as old, not really. She's simply a grown-up, and all grown-ups are essentially the same age to Abby.

Sophie, for her part, is the only person who treats Abby like she is really there, and her light-filled house is a haven where Abby can escape the sullen silences that often descend over her house in the years before her parents' divorce. Everyone else acts around Abby the way grown-ups always act around kids—like they're watching a particularly clever animal that's been taught to do a trick. But Sophie listens to Abby as if she's a grown-up herself, and talks to her like she's a person.

When Abby is twelve, she finds Sophie on the floor of her back porch, a jar of preserves shattered on the floor beside her head making a growing, spreading stain that stops Abby's heart for just a moment. She's the one who calls 911 on the rotary phone in Sophie's kitchen, the way her mom taught her to.

After that, Sophie goes to live at the nursing home, a long, low building of orange brick where old people sit and wait for Death to come. Abby still goes to visit her, but not as often as she used to. Instead of just two doors down, the nursing home is fourteen blocks away, across the wooden footbridge that spans Tucker Creek and past the graveyard where many of the people from the nursing home will soon end up.

It isn't until after she's in the nursing home that Sophie finally tells Abby the story. "When I was a girl," Sophie says, "the circus came to town. It wasn't really much of a circus—it was more what they used to call a ten-in-one, what these days we'd call a freak show—but it was more circus than I had ever seen. It didn't come on the train; it came on trucks with wooden sides, each one painted up like a billboard for what was inside. I remember the dirt of the fairgrounds packed hard by the truck tires and the feet of the roustabouts, the smell of hamburgers and waffle cones.

"It wasn't a proper ten-in-one, because there wasn't one big tent, just a lot of little ones, a barker out in front of each, exhorting you to come on in. There was a scrawny lion and an alligator in a long trough that they advertised as 'a beast from the mists of prehistory.' There was a bearded lady and a strongman. I don't remember what else. All I remember is him."

It is at this point that Sophie takes out an old cigar box. It is wrapped and tied in ribbons, carefully, lovingly. The logo has been partly covered over in silver paint, etching stars and moons and crude drawings of fish. "The sign on the side of his truck said that he was a 'Man from the Sea,' and it showed a picture of something like a fish that had stood up on two legs, its fins making robes around it, like a priest. They kept him in a big glass tank, the kind that Houdini used to escape from, stood up on its side and full of water so blue that it seemed to almost glow. Or maybe it was him that glowed; I can't seem to remember anymore.

"He didn't look anything like the picture on his sign. He was slender and scaled, with a ridge that ran up his back and along his arms. His hands were webbed, like baseball mitts, and his gills like flowers. He was the most beautiful thing I had ever seen. I think now that I was in love with him, but I was a child then, and didn't know what love was.

"I remember walking up and putting my hand against the glass of the case. Later, my father would tell me that he wasn't real, that it was just a person made up to look like a fish, but I always knew better. When I put my hand against the glass, he looked at me, and I know that he saw me, saw into me, and his big hand came down, pressed against the glass on the other side of mine."

As she talks, Sophie has been slowly, almost absently untying the ribbons that hold shut the box, and when she stops, she opens it reverently, the way a religious person would open up a holy relic, and hands its contents to Abby. Inside are papers—a handbill that has been folded and re-folded time and again, photographs that are faded with age—and a single scale that glitters with all the colors you can find on the inside of a shell.

"The circus came all the way from Florida, at least that's what the barkers said, and that's where they claimed to have picked him up. When I was a grown woman, I convinced Charley to take me to Florida for one of our anniversaries, though I never told him why. I went looking for the town that the circus came from—it had been written on the trucks, and on the handbill that I folded up and kept in the pocket of my skirt—but when I found it I couldn't learn much. There was a spring nearby, though, full of beautiful blue water, like the water in his tank, and I knew somehow that he had touched it, that he had been there. I kept a bottle of that water for years, but it eventually dried up, even with the cork in tight."

At the bottom of the stack of papers is a postcard with the words "What is IT?" surrounded by crude drawings of shrunken heads and scorpions and what Abby will eventually learn is called a bishop fish, and on the back a map drawn in blue ballpoint pen. "They'll take these things away from me eventually, if I keep them here," Sophie is saying. "I want you to have them. I found out where he is, finally, where they took him, but I never made it there. He comes to me at night now, in my dreams. He needs my help. But I've gotten too old, while he just stays the same."

The station wagon rolled, crunched to a stop in the shadow of tall trees. It was dark down where Abby was, but up high the sky was

still blue, the stars only just coming out. The headlights showed
the gate up ahead, corroded iron pipe plastered with signs from
the state warning against trespassing and the dangers of the tides.
When Abby got out of the car, she could hear the sound of the
ocean way off, like wind in the trees.

She had driven much farther than she needed to, always heading north and west. Somewhere near Reno she had seen a symbol
of a Jesus fish spray-painted onto an overpass—the one that is just
two curving lines that intersect—but to her it had seemed like a
symbol of something else, an omen or a portent, telling her that
she was going the right way. Why she had felt the need to come
to this secluded stretch of beach just a few hours' drive south
of where Sophie's daughter still lived, when there were miles of
coastline to the south, Abby couldn't say, but here she was.

The bolt cutters were in the seat beside her now, there wasn't
any more room in the back. The body wrapped in the army blanket took up all the space back there, the station wagon turned
impromptu hearse. She had wanted to keep the case that held
him, but hadn't been able to move it.

Death had rendered him unlovely—he was a mummy now,
not a merman, his skin dry and flaking, his scales dull gray—
but there was no mistaking him. Those enormous webbed hands
that Sophie had compared to baseball mitts, those gills, like dried
flowers now. Sophie had known about his condition, had warned
Abby of what she would find.

Sophie's whole life had been spent finding him, tracing his
movements, even as she married, had a family of her own, grew
old. Using her spare time to track down the heirs and surviving
members of the carnival that had passed through her little town
when she was a girl, finding out what had been done with him.
She learned that he had died, his body preserved, passed around,
sold as an oddity, to eventually come to rest in the low yellow
building in the middle of the desert, so far from where he be-
longed. And then, when she finally knew where she had to go,

what she had to do, to become too old, too fragile to do it.

Abby felt the weight of that responsibility in the chill evening air that blew in off the sea, the burden of it and the warmth. That Sophie had loved her, had trusted her enough to leave with her the one task that mattered most. It had pushed her to keep going, even when she doubted her mission, when she assumed that at the end of her trip she would find only an empty building, or a Feejee mermaid cobbled together from fish parts and human cadavers.

She had driven across hundreds of miles with the body in the back of the car, stopping only to fill up with gas and grab snacks from the convenience stations along the way, and as she drove she noticed his smell. Not like fish, and not like dust; not the spicy smell that books had taught her to associate with mummies. He smelled like a flower that blooms at the bottom of the sea, that's what her mind told her, even though she had no idea what a flower like that would smell like, or how she would smell it down under the water.

The bolt cutter snipped the chain on the gate as easily as it had the one on the door to the low yellow building, and Abby swung it wide, the headlights now shining out into deepening darkness, the ocean murmuring its lullaby somewhere up ahead.

When Sophie dies, her daughter flies down from Seattle to take care of things, and Abby stands far away in the cemetery and watches them lower the casket down. She wishes she could get close enough to drop the glittering scale down into the coffin, but she is too afraid. She imagines Sophie telling her that it's okay, that she'll be going to see him soon.

Toward the end, Sophie was having dreams. She told Abby about them. Dreams of a city down under the sea, someplace rich and strange, and the people who dwelt there, all of them rich and strange too, and eternal like the city, like the sea. "They say that we all came out of the sea once upon a time," Abby told her, and

Sophie smiled and put her light, papery hand atop Abby's. "Then maybe it's time for me to go back," she said.

Abby is sad that Sophie's body is going into the ground, rather than into the sea. She thinks that's what Sophie would have wanted. To be dropped into the ocean, her ashes scattered over the waves. But maybe it doesn't matter. Sophie believed, right up to the end, that her merman was waiting for her somewhere on the other side of dreams, on the other side of death, in the only place where she could be as eternal as he was. Maybe she was with him now.

With the station wagon parked in the sediment of the beach, Abby unloaded the body from the back and laid it on the sand. She unwrapped the army blanket from around it, because it didn't seem right to carry it to the water that way. Not twenty feet from her, the waves beat against the nighttime shore with a sound like muffled hammers.

When she lifted him in her arms, she was surprised anew at his lightness. He was big, his body slightly longer than a normal man's, and if he had not been shrunken from desiccation he would have stood more than seven feet tall. It seemed, then, that even his bones should have weighed more than the burden she now carried, but what did she know about his bones? Maybe they were hollow, like a bird's, or were made of cartilage like those of a shark.

She felt the spray from the waves hitting her face like a soft rain, and she thought that he was growing more colorful now than he had been in the desert, though she had nothing but the lights from the car and the stars by which to see.

Even as she waded out into the water, felt it close like a cold vise around her ankles, her calves, felt it soaking the hem of her shirt, she expected this to be nothing more than the burial at sea that she had never been able to give Sophie. Though she had admitted, there in the desert, that what she found in the case in that low yellow building was not a patchwork construct but a real and true fish person, still, she had believed, ultimately, in the finality of death. That ashes turned to ashes, and dust to dust. She had driven this far because it had been a way for her to say goodbye to Sophie, and because she had nothing else to do, nothing to leave behind.

So she was surprised when they came up from the waves and surrounded her. They were wondrous in their variety, no two of them alike. One came hooded, like the bishop fish she had seen on the postcard, another moved across the sand on two twisting legs like serpents. They were horned and finned and scaled, sampling from every creature that swam beneath the waves, but copying none of them. And each one glowed with their own light, and passed that light on to the water around them.

Abby expected them to drown her—that was, after all, what fairy folk did in every story she knew, and she had already seen too much—but she wasn't afraid, as she would have imagined, and when they took his body from her arms, she surrendered it silently.

Then she watched them go, and she saw, as they departed, sank back into the deep dark, that he went with them. Carried at first, then supported, and then swimming alongside the others, gradually dimming, his glow the last thing she saw as she was left behind.

And in that moment she *wished* they had drowned her, had dragged her down with them to whatever lay beyond. She wanted so badly to follow, to dive down into the dark and find the cities that Sophie had seen in her dreams. To leave behind the solid land and its disappointments, her going-nowhere job, her deteriorating relationship with her own dying mother, her string of listless attempts at romance. She longed for a place down in the deep, where none of those things had any meaning. But no matter how hard she wished, her feet remained clay.

Author's Notes: Believe it or not, I wrote this one long before *The Shape of Water* came out, for a monster-themed anthology that never came to pass. It isn't what I had expected to write for a monster-themed anthology, either, but it is a story that had been bouncing around in my head in one form or another for many years. Inspired by the kinds of circus freak shows and roadside attractions that no longer really existed by the time I was alive, what possessed me to write the story with the tenses shifted so that the past became present tense and the present became past I couldn't tell you, but it seems to work.

This is its first time in print.

INVADERS OF GLA'AKI

You remember the game, don't you? When it first showed up at the Qwik Stop up the road, past the supper club and the big empty parking lot, up at the top of the hill. Mr. Kent had given us a big jar full of loose change for washing his old Thunderbird, and we were taking it up there to get quarters so we could play *Street Fighter II* all afternoon. But when we got there, *Street Fighter II* was gone, and that game was in its place, next to the front windows, across from the beef jerky and the rack of magazines.

We were pissed off at first, remember? *Street Fighter II* was our favorite game, and we'd been coming up there to play it every time we had any spare change between us. Neither of us could afford a Sega Genesis or even a Nintendo at home, though your family had an old Atari, one that you had to share with all your brothers and sisters. But the graphics on the Atari were terrible, and *Street Fighter II*, well, it was something else, right?

The game that was in its place caught our attention, though, and not just because, well, what other option did we have? The only other gas stations within walking distance of the trailer park didn't have arcade machines in them, and while we sometimes convinced my mom to drive us up to someplace like the Copper Cue, and you'd once had a birthday party at Chuck E. Cheese—remember,

I got you a new Teenage Mutant Ninja Turtles figure, Leather-head—our options were pretty limited. But no, the game looked interesting because of the weird name, and the big monster paint-ed on the side. It was sort of a giant slug with a round mouth like the lampreys I'd seen pictures of in my school books and a Conan comic. It was covered in multicolored spines, like a porcupine, and it had three eyes on stalks. Even if the background hadn't been a starry sky, filled with swirling galaxies and weird-colored planets, we'd have known it was an alien right away.

The title of the game wasn't anywhere on the side, just a painting of that weird monster. The title was only on the overhang above the screen, written in red in weird-shaped letters, like the names of heavy metal bands on their album covers: *Invaders of Gla'aki.*

"What the hell's a Glaaki," you asked, remember? And I told you that I didn't know, maybe it was another planet.

We watched the game play itself for a while, rotating through the usual title screen followed by snippets of gameplay. It was a side-scrolling shooter, like Darius or R-Type. The players were tiny ships—or maybe they were aliens themselves; they looked sort of like bugs, like the water beetles that showed up in the drainage ditch during the summer. They flew through the air, through space initially, and then through some very odd-looking planets or cit-ies, blasting at equally odd creatures.

We took our jar of change up to the counter, and Kameron, the guy who usually worked in the afternoons when we came by, rolled his eyes at us. "You really expect me to count all that?" We told him he could count while we played, if he'd just set us out the quarters as he came to them. We promised to buy something from the store for his trouble, and since we always did—grabbing snacks to eat while we played, and liters of Mountain Dew—and since the station was never busy in the afternoons, he sighed and started dumping the change out onto the counter, shoving two quarters our way.

Do you remember any of this? I hear you, on the other side of the door, moving around. You know why you can't come out, you saw what happened, so just stay there and wait. It'll be dark soon. And look, talk to me, let me know that this is ringing any bell at all?

The game had a two player option, so we each dropped in a quarter. The first thing that popped up after the title was a black screen with words written on it in red letters: *Do you dare to stop the City of Glaaki* (it seemed like the game couldn't remember whether there was an apostrophe in the name or not, you pointed it out) *from reaching earth?* I suppose it assumed we dared, since we'd already deposited our quarters, and the next screen said:

World I
Shagai

First our ships or bugs or whatever were flying through outer space, the stars moving in that weird jerky way they always seemed to in space video games, and then we were hurtling toward a green planet, and dropping into a weird backdrop of what looked like giant mushrooms and bulbous, misshapen plants. You know bulbous, we learned it from that song, right? Anyway, the enemies in that first level were pretty simple. These sort of purple-and-gray cube things with lots of legs, and weird stumpy monsters that were just feet and teeth. They mostly kept to the ground, though occasionally they fired at us, and there were also big, brightly-colored plants that had waving stems or tentacles that ended in red hands, and their blooms fired spreading shot that was maybe supposed to be some kind of pollen. When it hit us, it did damage, but also slowed us down.

That day, we played for a couple of hours and spent probably ten bucks in quarters, but only got to about the fourth or fifth world, which was called something like "Tond of the Dead Star Balabo," where we flew through cities made out of what looked like shiny blue metal and fought these big guys in robes with heads that were shaped like flowers or something that unfolded to fire sprays everywhere. Then it was time to go home because your mom would be pissed if you weren't back in time for dinner. On the way back down the hill, across the parking lot in front of the supper club, you asked me if I wanted to come over for dinner, and I said that I'd check with my mom. You have to remember some of this?

When we got to your place, your uncle was already home. He works at the meat plant on the other side of the railroad tracks, do you remember that? He has those same boots he wears every day, the ones so saturated with blood that your mom won't let him bring them in the house, so he keeps them in a big Rubbermaid bin on the porch, because otherwise the ants would eat them.

I like your family. At my place, it's just my mom and Rob, her boyfriend. And they're nice enough to me, I guess. Mom works nights at a club, you know what kind, and you never made fun of me for it, which I appreciate. And Rob's a guard at the prison. Mom always tells me that we're only staying at the park until he gets a different job, but I know that it's really until he gets fired, or goes away, like all the others.

Rob and my mom are nice to me, but your family always seemed more like a family, maybe just because there are so many of you. Your mom and your uncle and your older sister and your two younger brothers. I guess, in case, I dunno, in case you stop being able to understand me soon, I should tell you now that your sister was the first girl I ever kissed. It was the day after *Big Trouble in Little China* was on TV, do you remember that? We were crawling through the culvert under the highway, and I was pretending to be Jack Burton and she was Gracie Law and we did that "thrilled to be alive scene," y'know? Afterwards we pretended that we hadn't liked it, that it had just been part of the game, but, because it's just you and me now, I can tell you that I did like it. I'm sorry if I shouldn't have.

I don't remember the other times we played *Invaders* as well as I remember that first one. Maybe you do, if you remember any of this. I know that we played it a lot, more even than we'd played *Street Fighter II*, though I'm not sure I liked it as much. Sometimes we played two-player and sometimes we took turns, because that actually seemed to get us farther. We got to levels with names like "The Maze of the Seven Thousand Crystal Frames" and "The Fifth-Dimensional Gulf," and the longer we played the weirder the levels got. On the dark side of the moon we fought pale, pacing things that came out of black buildings.

I was happy playing the game, because I was playing it with you, mostly, but the longer we played, the less I liked it. It creeped me out, and I started having weird dreams about it. In the dreams, I was walking alongside the drainage ditch that separated the trailer park from the hill, and I could hear this weird sound, like the engine in Mr. Kent's Thunderbird, and I felt like something was pulling me along, I didn't know where, and when I woke up, it felt like the image of the thing from the side of the arcade cabinet was burned into my eyes.

I wanted to ask you if you'd been having weird dreams, too, because your eyes started to get dark circles around them, and you were in a bad mood a lot. I kept trying to suggest other things we could do besides play the game, read comic books on your floor or watch some of the tapes that my mom occasionally let me buy out of the bin at the video rental place. I had *Masters of the Universe* and *Willow* and *The Dark Crystal*, but you didn't seem interested. All you ever wanted to do was go play the game, and it seemed like you always had a pocket full of quarters to do it. I even caught you playing it sometimes when I wasn't there. My mom would send me up to the Qwik Stop for a quart of milk or something, and there you'd be, hunched forward, and I swear, at least once, you were talking to the game, but I couldn't figure out what you were saying.

If you would talk to me, maybe you could tell me more about what happened last night. I know that I woke up because your sister was in my living room, talking to my mom real quiet. She was asking if I was home, if my mom knew where you were. She sounded really scared. I looked at my clock and saw that it was after midnight. My mom came and peeked into my room, but I pretended to be asleep. I didn't say anything, because I didn't want you to get into trouble.

I waited until your sister left, and until I was pretty sure that my mom was conked out in front of old reruns on TV, and then I pulled on my shoes and slipped out my window and headed to the place where I knew you would be. There were cars parked around the supper club, which always looked closed but I knew wasn't. It should've made me feel safer, I guess, like I wasn't out there all alone in the dark, but it didn't, it just reminded me that I was in a different world, one where I didn't belong.

I climbed up the hill, staying out of the glow of the streetlights. I went through the vacant lot off the side of the frontage road, running from one big chunk of broken-up concrete to the next. I had that feeling, that thrill up and down your back that makes you feel light-headed, the one you get when you know you're doing something wrong, something that could get you in trouble.

There was a different guy behind the counter of the Qwik Stop. He had bleached blond hair and bloodshot eyes and he looked pale and nervous, not nearly as friendly as Kameron. The only other person in the store was you, and you were hunched in front of *Invaders of Gla'aki*, right where I'd known I would find you. Maybe it was just the light from the screen on your face, but you looked like you'd been sick, your eyes looked sunken and dark, your skin looked clammy, like when you have a fever. And maybe you did have a fever.

I don't remember what I said to you, maybe you do, if you remember anything. I remember what you said back, without looking up from the screen. You told me to hold on, said, "I'm almost at the last level." On the screen there was a comet, and I could see that the comet had a city built on top of it somehow, one with weird black steeples and ruined buildings. It was burning up as it entered the atmosphere of some planet, and your little bug ship was following right along behind it.

"I guess you didn't stop the city from reaching earth," I said, trying make it sound like I was ribbing you, to soften the blow of what was going to have to come next, me telling you that you had to come home, that your mom was looking for you, that your sister had come to my house. But you didn't look up, and you didn't laugh, just said, "No, I couldn't."

The comet struck the surface of a planet, and it made a huge crater someplace that was surrounded by trees. The screen went black, and words came up:

World XI
The City in the Lake

Except when your ship was racing along again, you weren't in a lake. You were flying in front of trees, big and dark and growing close together. On the ground ahead of you, spaced evenly apart, were odd stone urns or something, shaped sort of like coffins turned upside down. As you approached them, their lids lifted off, and greenish hands with long nails poked out, followed by bodies that looked like people, but also were clearly zombies. They were weirdly large, in comparison to your ship, and they raked at you with their claws. Your regular shots didn't seem to do much against them, just made their claws get longer, but then you hit the button for your special weapon, and a big cone of light, like a flashlight beam, came from the front of your ship. The zombies that it hit drew in on themselves, and then they seemed to grow over with moss or something, and crumbled to the ground in a pile of goo, like Gremlins who got hit with sunlight.

As your ship cleared the trees, you were flying over the surface of some big body of water, with more trees in the background. The water looked black, and then your ship dipped below it, dropped below the surface. It had obviously been a while since the comet dropped to the planet, because not only was the lake above it filled with water, but long plants like seaweed grew up from the bottom of the lake and partially obscured the ruins of the city that had been on the back of the comet. I could tell it was the same city from the dark spires and the ruins, and now that you were flying through it, I could see that the streets were littered with strange-looking corpses, all red and shiny and covered in growths that looked sort of like trumpets.

"Did you have to fight those things earlier?" I asked, but you didn't answer. All you said was, "I'm getting close. Can you see him?"

I couldn't, but then I did. Ahead of your ship was a sort of trap door set in the bottom of the city, a trap door that looked like it was made of glass, and through it I could see three circles watching, like eyes. As your ship got closer, the glass door opened up, and a thing like the alien painted on the side of the cabinet rose up from underneath. I figured this was the final boss, and it certainly moved like one, and I was opening my mouth to tell you to aim for the eyes, which seemed like the most likely weak point, when suddenly the screen went dark, and was replaced by a few words: "Are you ready to receive the Revelation? YES/NO"

And this I'm sure you don't remember, but I do, even though it happened so quick that it's hard to say, even now, exactly what it was that *did* happen. Something came out of the quarter return slot. It looked like a knife, or like a snake, I don't know, it happened so fast, like it was propelled by a spring. Whatever it was, it was shiny, and it went into your chest and stuck there. You stumbled back, and I reached over to pull it out, but it was already gone, already sunk or wriggled or whatever it did into you, and there was only a sort of hard spot under your skin to mark where it had been, and then weird reddish-white squiggles radiating out from that point, like poison in a movie. I thought I'd maybe have to cut it, to suck the poison out, but I didn't have a knife, and the spot where it had stuck you was too hard now to cut anyway.

You couldn't stand up straight anymore, and you fell back against the magazines. I grabbed you by the arm, and helped you over to the front counter. "Please," I said to the unfamiliar guy behind it, "we need help. My friend got hurt. Call a doctor?"

"Not here he didn't," the guy replied. "Now get the hell out before I call the cops."

Even I don't remember how I got you home, down the hill, past the dark-windowed supper club, over the drainage ditch and into the trailer park. Your arms and legs were already getting stiff, but you could still walk, just not well. I wasn't sure where to take you. The sun was starting to come up, and when a beam of it hit your arm it seemed to wither, curl up like a dead plant, turn green.

I knew that your mom would be worried sick, that she would probably know how to treat you, would maybe even take you to the emergency room. But I couldn't explain what was happening to you, and as I helped you to stumble across the drainage ditch you grabbed my arm with surprising strength and croaked, "No. Not home, I'll be fine, I just need time. Please, hide me."

I don't know why I listened to you, but I did. I took you back to my house, helped you in through my bedroom window, and locked you in my closet. Surely you remember that. It's where you are now, and I'm right here, just outside the door. I'd stay in there with you, but you tried to hurt me. I'm sure you *don't* remember that, wouldn't do it if you were thinking straight, but the scratches are here on my arm, and maybe I'll show them to you when you're feeling okay enough to come back out.

I'll admit it, I'm scared to let you out. It's daylight now, and I know I *can't* let you out in the daylight. The daylight would hurt you, like it hurt your arm, like it hurt those things in the stone coffins in the game. My mom came in to check on me after Rob left for work. I pretended I wasn't feeling well, which isn't completely a lie, and told her not to worry, that I just needed some sleep. I should have told her what happened, but I couldn't. I'm afraid that you're really sick, and that they'll take you away. I already lost you once, to that game, I don't think I could lose you again.

Mom said she was going out for some errands before work, that she wouldn't be back til late but that there was a microwave dinner in the freezer. She said that Rob was going out with some of his friends after work, so it'd probably be after my bedtime before anybody was home. I told her that was fine, and promised to call her or Rob if I got to feeling any worse. Then she left, and now it's just you and me.

I can still hear you moving around in there, really quiet, and I really wish you'd talk to me. I don't know what that game did to you, but I've gotta believe we can figure it out together. So this is what I'm going to do. If you can just stay quiet in there, and just try to remember what happened, try to remember that we're friends, and that I'm going to help you, then as soon as it gets dark again I'll open the door and I'll let you out. Then maybe we can figure this out, you and me. At least, I hope we can.

Author's Notes: As someone who publishes in a lot of Lovecraft-themed anthologies, I generally try pretty hard not to write stories that actually take place in Lovecraft's mythos. I go out of my way *not* to pepper my tales with mentions of Cthulhu, students of Miskatonic University, or copies of the *Necronomicon*. But when I was invited to write a story for *The Children of Gla'aki*, a tribute specifically to Ramsey Campbell's contribution to said mythos, edited by Brian M. Sammons and Glynn Owen Barrass, I couldn't really see a way to avoid it, so instead I leaned in, and leaned in hard.

I'm not sure where the idea to recast the plot of Campbell's "The Inhabitant of the Lake" as a side-scrolling arcade game came from, besides that "Gla'aki" just sounds like something from an old space shooter. The trailer park where the two boys live and the convenience store where they play are both inspired by real places from my childhood, and we really did go up there to play *Street Fighter II* pretty frequently.

BARON VON WEREWOLF PRESENTS: FRANKENSTEIN AGAINST THE PHANTOM PLANET

B aron von Werewolf comes out to a clap of thunder, like
he always does, and the painted lightning bolt outside the
window flickers behind him. You can tell that it's painted,
that it's fake, but that doesn't matter, doesn't affect how much you
believe in it.

"I've got a special treat for you tonight, kids," Baron von Werewolf says as he walks into the library, with its candelabras and
its wall of books and the window overlooking the painting of a
graveyard, complete with skeletal trees that claw at the cloudy sky.
He always says "tonight," even though when you watch him it's
always Saturday afternoon. You don't know why he says "tonight;"
if it really is night where he is, or if he just says it because it sounds
better than "this afternoon." It *could* be night where he is. You
learned about time zones in school; maybe he lives a long ways
away. Or maybe it's always night wherever he is, like on the dark

side of the moon.

He walks over to the big wall of books—they're all what your mom calls "foe leather," in reds and greens and blues—and pulls one down. Today's book is purple, and the camera zooms in as Baron von Werewolf strokes his long black nails along the cover, past a silver picture of a planet surrounded by stars.

Every time you watch him, he's dressed the same way, in a smoking jacket and cravat—you saw them in so many movies that you asked your mom what they were called—and a top hat that he always sets aside on the desk before running a long-fingered hand through his mane of wavy brown hair, hair that seems to crawl down his head to become the beard that covers much of his face. He's got an eye patch over his right eye, something he never mentions, though you've occasionally noticed his hand straying to it, like maybe it itches. His other eye is a dark spot that stares out from all that hair, catching the light from the big cameras that you can't see but that let you see him.

You know that it's a TV show, even though your mom, concerned, once asked you if you knew that movies weren't real. She'd been reading something in the paper about kids and TV violence. *Of course* you know that it's just a show, that the movies aren't real. It wouldn't make any sense otherwise. Baron von Werewolf shows you the movies, after all, talks to you about them and how they were made. You recognize actors, sometimes, from one movie to another. That couldn't happen if the movies were real.

But Baron von Werewolf is real. Oh, not a real werewolf, probably, and not in a real castle, you can tell that much. But he's a real person somewhere. A person who gets dressed up and shows you monsters. That's the only reality that matters.

Normally, Baron von Werewolf would sit down behind the desk, open the book, and start to tell you about today's movie, but this time he paces in front of the desk instead, his hand resting on the book, looking down at it, like your mom sometimes does when she forgets what she's doing in the middle of cooking. "I know that you kids have all seen *King Kong*," Baron von Werewolf says when he's walked back across the length of the library. You smile and nod, even though he can't see you. You've seen *King Kong*, and you've also seen *King Kong vs. Godzilla*, which you liked better because it was in color and had Godzilla, who is cooler than King Kong.

"Well, *King Kong* has always been a favorite of mine," Baron von Werewolf continues. He seems a little sad, and you kind of feel bad for him, which is a weird feeling to have. "It was made by a man named Willis O'Brien, and Mr. O'Brien had a dream after he finished it. He wanted to make a sequel, not the one that actually got made, but one where King Kong fought Frankenstein's monster."

Now *that* sounds pretty cool, but also kinda dumb, because Frankenstein's monster wouldn't last long, would he? He's just the size of a regular guy, while King Kong is huge. But then again, Godzilla is a lot bigger than King Kong, but they were about the same size when *they* fought, too...

"He drew up a bunch of sketches and tried to get the movie studios to let him make his movie, but nobody wanted to put the money behind it." Here, Baron von Werewolf rubs his hairy pointer finger and thumb together, making you chuckle. "His efforts to get his movie made eventually led to *King Kong vs. Godzilla*," and you smile again, because you were *just* thinking about that. "But Willis O'Brien's project never happened. However, that's not the end of our story..."

You love it when Baron von Werewolf does that, when he seems like he's coming to the end of something, but then it turns out that it was just a...what does your mom call it...a prologue?

"You see, Mr. O'Brien had a protégé, that is, an assistant, someone who helped him out but also learned from him, the way you kids learn from your teachers at school. Actually, he had several, and one of them was someone you kids will probably recognize—Ray Harryhausen." You *do* recognize Harryhausen's name. You've seen *Jason and the Argonauts* and *7th Voyage of Sinbad* and that weird one where Sinbad fought a statue with a bunch of arms and a centaur with only one eye.

"But Mr. Harryhausen isn't who we're here to talk about tonight either, kids. Instead, Mr. O'Brien had another, lesser known protégé, a young woman from Mexico City who came to Hollywood and wanted to be a stop motion animator, just like O'Brien and Harryhausen. You all remember what stop motion is, right?" You do, because Baron von Werewolf has talked about it before. He says that the movie people make it happen by repositioning tiny models over and over again. Like when you play with your action figures, but very, very slowly. Then, when they play all the pictures together really fast, it looks like the models are moving.

"If any of you have ever seen *Son of Kong*," Baron von Werewolf continues, "some people say that she worked on the cave dinosaur and the giant statue in that movie, though she's not officially credited. Her name was Gabriela Moreno, and her only actual credit is tonight's film, which she wrote, directed, produced, and created the special effects for. There's some question as to how she got the financing, and there are stories that say that she turned to… unorthodox sources."

Baron von Werewolf seems to realize suddenly that he's still standing, and he steps forward in front of the desk, turns more toward the camera, the book still closed in his hands, pressed between his palms. "Tonight's movie was shot in Mexico, and released to a handful of theaters in 1967, but it disappeared from circulation almost immediately afterward, and is considered to have been lost. Some people claim that it never existed at all, but I saw it once, at a tiny theatre that was about to close down. When I decided to track the movie down, I tried to find the owner of that old theatre, but he had disappeared, and I soon learned why. It seems that getting a copy of tonight's film requires that you do what you kids might think of as a favor in return, and it's got some pretty steep penalties. In spite of that, I've got a copy, just one copy, which I'm going to show to all of you tonight."

Once again, you find yourself squirming a little bit. Baron von Werewolf is acting weird, like your mom sometimes does when a stranger asks about your dad. Baron von Werewolf has always seemed real to you, but the way your teacher seems real. He's never seemed like you, or like your mom, but today he does. "I've read your letters, and I know that you kids out there are the best fans that someone like me could ever have," he says, and you smile, because you've written him lots of letters, with your own ideas for monster movies and drawings of what you think the posters should look like, and it's nice to think that maybe he's talking about you. "This is an important movie to me, kids, and I had to agree to pay a high price to get it, so I want you to give it a chance, even if you find it a little bit confusing at first, okay?"

You smile, and nod, and scoot closer to the TV as Baron von Werewolf fades out and the movie begins...

It opens with some words in white on a black screen, first in another language that you guess is maybe Spanish, and then underneath that in English: In Justice for Willis O'Brien.

Those words fade out and are replaced by the title, which makes you sit up a little bit straighter and put your bowl of cereal aside, because it sounds *awesome*.

FRANKENSTEIN AGAINST THE PHANTOM PLANET

There aren't any credits or anything like there would normally be, and the title fades out and is replaced by a picture of a big radio tower that looks kind of like the water tower on the edge of town. The radio tower is sending out little animated lightning bolts while an announcer delivers a fake news broadcast about a comet that is going to pass near earth. The picture is black and white, and the news broadcast seems to cut in and out, so you miss bits of it, but you get the gist. It's a really big comet, and one that "doesn't show up on normal instruments." The announcer continues that scientists and military forces are encouraging people not to panic and to "stay in your homes, as the proximity of the comet could lead to unexpected atmospheric disturbances."

Then that picture fades out, too, and is gradually replaced with the inside of a courtroom. Outside the windows, you can see what is clearly a painted backdrop of New York City. You're disappointed to see that this part is in black and white, too. You don't normally like the black and white movies as much as the color ones, and you consider getting up and leaving, or changing the channel, but then you remember Baron von Werewolf saying how this movie was special, and how you were the best fans in the world, and you remember how it felt like he was talking right to you, so you settle back down to watch.

The people in the courtroom all look pretty much alike, but one guy is standing up in front, facing the judge, while everyone else sits down. The judge is talking, but the camera gradually zooms in on the guy, instead. He has his arms behind his back, and his chin up, looking very brave, while the judge refers to him as "Doctor" and says how he has been found guilty of "willfully creating the monstrosity that has laid such waste to our fair city." The judge goes on to say that the Doctor will be remitted to Devil's Island— a name that you've heard before in old movies, so you know that it's a prison—but that since his creation can "by no earthly weapon be destroyed," other plans have "perforce" been made.

You start to get up to get a pencil and a piece of paper so you can write down that word, "perforce," and ask your mom what it means later, but then the scene changes again, and what it changes to stops you in your tracks. It's a big open area, like a town square, and there are dozens of people, maybe hundreds all crowded around. In the center of the square is an enormous throne made of metal girders, and sitting on it is a giant. For just one moment it looks like a statue, but then it moves, straining against the chains that hold it down.

Even though the judge never said the Doctor's full name, you know who he is, just as surely as you now know what this is: the Frankenstein monster, even though it doesn't look much like any of the costumes of the monster that you've seen at Halloween, or the way the monster looked in any of the old movies. It's huge, for one thing, every bit as big as King Kong ever was, making the idea of them fighting suddenly not seem so silly. But it also doesn't look like Boris Karloff, even under a lot of makeup. There are no bolts in its neck or stitches across its head. Even moving around it still looks like a statue, but one that hasn't been carved very well, its skin a sort of midway point between stone and an elephant's hide. Its shoulders slope, and its arms are long enough that they would hang down to its knees, if it were standing up instead of chained to a chair. Its struggles have the same uneven, jerky motions as King Kong and the skeletons in *Jason and the Argonauts* and the cyclops in *Sinbad*, so you know that it's stop motion.

Once you drag your attention away from the monster in the throne, you notice two things. The first is that there's a comet in the painted sky in the background. It isn't moving, because it's just a painting, but it could also be because it's very far away and so it doesn't look like it's moving. The moon and stars are constantly moving through the sky, you know that from school, but you usually can't tell they're moving just to look at them.

The second thing you notice is that there is a crane or something lowering a rocket ship down over the throne where the Frankenstein monster is sitting. Bit by bit the rocket covers the monster, until he is completely hidden from view and with a metallic clank the rocket locks into place.

The next thing you see is the rocket ship flying through space toward the comet. The comet is huge, and as the rocket ship approaches it, you can see designs on its surface that might be drawings of buildings or trees or something, like maybe someone had painted the comet over an old map. Then the rocket strikes the comet and the screen goes black.

THE PHANTOM PLANET

When the picture fades back in, there's been a change, a drastic one. The movie is in color now! And not just color, but vivid, candy-bright color. It reminds you of the colors in *Planet of the Vampires*, which Baron von Werewolf showed you one time. Just like in *Planet of the Vampires*, the weird colors are part of an alien world—the comet, obviously, which must also be the Phantom Planet—a world of black dirt and strange plants where the rocket ship has crash landed. There are bright pink and purple bushes, and mushrooms that reach taller than trees and seem to be lit from inside.

From out of the wrecked rocket comes the Frankenstein monster, and he is the only part of the movie that still seems to be in black and white. You guess maybe that's just what color he is, all shades of gray, like stone or an elephant after all. He moves sort of like an elephant, too, like his arms and legs are heavy.

He looks around, taking in the surface of the Phantom Planet as if maybe he's never seen color before, either. You sort of like that idea; that earth is all in black-and-white, but that the Phantom Planet is all the colors of a box of crayons. That seems right somehow.

As the Frankenstein monster starts to move away from the rocket ship, something else comes from off the edge of the screen. For a second you think they're people, but they're definitely not. Smaller than the Frankenstein monster, but still not as small as the people were in the earlier shot, they appear to be robots with four mechanical legs and little short arms that are holding long sticks with tuning forks on the ends. They don't really have bodies, just legs and arms jutting out of a square box, and then on top of that a clear dome through which you can see their glowing brains. The way they move lets you know that they're stop motion, too.

They scuttle like boxy crabs onto the screen. Two of them, then three, four, until they surround the Frankenstein monster, trapping him against the wreckage of the rocket that brought him here. They make some kind of noise. Clicking, and these sounds like the beep at the end of an answering machine, only shorter, as they jab at the Frankenstein monster with their long sticks. Every time one of the tuning forks touches him, there's a little spark of blue electricity, and he draws back, seeming more startled than hurt.

At first he just tries to back away, holding up his big arms so that the tuning forks shock his elbows and forearms instead of his torso. Finally he roars, lashing out and smashing one of the little robots apart. Bits of metal go flying everywhere, the glass dome shatters, and you see the thing that you thought was the robot's brain crawling away, dragged by a bunch of narrow tendrils. It doesn't get far, however, before the Frankenstein monster brings one of his big elephant feet down and smooshes it, leaving behind something that looks a lot like grape jelly.

It seems like the Frankenstein monster is going to make short work of the alien robots—you realize that you've been thinking of them as Martians, which isn't right, since they're not on Mars, they're on the Phantom Planet. So…Phantomites? But then more Phantomites show up, rolling out this new thing. It looks sort of like a wagon, but it has big knobby wheels, and in the middle of it is a ball with a ring around it, like a flying saucer, or like Saturn seen from the side. As the other Phantomites try to hold the Frankenstein monster off with their long sticks, the ones pushing the wagon operate a lever on it with their short pincer arms, and the ball shoots off into the air. It only goes up a little ways, and then it hovers in front of Frankenstein's monster at about eye level, suspended on a wire that you can sometimes see against the black backdrop.

The ball part pulses red, then blue, then green, then red again. The Frankenstein monster stops struggling and just stands there, his long arms dangling limp at his sides, and you know that the ball has hypnotized him somehow! You saw somebody hypno-tize Vincent Price like that once, with a multi-colored lamp that turned.

In a trance, the Frankenstein monster follows the Phantomites across the black desert filled with the strange, unearthly plants. They pass an odd lizard with bulging eyes and only two webbed feet that drags itself off a rock and disappears as they approach, and another time a bunch of things that look like purple spiders but with all their legs shoved to the back scuttle out of the path in front of them. Through the air, odd things like round bats with four wings flap, and everything is some color that animals aren't on earth, like the drawings that younger kids sometimes color at school.

After walking for a while, the Phantomites and Frankenstein's monster reach a building. It looks like it was once someplace grand; a palace or something, with a wall around it, and a huge dome. But it has fallen into disrepair, and now vines grow up it that sprout bright flowers in colors you'd have to dig through your crayon box to name. As you watch, the flowers open and close, like mouths.

Inside, the dome is cracked open, so that the black sky shows through on the other side, and there are lots more Phantomites, some of them bigger than others, their robot suits almost as large as the Frankenstein monster himself. In the background you can see hundreds more, painted so they don't move, all gathered around to watch, like in a colosseum in old gladiator movies. In the middle of the building there is a hole in the ground, and above that a huge mechanical thing with four screens on it, like giant TVs.

The Phantomites get out of the way as Frankenstein's monster walks forward, following the glowing ball until it passes over the pit, and you leap up to say something, even though you know he can't hear you, as Frankenstein's monster steps over the lip of the pit and then he's falling, falling, falling.

He hits the bottom like a dropped toy and for a moment lies in a heap before slowly rising, shaking his head. You can tell from the way he moves that he's no longer in a trance, and you creep closer to the TV, wondering what the Phantomites want with him, and what he's going to find down in this hole, but then, all of a sudden, the picture cuts to a commercial.

You get up to refill your cereal, and when you get back Baron von Werewolf is back on the TV. He's saying something about the next sequence of the movie, how it's pretty scary, so you may want to close your eyes through some parts of it. He says that there was once a "spider pit" sequence in the original *King Kong*, but that it got cut out of the movie for being too scary, and how he's pretty sure some of what you'll see in the next part of the movie is actually left over from that.

Then he says, smiling just a little, "Well, we warned you," and the movie starts back up.

When it does, it seems like maybe something has been missed, because it's not quite where it was before. Frankenstein's monster is already up, and he's in a different part of the cave, one where it's all lit in purples and greens, and big glowing crystals stick up out of the ground and out of the walls. He's also being surrounded, gradually, by all sorts of weird creatures.

There's a thing that looks like a tick, but instead of legs it has tentacles; there are giant skeletal crabs, and spiders with big bent legs, and others, huge and hairy, that are just shadows in the background. All of them are moving at once, converging on Frankenstein's monster. From behind him a shadow rises up, a big worm thing with arms and bulging eyes that glow. It grapples with the Frankenstein monster and manages to wrestle him to the ground as the other creatures close in.

The scene shifts, and you're seeing the Phantomites up above, watching all this on the four big TVs suspended over the pit. The thing on the bottom of the TVs is projecting a beam of light down into the pit, and you guess maybe recording what's going on or something, so that they're watching it, just like you are. But you're rooting for the Frankenstein monster, while you're pretty sure they're not.

On the TV screens, you can see Frankenstein's monster struggle back to his feet, raising the wriggling worm thing up into the air and bringing it down onto his knee, like you've seen wrestlers do. The worm twitches a few times, and then is still, the light going out of its buggy eyes.

After that the other creatures sort of draw back, and the Frankenstein monster starts to make his clompy way across the floor of the cave. The various monsters get out of his way, scuttling back into holes and stuff, but then suddenly it becomes clear that maybe it's not him they're avoiding, as something else comes out of a really big hole in the side of the cavern. At first all you can see are its eyes, which come on like Christmas lights, glowing bright blue. But then the rest of it follows. A big lizardy thing, somewhere between a brontosaurus and an alligator, but where the other lizards you've seen so far on the Phantom Planet only had two legs, this one has six, and a long snaky tail. The eyes pop out of its head like those plastic bubbles that toys come out of quarter machines in, and its snout is long and toothy.

It charges the Frankenstein monster, its mouth open wide to bite, and latches onto his forearm. They wrestle around for a bit, with first the dragon—for so you immediately think of it—and then the Frankenstein monster getting the upper hand. At one point he wrestles its body to the ground and sits astride it, pounding on its head with his huge fist while it lashes its tail and continues to bite him.

Finally, the dragon rears up onto its back two pairs of legs and rams the Frankenstein monster with its head and its front feet, knocking him to the ground, where he lays still and doesn't move. You slide forward again, closer to the TV, your cereal forgotten. You know that this can't be where the Frankenstein monster dies, that would be a terrible movie, just as you know that he is bound to die, because the monster *always* dies, no matter how much you want him to live.

The dragon stomps around the body twice, waving its head and roaring, and then it starts to move away, back into the dark cave, when you see the hand of the monster twitch. With a sudden movement, he grabs the dragon's tail, and the next thing you know the Frankenstein monster is on his feet, hauling the dragon back toward him hand-over-hand, like he's playing tug-of-war.

When the dragon gets close enough it circles back around to bite again, but the Frankenstein monster punches it on the head and then grabs it in a headlock, dragging it backward until you hear the snap of its neck and it lies still, at the monster's feet. Not content to let it make a comeback like he did, the Frankenstein monster brings his foot down on its neck and keeps pushing until it goes all the way through.

The film seems to skip a bit here, and suddenly the Frankenstein monster is climbing the wall of the cavern, presumably climbing out of the pit and up to where the Phantomites are waiting. And you're eager to see him get to them, to see him smash them up for tricking him into the pit. But he doesn't make it all the way up, not yet. Instead, he finds a ledge, and on it a smaller tunnel, which he goes through.

On the other side, the tunnel opens out, and you see maybe the weirdest thing you've seen in the movie so far, which is saying something. The room that Frankenstein's monster comes into is filled with machines that don't seem to make a whole lot of sense. Lots of big pipes, lots of glass cylinders filled with colored liquids that bubble and rise and fall. And at all of the machines are mushroom people.

Baron von Werewolf once showed you a movie called *Attack of the Mushroom People*, and the mushroom people in it looked almost just like these, although, like everything else in *Frankenstein Against the Phantom Planet*, these are more brightly colored and seem to glow faintly. They stand at every machine, making a constant sort of murmuring, purring noise—like the tribbles in that one episode of *Star Trek*—and operating levers and turning knobs.

When the Frankenstein monster walks into the room, the closest mushroom people start to run away, or waddle away, since that's about all they can do, but then the weird little collars they wear around what would be their necks if they were regular people light up and they stop suddenly, and then trudge back to their places at the machines. The light-up collars remind you of the ball that hypnotized Frankenstein's monster, and you realize that the fungus—you learned that word in school—people are slaves to the Phantomites above, and you can tell that the Frankenstein monster realizes it, too. Given what you know about the story of Frankenstein, you don't think that the monster will take very kindly to things being slaves.

You don't seem to be wrong, either, as the film jumps again and in the next scene the Frankenstein monster is above ground, inside the huge dome from before, smashing Phantomites. They fire bolts of lightning at him from things that look like glass balls on top of pyramids, but they hardly slow him down. Then, he knocks down the wall of the dome, and from the outside you can see the model building falling apart, no doubt crushing the Phantomites.

The big fight comes when the Phantomites send a huge version of themselves—one with bigger pincer arms than the others, and an enormous translucent brain inside a glass shell—to fight the Frankenstein monster. The two grapple, and it looks like the Frankenstein monster is done for, as the other Phantomites crowd in and distract him by zapping him with the tuning forks on the end of sticks that they had earlier. But then the fungus people come streaming up out from the underground somewhere, and they start to fight the smaller Phantomites, freeing up the Frankenstein monster to concentrate on the big one.

He manages to tear off one of its pincer arms, and then he uses it to crack the glass dome that encases the actual Phantomite brain thingy. After that, he pushes the whole thing over into the same pit that the Phantomites tricked him into earlier. You don't see what happens to it when it falls, but you know that it can't be very good.

The movie ends abruptly, with Frankenstein's monster sitting on a big throne, like he was at the beginning. This time, though, there are no chains, and he's surrounded not by an angry mob but by the fungus people, their mushroom heads all bowed. As the screen fades out, it is replaced one last time by titles:

FRANKENSTEIN, KING OF THE PHANTOM PLANET

After that there's a commercial, and when Baron von Werewolf comes back on he's smiling, but he also seems nervous, his good eye glancing around a lot rather than looking right at the camera, and therefore at you. The book is lying on the desk now, and he's pacing in front of it. Not for effect, like he sometimes does, but just pacing, like someone waiting to be called into the principal's office.

"What did you think of that, kids?" he asks, again seeming to force his smile. "I know that it's a little shorter than some of the other things we've seen on here, and I've got more in store for you, so don't change the channel..."

He's probably going to say more, you figure he is, but instead he stops his pacing. He's not looking at the camera, but he's also not looking at what's behind him, where the camera is pointing. You are, though. It seems like the library has gotten darker, without you really noticing, and most of that dark seems to be gathered in one corner, the corner directly opposite the camera.

In fact, that corner has gotten so dark that you can't see it anymore. The painted stones of the castle wall are gone, and the candles in the nearest candelabra have started to dim, their flames suddenly burning blue. Baron von Werewolf still isn't looking in that direction, he's staring off the screen, his arm half-raised, and you can see his breath in the air all of a sudden, like when you go outside on a very cold day.

The shadow in the corner is getting darker yet, thicker, and it seems like it's getting more solid, somehow. At the edges, it looks almost tattered, like instead of a shadow it's a bunch of dark cloth, or black spider webs. Somewhere up high in the dark, too high for a person's head, unless they were standing on a ladder, you notice that there are two eyes. Or maybe they're not eyes, though it's the first thing you think to call them, because of how they're spaced apart. They don't really look like eyes, though. They look like metal, or maybe like glass, with something moving on the other side of them. It's one of the neatest effects you ever saw.

"No," Baron von Werewolf says, very quietly, still not looking into the shadow that's getting thicker by the minute. "Please. Not in front of the kids?"

The shadow reaches out an arm, a sleeve of darkness with just the echo of fingers jutting from the cuff, and then the picture is gone, replaced by a piercing whine and a bunch of colored bars, like when they test the Emergency Broadcast System.

You stare at the colored bars for a while, and then they're replaced by a commercial, and then the news, which never shows at this time on Saturday afternoon. Finally, you turn the TV off.

You're worried about Baron von Werewolf at first, but then you remember that it's just a show, like your mom is always saying. What you saw had to be a special effect, like the stop motion in the Frankenstein movie. They wouldn't have put it on TV otherwise, right? So instead of worrying, you go outside, under the bright blue September sky, with just a handful of clouds overhead. Under your feet the yard is full of dead leaves and the branches of the tree are already almost bare.

You know that the movies are fake, but you also know that they teach you something real. Just as real as the things your mom tells you, or the things you learn in school. How to look past what's actually there and see instead what *might* be. That's what you're thinking about, as you look up at the sky.

You learned about space in school, too. How just because you can't see it when it's daytime, doesn't mean that it isn't there. You know that just beyond the blue, blue sky, stars and phantom planets are tumbling through the dark, so you stand there in the yard, looking up, past what you can see, and try to imagine what might be waiting on the other side.

for Willis O'Brien and James Whale,
and for all the horror hosts everywhere
past, present, and (hopefully) future.

Author's Notes: Creating a horror host named Baron von Werewolf is something that I've been talking about doing for years. I think the name probably comes from me misremembering the title of the old anthology horror comic series *Baron Weirwulf's Haunted Library*.

The structure of using a horror host as a framing device for a story that then actually becomes the crux of the story's climax is probably borrowed from the Tom Noonan portions of the 2005 Ti West film *The Roost*, while the details are provided by my own memories of watching monster movies on Saturday mornings as a kid.

What about the movie that Baron von Werewolf is presenting? *Frankenstein Against the Phantom Planet* is inspired by my favorite movie that never got made, Willis O'Brien's proposed *King Kong vs. Frankenstein*. When Ross Lockhart invited me to submit something for his Frankenstein-themed anthology *Eternal Frankenstein*, I was struck by the daunting notion of trying to tell a Frankenstein story that hadn't been told a million times before. So instead of going to the Mary Shelley novel or the great James Whale film as my source material, I looked up the sketches Willis O'Brien had done to try to sell *King Kong vs. Frankenstein*. That giant homunculus became my version of Frankenstein's creation, and because I had no budgetary limitations, I transposed him into a purely stop-motion world of monsters and weirdness of the kind I would have loved to see O'Brien or his protégé Ray Harryhausen turned loose in.

THE CULT
OF HEADLESS MEN

Kirby Marsh pulled up in a devil-red Alfa Romeo Spider
because he was *Kirby Goddamn Marsh*, that's why. That
the car was on loan from an actor friend who kept a place
in London due to the fact that Kirby was, presently, as his British
acquaintances would put it, skint, was beside the point.

For now, his creditors were an ocean away and, if Angela did her
job and kept those lovely lips of hers buttoned, they wouldn't have
any idea that Kirby had decided to accept an invitation from an
old friend to spend a few weeks in England.

The house he pulled up in front of was the kind of place that
would normally have been a matte painting in one of his pictures—the British ancestral manor, through and through, with a
hexagonal tower to one side of the broad front door, and a fountain in the middle of the drive peopled by the usual malformed
fish, like decorations from the corners of old maps. "Here there be
monsters," he said to himself as he stepped out of the Spider and
onto the gravel drive.

He had seen houses just like this in some of his competitors'
films—the ones that were coming out of the British Isles today, from companies like Hammer and their ilk now that the

all-but-official ban on horror films in Britain had been lifted following the war. Yes indeed, if he was going to try to horn in on the growing market for British shockers, this certainly seemed the house to do it in. Hopefully his old friend was on the same page. And if he wasn't, well, Kirby hadn't made almost forty movies in ten years by not being persuasive.

As if summoned by Kirby's cogitations, Sir Joseph Drake, as of his father's death a few months prior now the Eighth—or was it Ninth?—Lord Whitley, stepped out of the front doors of Whitley Manor, which, Kirby had to admit, somewhat spoiled the illusion. Not that Drake wasn't a fine specimen of English aristocracy. He didn't seem to have aged a day in the, what, eleven, twelve years it had been since they last met. His hair was still dark and full, and he had grown out a beard, practically a Van Dyke, immaculately kept.

Drake's suit was undoubtedly more expensive than Kirby's, who had gone as natty as he felt comfortable, trying to look less the Ugly American, though his shirt collar was still a bright paisley and he eschewed the tie that Drake was sporting. In one glance, Kirby had cast his old friend as a dashing, charismatic warlock, though from Kirby's recollections, Drake was actually as congenial as you'd like, and meek as a kitten in most situations.

"Kirby," Drake called out in greeting as he approached the car, skipping all the Cheerses and What-hos and other Britishisms that would have, once again, helped to better sell the whole scene. Perhaps that's what almost a decade of schooling abroad did to a fellow. Kirby stepped forward to meet him, swinging his arm around to clasp Drake's handshake, only to be pulled into a half-hug. "It's been too long, old chap." At least there was that, "old chap." It would have to do.

"Drake," Kirby said when the hug was broken and both men had stepped back, "how'd you get yourself roped into this dump?" With a gesture that encompassed the entirety of the sprawling and ancient pile, he added, "Do you want me to help you sell it, or just rent a bulldozer?"

"It's the family homestead, don't you know. I grew up in this ridiculous acropolis, if you can imagine that."

"I really can't," Kirby replied, and he meant it, remembering the two-room apartment in Brooklyn that had dominated much of his own childhood. "Did you get all your exercise just hiking to the commode every morning?"

Laughing, Drake turned to look up at the house, maybe trying to see it through Kirby's eyes. "It'll be perfect for what you're looking for, though, don't you think? Anyway, come on inside, it's too damned hot and bright out here. I know that you're from California, but we English aren't accustomed to this sort of weather."

Which was also true enough. Kirby had been to England several times before, and every previous visit it had been either raining or choked with clouds from dawn til dusk. This trip had been nothing but balmy weather and bright sunshine from the moment the plane touched the tarmac, in spite of the fact that they were headed into fall. Was that some sort of omen, he wondered, and if so, was it good or bad? Was this the British equivalent of the clichéd "dark and stormy night?" Unseasonable sunshine and warm breezes?

Had he found the weather outside too clement for his tastes, as Drake seemed to, then the inside of the house held the cure. The first thing Kirby noticed was the dimness, which forced him to remove his sunglasses as soon as they stepped through the big wooden front doors, all carved with creeping vines and bunches of grapes and grotesque figures like the ones in cathedral carvings peering out from amid the faux foliage.

Those few windows that Kirby could see were small and leaded, and the walls seemed to suck up what little light they admitted. Everything within the manor was cool shade, even in the middle of the afternoon. His first thought was, "great atmosphere." His second: "We'll have to light the piss out of this place if we're ever going to film here."

There was also a smell, not exactly unpleasant, but some odd combination of dusty and damp. The smell, Kirby imagined, of an old house that hadn't been used much or aired out often in decades.

"Shouldn't you have servants to open doors and wipe your ass for you or something?" he asked his host as they descended deeper into the dim interior of the house.

"We still keep a few servants around, but I prefer to do things myself when I can. I'm not my father, thank Christ." Drake said it over his shoulder as he led the way through the front hall, and Kirby had to admit to himself that it was a fact. Though he had never actually met the previous Lord Whitley, Kirby had seen enough pictures of him to know that he had been all good old English stock, with high-collared suits and shining cufflinks and carefully knotted ties, his features pale and bloodless compared to his vivacious offspring.

Kirby followed his host deeper into the house, past a sweeping staircase of the kind that would nicely showcase expensive gowns—on loan, of course—and also throw ominous shadows with the proper lighting setup. They stopped in a sitting room where booze had been placed in crystal bottles on the sideboard, Drake keeping up a steady stream of light chatter throughout. His voice was as jocular and cheerful as it had been when Kirby had known him years ago, but there was a touch of brittleness in it, too. Well hidden, but there for Kirby to spot because, when you stripped away all the glitz and glamor, Kirby's whole job pretty much boiled down to dealing with phonies all day.

But Kirby didn't say anything about it, not yet. Instead he accepted Drake's offer of Scotch and made small talk while looking around the room, peering out the windows at what he could see of the grounds, mentally sizing everything up, Drake included.

His old friend wasn't wrong. The house was perfect, exactly what Kirby was looking for, a gift dropped right into his lap at the moment he needed it most. And Kirby hadn't gotten to where he was by looking gift horses in the mouth, though he also hadn't gotten there without learning that nothing in this world came for free, or without a lot of strings to get tangled up in. There was something Drake wasn't telling him, but that was okay, he'd figure it out in time, and there were things he wasn't telling Drake, too.

Like the creditors that he'd left behind in the States, or the fact that he hadn't much more than a penny to his name. Natty or not, the suit he was wearing was one of only two suits he still had on hand, and his dry cleaning was being done for free by one of the girls at the hotel because she had recognized his name and he had promised her a part in his next picture. Like the borrowed car, these weren't the things that really mattered. Kirby had learned *that* a long time ago, too. It didn't matter what you really had, or who you really were. What mattered were appearances, and those he always had a way of keeping up.

So he sat in the gloomy sitting room—because that's what it's for, it's right there in the name—under the disapproving portrait of some pale, long-dead relative and drank expensive Scotch and reminisced with Drake about old times while waiting for the other shoe to drop. Eventually Drake asked, "Do you want the grand tour?"

And Kirby said "sure," partly because he did, and partly because he'd been to enough fancy houses over the years to know that the grand tour was where things happened, whether those were handshake deals for financing, steamy trysts in back bedrooms, or unfortunate revelations about your host's ulterior motives.

The house was bigger inside even than it had appeared from without, and before they got to the unfortunate revelations part of the tour they passed through innumerable dimly-lit corridors hung with creepy portraits which seemed to loom up suddenly from the shadows, and tapestries where furtive shapes cavorted. After several twists and turns that Kirby could never have retraced, they came out one of the manor's many doors and into the family cemetery, a garden-like patch of dirt on a slight rise out behind the house, bordered by holly trees and overgrown with creeping vines.

The river could be seen flowing off in the distance, and closer to hand headstones canted at odd angles around the central figure of the family crypt, a squat, gray temple to the dead. Kirby couldn't have framed the shot better if he'd had the set built himself.

"I'd offer to show you the inside of the crypt," Drake said, "it seems like it'd be right up your alley, lots of cobwebs and candle sconces, but I'm afraid that it's padlocked, and the key seems to have gone missing ever since Dad's funeral. Thus far, I haven't had the heart to take the bolt cutters to it."

"I can see why," Kirby said with a low whistle. The doorway to the crypt was huge, wide and tall enough to drive a camera truck through, blocked by an enormous iron door decorated with rivets and the wrought shapes of some sort of creeping ivy. A chain wound round the handles of the door, secured with an ancient padlock the size of a human head, the sort that looked like it probably took a real-life skeleton key.

"So did they bury your whole damn clan in this barn?" Kirby asked. Though he was, of course, familiar with the concept, he found it difficult to imagine, his own father little more than a dim memory of a loud, angry voice and the scent of whiskey and cheap cigars. His mother's grave he had moved to Colma when he still had money, and given her a much nicer headstone than the spare, small one she'd had in Jersey.

"Well, mostly," Drake replied. "Everyone's got a plot, anyway, even if a few of the bodies are currently missing somewhere over in the Holy Land or some such place. In those cases, there's just an empty box in the slot. But everybody who *had* a body to bury is buried right here, or stuck in that tomb. I guess I'll be the last, unless some bird comes along and makes me respectable. That's always assuming that I've still got the place by then..."

So there it was, that other shoe. "Thinking of selling?" Kirby asked, already knowing the answer, but knowing also that Drake needed to come at it in his own time, his own way.

Drake smiled, as if he knew that Kirby knew, and shook his head. "Thinking of *losing*. Kirby, old sport, I've got a confession to make. When I asked you to come stay here for a bit, it wasn't just because I thought the old homestead would fit right into your pictures. It was, in fact, because I was rather *hoping* that it would. You see, when the old man passed on, I inherited more than this place and his title. I'm afraid I also got a look at his books for the first time and, well, not to put too fine a point on it, I'm flat broke."

That was something of an onion in Kirby's particular ointment, as he had rather been counting on talking some funding out of his high-born friend, and yet he almost smiled himself at the irony of the situation. Most people would probably find it hard to imagine someone being broke while still occupying such a sprawling mansion, but Kirby understood it all too well. Appearances, again, mattered more than truth, and always had, and always would.

"So," Kirby said, "you're thinking we film a picture here—or, hell, why not make it two or three or four, film them back to back, use the same setups where we can—and then you get to keep the family home, and I get a few more movies under my belt? Is that the plan?"

"Well, *plan* might be too strong a word, but that's certainly the idea, yes."

Kirby looked around once again, turning the new information over in his mind. "The place has certainly got the right mood," he said. "We'd hardly have to do any set dressing at all to make it passable, and hell, there should be plenty of crew available to hire out from under those chaps at Ealing and Bray."

"They've probably already been making your kinds of movies, from what I hear."

"Well, maybe not *exactly* the same," Kirby replied. "My films haven't always been as classy as the stuff your countrymen have been turning out up to now. But times change, and I didn't weather them this far without learning how to change with them."

It was part of the reason he had agreed to come to England in the first place, besides the creditors and everything else. The British film companies were producing smart science fiction films and Gothic chillers with low-cut blouses and bright red blood, while he was still churning out black-and-white flicks about giant mollusks and dragstrip kids finding trash bag monsters in haunted shacks and haunted caves, and he knew that couldn't last. The days of atomic panic and kids in hot rods ruling the drive-ins were coming to a close, and while the Sixties had only just started to swing, Kirby could taste the change coming in the air, and he planned to get out in front of it, rather than be left behind.

There were some logistical hurdles to get by before they could start filming. The first one—and the one most likely to trip them up completely—was funding. Kirby admitted that he was every bit as cash-strapped as Drake himself, and that he had been planning to hit his old friend up for funding to finance the first couple of pictures, and then using the money they made to get the next ones rolling.

"Since you're a bit flat yourself, though," he said, "we'll have to look elsewhere. Fortunately, while you might be broke, I figure that being the Eighth or Ninth Lord Whitley ought to carry a certain social cachet that can get us both into some of the right parties. The kind where there are plenty of people with money to spend. And if you don't mind using your family name to get our foot in the door, I like to think that I've got a certain charm—or at least a way of parting fools and their money—that should be enough to get someone to pony up the dough."

According to Drake, the next party where the "right sort" would be in attendance wasn't for a couple of days, so that first night the two of them ate an exceedingly bland dinner in the manor, one that would have tipped Kirby off as to the absence of many servants on the premises, even if Drake hadn't already told him as much. They didn't eat alone, though. That was where Kirby met the Professor.

Drake introduced him by name, something suitably unassuming and British. Professor Edward Mosby, something like that. But after that first introduction, Drake just called him the Professor, and so Kirby did, too.

He had been a friend of Drake's father since their college days in Eton or wherever they had gone, and the two men had served together during the war. The previous Lord Whitley had always bankrolled the Professor's various expeditions, and it had been included in his will that the Professor would retain his living space and laboratory in the old carriage house out beyond the family cemetery until his own demise, which didn't seem like it could be all that long in coming.

"He was never the same after the war," Drake confided. "At least that's what I'm told. Can't say I really remember much from beforehand."

The Professor was an older man, balding, which made his head seem somehow small for his body. Or perhaps it was that, though skeletally thin at the wrists and ankles, he was nonetheless surprisingly broad of shoulder and chest. His hands and face had that waxy pallor that one associates with corpses and small, bookish men who seldom see any natural light, and when Kirby shook his hand upon being introduced, it was as chilly as the handle of a cold spoon. He wore his collar buttoned all the way up to the neck, and a black silk bowtie speckled with matte black spots.

He appeared perpetually startled and distracted—as though he was listening for something, or, whenever he wasn't speaking himself, he forgot that a conversation was going on around him, and each exchange came to him like a gunshot in darkness—but his voice wasn't the thin, reedy thing that Kirby would have expected. Instead it sounded deep and hollow, like he was speaking to them from deep inside a barrel, a trait that was only enhanced when Kirby asked about his work.

Apparently some sort of anthropologist, the old man initially declined to talk about it, bobbing his too-small head and raising a pallid hand to ward off the question, warning that Kirby would find it "frightfully dull." But Drake was having none of it. "Oh come now, don't be modest, old man!" he said, putting down his own fork. "The Professor has been all over the world. He and my father even discovered some island during the war, down near… Borneo, was it?"

"No, not quite," the Professor replied. "It's a little South Seas island; we never gave it a name. In the dialect of the nearby island-ers it's called the Island of the Headless Men, roughly translated."

"That could be the name of one of Kirby's films," Drake laughed, pointing out just what Kirby had been thinking.

"Oh, it gets better," the Professor said, suddenly warming to his subject, as Kirby imagined he must do when lecturing, if, indeed, he was the sort of professor who lectured. "The natives who dwell on this particular island are uniquely feared and shunned by their nearest neighbors. They have no name for themselves, for from their perspective they are the only people, and all other human animals are simply a food source. To some of the neighboring is-landers, they are known as Tcho-Tcho. What this name signifies, I have so far been unable to ascertain, but it is said always with a certain dread and awe. These men have been my primary field of study since the war, and I believe I am near to publishing the first scientific treatise on their culture. Mr. William Seabrook wrote of them briefly, but he had heard of them only through hearsay."

"Now *that's* a name I know," Kirby said, gesturing to Drake with his fork. "He's the fellow who wrote that book about Haiti that popularized voodoo and put so many zombie pictures into pro-duction back in the '30s and '40s. Hell, I even made a couple. *I Married a Zombie* was probably the biggest, though I don't think it ever made it over here."

He turned back to the Professor, "So these natives, they're can-nibals, right? That *does* sound like one of my movies. But why the 'Headless Men' thing?"

"That remains unclear," the Professor said. "It's possible that the

Tcho-Tcho are headhunters, whose witch doctors make and keep the shrunken heads of their enemies. I also believe that their warriors may paint their bodies with a kind of chalk made from the ground bones of their victims and dyes they extract from local plants, drawing crude, demonic visages on their naked torsos. In the pictographs of the neighboring islanders, the Tcho-Tcho are always depicted as monsters, men without heads but with faces in their chests and mouths in their stomachs."

"That seems familiar somehow," Kirby said.

"I remember Sir Walter Raleigh writing about a similar tribe in Guiana, if I'm not mistaken," Drake said, glancing at the Professor, who nodded.

"Yes, he called them the Ewaipanoma. But he was certainly not the first. Herodotus and Pliny the Elder both tell us of the Blemmyes, headless men whose faces are in their chests."

"Didn't the Hindus have a headless demon, too?" Kirby asked.

Again, the Professor nodded. "Kabandha, whose single eye and mouth are in his torso. And contemporary students of the occult have long whispered of a headless deity known as Y'Golonac, god of perversion and depravity. Even the Bard himself spoke of 'the Anthropophagi, and men whose heads do grow beneath their shoulders.'"

At that moment there was a sound from outside, an echoing clang, like metal crashing against metal. The lights in the house all dimmed momentarily before resuming their usual brightness. "What the hell was that?" Kirby asked, and Drake shook his head.

"It happens sometimes. I haven't yet been able to pin it down."

Whatever it was, it had shaken the Professor. He seemed even paler than he had before, if that was possible, and his eyes were wide, the whites around them showing like a frightened horse. His mouth gawped open and closed like a fish for a moment, and a sound came from his throat, something hideous and creaking. Drake leapt up and slapped the old man on the back, and the Professor coughed, drew in a long, shuddering breath, and then lifted his napkin with a shaking hand, holding it over his mouth.

"I'm sorry," he said. "My nerves, you know?" Both Kirby and Drake assured him that they understood, and the Professor excused himself, demuring Drake's offer to see him back to his rooms in the carriage house.

"So, he seems damn creepy," Kirby said, when he was confident that the old man was out of earshot.

"The Professor? I guess so, though I never really thought of it before. He's been around for as long as I can remember, and I always thought of him as sort of like an uncle. Though now that you mention it, I remember something from when I was a kid. I couldn't have been more than a few years old, it was right after he and my father got back from the war. They had this crate with them, something that they must have brought back from that island. It couldn't have been more than this big," and Drake held his hands up a couple of feet apart, "but the Professor and my dad were both really excited about it. They wouldn't let me see what was inside, but I saw the crate. It smelled old and stale, like how I imagine a mummy would smell, and I'm sure it was just my imagination, but I swear to god that I heard a scratching sound from inside, like rats were in there scurrying around."

"Has he always been so jumpy?"

"Pretty much. He's always been very secretive—I was never allowed to go into his rooms when I was a kid, they told me that there were delicate artifacts that weren't safe for little hands, you know—but he's gotten worse since Dad died. He says he's preparing a monograph on those natives to present before the Board of the British Museum."

"And he's worried that someone's going to get the scoop on him?"

"I guess so. I'll tell you another one, Kirby, because it seems like something from one of your pictures, but this is just between you and me, right? I had a dream, right after my father died. We had laid him to rest in the crypt earlier that day, and that night I had

this dream that the Professor went out to the crypt in the middle
of the night. In the dream, he had this thing with him that looked
like a spider, but it was as big as a horse. Gave me a bad case of the
heebie-jeebies, I don't mind admitting."

Kirby shook his head. "You've been watching too many of my
movies, old sport. Still, those headless fellows of his wouldn't be
too hard to do on film, I wouldn't think. Maybe we can even get
the Professor to do an introduction, after he's published his monograph of course. One of those things where he assures everyone
that our stupid rubber monster is really very scientific, he swears."

The next few days were a flurry of very dull parties—if dull things
can, indeed, happen in flurries—which was just fine with Kirby.
In his experience, there were two kinds of parties: the kind where
you had any fun, and the kind where you got anything accomplished. Right now, he was much more in need of the latter than
the former. That there was a third kind of party, the kind that was
no fun *and* didn't get you anywhere in business, he didn't care to
contemplate.

Over the course of them, he met piles of old British gentlemen and ladies, with Sirs and Madams and Lords in front of just
about all of their names. He shook lots of clammy, pale hands,
and decided that maybe seeming a bit like a walking corpse just
came with the territory on these usually very overcast British Isles.
Ultimately, though, he and Drake were able to convince a handful
of landed gentry to invest the capital that they would need to get
at least three productions up and running almost simultaneously,
all of them using Whitley Manor as their primary setting.

Kirby hired a young playwright that he knew in London. The kid's
name was Irving Drayvon, so he at least had that going for him, and
he was all-too-happy to trade some of his pay for free room and
board at Whitley while he worked on the screenplays, since he was
just about to get kicked out of his flat or garret or wherever he lived
on account of being four months behind on the rent.

They gave Irving a room down the hall from Kirby's, and before long several other key members of cast and crew were also holed up at the manor, though the majority of the crew didn't stay on-site but were, instead, occupying all the available beds in the nearby village. Kirby's room was at the back of the house, shielding him somewhat from the comings-and-goings that now took place at all hours of the day and night, and looking out over the graveyard and the carriage house where, Kirby noticed, the Professor also tended to come and go at odd hours. Looking out his window, he sometimes noticed lights on in the carriage house late into the night, and he could imagine the Professor in there, bent over his desk, hard at work on that monograph.

Most of the time, Kirby didn't pay much mind to the Professor's activities. He had his own things to worry about, rounding up cast and crew and getting production underway. The first event which really drew his attention happened when they were already into post on *Beneath the Blighted Moors* (working title) and about two weeks out from wrapping *Vampires of the Scarlet Coven*. The third film was having problems, though. The title had changed three times already and it hadn't even so much as gone in front of cameras yet. The various delays were tying most of the crew in knots, and Kirby found himself staying awake long into the night, reading over Irving's latest draft of what they were currently calling *The Chiselhurst Conundrum*.

Kirby had pushed his desk up against one of the leaded windows so he could glance out at the moonlight on the headstones when he looked up from the screenplay, which he did from time to time to take a drink of coffee or of Scotch. One of those times, he saw a black sedan pull up in front of the carriage house, and saw the Professor get out. Kirby hadn't even realized that the old man had left, but now he was getting out of the sedan and unloading what looked like a heavy steamer trunk from the back, handling it like it was filled with batting.

"I wonder if he's got a mummy in there," Kirby said aloud, and jotted a note about it—"mummy in a steamer trunk"—into the margins of the script. It wouldn't fit into this picture, necessarily, but he was sure that he could put it in *something*.

The Professor's surprising feats of strength, coupled with the fact that it was almost two in the morning, were enough to distract Kirby from the, he had to admit, somewhat grim task of reading through the latest draft of what was rapidly becoming a nightmare project. So he found himself staring out the window instead of reading, even going so far as to turn off the lamp at his desk, plunging his room into darkness, the better to see the goings-on outside.

He watched as one light and then another came on in the old carriage house, and he imagined, with a director's eye, the old man shuffling about the rooms, unpacking shrunken heads and wooden masks, bone necklaces and fetish dolls pounded full of nails. Of course, in actuality Kirby had no clue what sorts of artifacts the Professor might have on hand, but he had made enough movies with tribal themes in his day to know what sold the notion to the people in Poughkeepsie.

It was because of this daydreaming—was it still daydreaming if it happened in the middle of the night?—that he remained sitting, staring out the window, when the Professor came back out of the carriage house. For a moment, Kirby expected him to head toward the manor, maybe for a bite of very late dinner. While there still weren't really any servants to speak of, Kirby had used the need to cater the shoot as an excuse to bring in a couple of decent cooks from the city.

The Professor didn't take the footpath that led from the carriage house to the manor, however. He walked about halfway and veered to his left, into the family cemetery where they were now letting the weeds grow rank because it added to the atmosphere, rather than because Drake couldn't afford to hire a gardener. A bright moon that was occasionally occluded by drifting clouds let Kirby pick out the man's bald head like a bright stone at the bottom of a stream as he made his way between the weathered monuments. Was he simply taking an evening constitutional, stretching his legs before turning in for the night? Perhaps, but midnight—or rather, two-in-the-morning—walks in the graveyard were Kirby's stock in trade, so he paid attention.

The Professor didn't dawdle, as a man might who had come out to enjoy the moonlight and the ambiance, and instead went straight to the door of the crypt. There, against the backdrop of the dark stone, the moon painted him in a starker silhouette, and Kirby was able to tell that he carried with him what looked like a burlap sack and, moreover, that the sack appeared to be *wriggling*. That was all he was able to tell, however, before the Professor had unlocked the door to the crypt—the one whose key, Drake had said, had gone missing some time back—and disappeared into the darkness beyond.

The scene reminded Kirby of the dream that Drake had recounted to him, the one of the Professor and the spider the size of a horse, and he firmly intended to keep watch until the Professor came back out, but at some point in his vigil the exhaustion of the past few days of long hours and late nights must have caught up with him, for suddenly the sun was coming up beyond the leaded glass and he saw that the crypt door was shut once again, the giant padlock securely in place.

The next morning, Kirby half-believed that he had dreamed the whole thing himself, prompted, perhaps, by the Gothic subject matter of his films and his recollections of Drake's earlier dream story, and so he didn't mention the incident to his host, though he did inquire casually after the Professor. "He's been keeping to himself lately. I think the film crew may all be a bit much for him. Nerves, you understand," Drake said, which Kirby already knew was the code that well-to-do British gentlemen used for everything from stress to alcoholism to stark, staring insanity. Kirby nodded his sympathy and didn't press the matter further.

What he *did* do, perhaps somewhat perversely, was start subtly pressuring Drake to unlock the crypt so that they could use its interior for shooting. "From the way you described it," he said, "there should be plenty of room in there to get cameras and lights and still have space for a couple of actors."

"Oh, absolutely," Drake replied. "It's as big as a ballroom in there. I'll talk to Abby, see if we can't turn up the key." Abby was the oldest of the housekeepers, one who had been there since Drake was an infant, and who stayed on through the financial straits of the family probably due to inertia, as much as loyalty. Kirby had his doubts about whether or not they would find the key, since a part of him wondered if maybe he already knew where it was, but for the moment he let the matter lie.

In the meantime, production on *Vampires of the Scarlet Coven* ran four days over schedule, and shooting started on what was now being called *The Chiselhurst Experiment*. Three days into *that*, when *Vampires* was now *six* days over, *Chiselhurst*'s lead actress, a curly-haired redhead with big eyes and bigger tits, left the set, saying that she wouldn't spend another minute in "that godawful house." It was Irving who told Kirby of her departure, and when he finally caught up with her just before she got into a waiting car in the front drive, all he could get out of her was that she had heard "strange noises" and "awful scratching" while walking the grounds.

So then it was a matter of trying to find a replacement actress, since Sophia Michaels, who had starred in both *Beneath* and *Vampires*, was already off filming something else at Pinewood or Ealing or somewhere. Kirby had to drive down to London to work that out, and also meet with some of the investors who, thank the great good Lord, seemed unfazed by the delays in production when he shook their cold hands, saying simply that they were happy to help, and that they knew the end result would be "a credit to us all."

The drive gave him time to think, and when he was on his way back, he had decided that, upon returning to Whitley Manor, he would press a little harder to try to get Drake to open up the family crypt.

He told himself that it was out of some sort of civic spirit, or at least a sense of duty to his friend. After all, if something unsavory or illegal was going on in the place where his ancestors were laid to rest, it seemed that Drake should know what it was. But ultimately, really, if he had to be honest with himself at all, Kirby was just curious. Ever since he had seen or imagined the Professor skulking into the crypt with that wriggling bag, his fancy had peopled the dark space with all sorts of boogeymen and horrors, and now he had to know what was actually going on behind that heavy iron door.

That was his plan, anyway, but like so many plans, it never had a chance to come to fruition. When he returned to Whitley Manor, it was to a shambles. A corpse had been found, naked, stuffed into a disused linen closet. It took some time for Kirby to ascertain why it was just "a corpse," and not Such-and-such Person's corpse. It seemed that the head and hands had both been cut off, and were nowhere to be found. What's more, as near as anyone in the house could tell, no one who should have been there was missing.

Of course, that stopped production dead on both *Vampires*—of which there was, at least, probably already enough usable footage from which to assemble an adequate cut, if it came to that— and *The Chiselhurst Disaster*, which, well, Kirby had to admit was probably just going to have to be a write-off. The police came out and questioned everyone what felt like half-a-dozen times—first the constables from the village, then actual inspectors from London—and most of the cast and crew got sent back to wherever they originally came from, with orders to make themselves available should they be needed.

The police took the body away for a post-mortem, but one of the inspectors confided in Kirby that a positive ID wasn't terribly likely. "Mobsters an' the like tend ta do this," he said. "Over in your country, too. Chop off the 'ead 'n' 'ands, an it's damn difficult to figger who a fella was."

Once the whole mess had cleared out, hardly anyone remained at Whitley Manor besides Kirby, Drake, the Professor, and a handful of help. Even the cooks had departed with the rest of the crew. Irving stayed on in his room down the hall, though, in spite of there not being any further need for script doctoring at the moment, because he said he didn't have anywhere else to go, and Drake was too kind-hearted to kick him to the curb. Besides, the Professor, surprisingly, spoke up in his defense. It seemed that the two of them had managed to find the time to play some games of chess when Kirby wasn't looking, and the old man apparently found the activity "soothing."

What Kirby found less-than-soothing was the notion of rattling around the big empty house again with nothing now to occupy his mind except how he was going to salvage this latest disaster. Possibly, once the police got everything cleared away, he could actually spin this mess into some gold. After all, a grisly real-life murder case couldn't possibly do anything but help the box office of a cheapie horror flick. He even considered working some details of the murder into another film, a crime picture that would cost even less to get rolling than the horror stuff they had been working on.

He spent his time making phone calls, but while the police investigation was still ongoing he found it impossible to get any wheels to turn, and he spent more sleepless nights than he would have liked staring out the window at the moonlight on the cemetery, the grass now turned brittle by frost. Several times he saw Irving walking out to the carriage house, his collar turned up against the growing cold. Out for some late-night games of chess, perhaps?

With little else to occupy his thoughts, he found himself obsessing about the Professor's strange behavior, real or imagined. He developed a theory that the Professor's unusual activities might be linked somehow to the murder. Perhaps the Professor had gotten involved in something illicit in order to fund his work when the elder Lord Whitley's coffers dried up. Kirby resolved to take his hypothesis to Drake, and then maybe to the police, but as with his earlier plan, he never got the chance to put it into action.

He was awake when he heard the scream, lying in bed and staring at the ceiling, exhausted but unable to drift off. The day before, for reasons that he himself didn't completely understand, he had gone out to the crypt and listened at the big iron door. And had he heard something on the other side, the scratching that the departing actress had mentioned, like thousands of rats in the walls?

The scratching may have been his imagination—"nerves," right, that's what Drake would have chalked it up to—but the scream was definitely real. It came from the carriage house, rising high and fast and then choking off. As he sprang to the window, he saw Drake fleeing down the path that led from the carriage house to the manor, painted fitfully in the moonlight like the heroine on the cover of a Gothic novel.

He rushed down those wide stairs that had so attracted him when he first visited Whitley Manor, and was at the kitchen door by the time Drake arrived. His friend's clothes were disheveled— maybe from the run, or maybe from some sort of altercation—his eyes wide and staring. When Kirby opened the door, Drake started back, then collapsed forward as he saw who it was that stood before him. He probably would have fallen straight to the tiled floor had Kirby not been there to catch him.

"It really *is* you, isn't it, Kirby?" Drake asked, and his voice had the edge of a sob in it.

"Last time I looked," Kirby replied, knowing even as he said it that his instinctive attempt at levity was out of place here, but unable to check it.

He guided Drake to the sitting room where his friend had first received him upon his arrival at Whitley Manor only a few short months ago. Drake collapsed into one of the scattered couches, and Kirby poured him a tumbler full of brandy. As Drake took a long drink of it, his hands shook such that he sloshed almost as much over the side of the glass as made it to his lips.

"Now what in the pluperfect hell is going on?" Kirby asked, then shook his head. "You know what, never mind. You take a couple more drinks, steady yourself a bit, and then we'll go out together and get the car, head into the village. You can tell me all about it on the way."

"I don't think that either of you should be in a hurry to be going anywhere," Irving's voice said from the doorway. But was it Irving's voice? It sounded different—like maybe it was coming from someplace farther away. But it was definitely Irving who stood in the doorway, a pistol dark in his hand. Or, again, was it? Had Irving been using his free time to work out? That would perhaps explain his broadened chest, which strained the buttons of his striped dress shirt. "Sir Drake doesn't look so well just at the moment. I think he should stay sitting right there."

"Irving," Kirby said, starting to take a step forward, and then remembering the black barrel of the gun trained on his chest, "what the hell are you playing at?"

"It was supposed to be you, Mr. Marsh," said another voice, this one from behind him, in the other doorway. The voice was familiar, so Kirby wasn't surprised when he half-turned to see the Professor standing there, his waxy flesh turned marble in the moonlight. "We thought that you would have more influence over young Master Drake here. But then that actress saw and heard things she shouldn't have, and you went running off down to London. Plans had already been put into motion, it was too late to call them off, and so Mr. Drayvon had to do."

"I don't know what you're into," Kirby said, his hands held up at about the height of his shoulders, his eyes sliding from one man to the other. "Communism, free love, some kind of cult. But I can tell you that swordpoint—or gun point, as the case may be—conversions went out of fashion ages ago. You get more devotees with honey than you do with bullets. Now, I can't speak for Drake here, but I'm not opposed to secret societies or political movements, not as a rule, and not if there's something in it for me. So let's put the pistol away and talk about whatever it is that's on your minds, gentlemen."

The Professor laughed, and it wasn't a human sound. A ratcheting cough, like the sound that he had made at dinner that first night. "A cult? Yes, I suppose that *is* how you would see it, given your limited understanding. 'The Cult of Headless Men,' eh? How little you know, and how much you could have been." The old man shook his head sadly. "But perhaps it's not too late. If the exchange hasn't taken hold too strongly, perhaps Mr. Drayvon could still be traded for you. Master Drake, you're being awfully quiet. Please speak up. Ultimately, it will be your decision that determines your friend's fate."

Kirby's eyes went now to Drake, where he sat still on the couch. The glass of brandy had fallen from his fingers and what was left in it was now a spreading stain on the upholstery. Drake's eyes were invisible in the dim light of the room, cast in pools of shadow by his heavy brows. "You're a monster," he said, the words falling from his mouth like food that he couldn't bring himself to swallow.

"Now Drake," Kirby said, taking a step, only to have the pistol raise a few inches, stopping him in his tracks, "let's not lose our heads."

At that, Irving—if it really *was* Irving, didn't the Professor imply that they had replaced him somehow, Kirby's thoughts turning to *Invasion of the Body Snatchers*—let out a laugh of his own, high pitched and somehow wrong, like a wild animal trying to learn to mimic human sounds.

"What did you do with my father?" Drake asked, starting to rise. His gaze was still on the Professor, ignoring Irving now. Something inside him seemed to have snapped, and Kirby was afraid that he would do something that would get them both shot. "What did your expeditions turn you into?"

The Professor laughed again, and when he spoke, it was as if his voice was gradually changing with each syllable. Like a recording that was breaking down. "You think it was always me," he said, and Kirby realized that his lips weren't moving. Ventriloquism? "Professor Mosby was in your father's platoon during the war. It was Lord Whitley who ordered the expedition to that island, to find the idol before it sank into the sea. But we were already here long before that. There are no Tcho-Tcho peoples, there never have been. It has always been us. The Headless Men, the Anthropophagi, whose heads do grow beneath their shoulders, they—we—are where we have always been. Here. Right here. In your cities, at the heads of your tables. Dig into your family's crypt, Master Drake, ransack their tombs, and tell me what you find. How many are missing their heads? How many had already been laid away for years before their funerals, before they were no longer of any use to us, and we abandoned their disguises to take on another. Just as I will soon shed Mosby's disguise. We have been with your family since the beginning. It wasn't I who initiated your father into the Cult, my boy. *He* initiated *me*."

Before the Professor could utter another word—if, in fact, he had been going to—Drake lunged at him, over the back of the couch that stood between them. Kirby, who had been waiting for just such a moment, dropped to a crouch and wrapped his fist around the handle of one of the fireplace pokers as a bullet buried itself in the mantel beside his head. Then he was up and swinging, expecting every moment to feel a hot bloom in his chest, but Irving didn't get off another shot before the poker took him in the temple, where it did something that Kirby hadn't expected. It knocked the young writer's head clean off.

What was left behind was the stump of a neck, almost smooth but not completely. Tendrils, like the hyphae of a fungus, strained up from the stump, wavering in the flickering light from the fireplace. The pistol swung toward Kirby again, and another shot rang out, this one burning across his bicep. Kirby brought the poker down on the hand that held the pistol, and found himself less surprised than he would otherwise have been when the hand came off like the hand of a mannequin. At the wrist, five questing tendrils quivered, their tips ending in snapping pincers.

Putting his palm against the back of the handle, Kirby drove the poker into the chest of Irving's body—or whatever it actually was—as hard as he could. He felt the poker bite against flesh and sink in, felt the weight of the body against him, felt it give back. And then he dropped the poker and dove for the pistol, putting two bullets square into the center of that striped dress shirt. The body stumbled once more, knocking into an end table and sending a lamp to shatter on the wood floor, before finally collapsing in a spreading red pool.

The Professor was kneeling atop Drake now, those pale hands around his throat. "Don't worry," he whispered, "not all of you will die. The rest will join your father, will join with me, with all of us."

Kirby didn't bother pressing the pistol to the back of the Professor's head—he wasn't certain at all that doing so would have much effect—and instead emptied everything that was left into the old man's broad back. For a moment, he feared that it hadn't accomplished anything. The two figures remained locked in their *danse macabre*, but then the Professor's body collapsed to the side and Drake pushed him away, coughing, dragging ragged breaths into his lungs.

"Thanks," he croaked, as Kirby extended a hand to help him to his feet.

"Don't mention it," Kirby replied. "Now who, or what, did I just kill?"

Without further preamble or explanation, Drake rolled the Professor's body onto its back, and tore open his shirt. Beneath was not the chest of an old man, or a young man, or anything human at all. It had the same basic outlines as a human torso, to be sure, but in place of ribs or pectoral or abdominal muscles were two eyes, vertical slits for a nose, and an almost round mouth filled with rasping teeth, like the maw of a leech.

"The Anthropophagi," Kirby murmured.

"Whose heads do grow beneath their shoulders," Drake finished. Perhaps they would both have laughed then, that strained, half-mad laughter that comes when terrible tension is terribly broken, but instead another sound stopped them. A deep rumble, the sound of stone grinding on stone, and it was coming from the graveyard out behind the house.

Without speaking a word, they followed the noise. The rumble was replaced with a rhythmic banging, a reverberating sound like the one that had interrupted their first dinner with the Professor. Only now was Kirby able to place what it had reminded him of all those nights ago, the sound from Poe's "House of Usher." He was not at all surprised that it was coming from within the crypt.

Side by side, the two men walked out into the moonlight, until they were standing in front of the tomb, their breath steaming in the cold night air. Kirby still held the pistol limply in his hand, though even had it still been loaded, he doubted that it would do him any good. With each new bang the crypt door shook, and gray dust trickled down from the stone walls around it.

The massive crypt door fell from its hinges with a resounding clang, and they saw what the Professor had brought back with him him from the island. At the time he had carried it in a crate no bigger than a bread box, but it had grown in the years since. As it rolled forth from the tomb, it looked at first like a giant boulder—maybe one of the *papier mâché* boulders that decorated Kirby's sets. But then as it came to a stop they could make out its features and they recognized it for what it was: a mummified human head, albeit one the size of a camera truck.

That would have been enough, of course. To freeze their blood, to send them running, but it wasn't the end. For a moment the grisly thing just sat there, resting on the place where its bottom jaw should have been, and they were allowed the blissful illusion that its movement had been a natural occurrence, the result of it becoming unsettled within the tomb. But then they saw one horrid eye peer at them from a gaping socket, and then retreat on some kind of stalk, as though it was not the eye of the head at all, but of some creature that dwelled within.

With a sound like the grinding of giant teeth, the skull began to rock back and forth, and they saw masses of human arms—of normal size, but as mummified as the head—scrabbling at the ground from beneath it. One by one, the gnarled hands found purchase, and then the head began to lurch toward them, pulled along by a tide of arms, like a hermit crab dragging its shell.

The thing, the idol of the Headless Men, the spider the size of a horse—grown even bigger now—that Drake had thought he dreamed, came toward them through the graveyard like a bulldozer, pushing tombstones aside as it advanced. Kirby raised the pistol in his hand, which he knew would have been a futile gesture, even had there been any bullets left in the chamber, but doing it felt better than doing nothing, better than collapsing to the dirt and clawing at it, better than going mad.

But then there was another sound, another rumble, larger and louder than the one that had come before. Off in the distance, a red glow, the bloom of a luminous rose the size of the moon, like a bomb had gone off somewhere out over the ocean. The ground beneath their feet shook and heaved, and Kirby imagined some even larger horror, one the size of Godzilla, pushing itself up from beneath the earth.

Instead, a fissure cracked the cemetery in two. Kirby could see coffins dropping out of the dirt and tumbling into the darkness as the chasm split open the ground. The crevice swallowed up the giant head, its numberless arms clawing at the air as it fell into the abyss. For years after, Kirby would have dreams in which he watched the thing tumble. In those dreams, there were always other hands down there in the dark. Grasping hands, blacker than the shadows from which they groped. He could never be sure if they had actually been there that night, or if his mind had conjured them later. Worse, he could never decide if they had been dragging the abomination down, or welcoming it home.

When they walked back into the house, both of the bodies they had left there were gone, as well as one of the cars from out front. Neither was terribly surprised. Drake never told Kirby what had happened to him in the carriage house, though Kirby had his suspicions. "It must have been what they brought back from that island," was all Drake said on the matter. "The one that sank into the sea. Whatever it was, I think they must have worshipped it."

"Made sacrifices to it," Kirby added, thinking back to the wriggling burlap sack.

In the days that followed, Kirby read an article in the newspaper while he was waiting for the plane that would take him back to America. It talked about a volcanic eruption that had occurred on that night of horror, more than a thousand miles away from where he and Drake had been standing. An eruption that was slowly forming an island. Too far away to have produced any seismic activity in the cemetery behind Whitley Manor, too far away for its blossom of fire to be seen in the sky, and yet...

Author's Note: Originally published by Jordan Krall as a chapbook for Dunhams Manor Press, this one got its start as a project I did with Michael Bukowski. He was illustrating avatars of Nyarlathotep, and he had asked a handful of contemporary writers—including yours truly—to contribute their own original versions. Mine was a couple of paragraphs from what would become the climactic creature reveal of this story.

But really, it had started long before that, when I first saw the movie *The Four Skulls of Jonathan Drake.* While ostensibly a fairly pedestrian 1959 drawing room shocker of the creaky old house variety, *Jonathan Drake* had a particularly weird turnaround in its final reel that helped inspire "The Cult of Headless Men," though it took years—and Michael's invitation—for the seed to bear fruit.

Even then, several more years passed between when I wrote the fragment for Michael's project—featuring one of my weirder monsters to date—and the actual completion of the novelette. When Dunhams Manor put the chapbook out, my only condition was that they get Michael to do the cover, bringing the whole thing full circle.

WHEN A BEAST LOOKS UP AT THE STARS

"What's the earliest memory you have of your father?" my therapist is asking. Such a tired line, something that a therapist would ask in a movie. I don't tell him the truth, of course. I cast around for an easy lie, the same one that I would give to Kenzie if she asked, though she never does. Tell him something about my dad wrapping Christmas presents in old shoe boxes, packing them in socks, a twenty-dollar bill stuck between two bricks, wrapped in faded paper. Something that could be cute but always felt mean-spirited.

My laptop case is lying on the floor of the office. In it is a letter on stationery from the Seldon Civics Committee or somesuch, a clipping from the *Seldon Herald*, complete with a grainy newsprint photo of the old Gorka Theatre, with its marquee like an art deco wave. I'm driving there from here, in a rented black Accord, but I thought it would be a good idea to get one last therapy session in before I go.

No, let me stop. That's a lie, and I know it. Kenzie thought it would be a good idea, and she's right, but I knew it would be a waste of time, and it is. I talk about Seldon, about my childhood, about my dad, but I skim over the surface, like I've taught myself

to do. A rock skipping across a deep, black pond, never touching
the water long enough to attract the attention of the beasts that
circle below.

I had written a book; nothing actually very respectable, one of
those "100 Films to See Before You Shuffle Off This Filthy Coil"
jobs, but it made it into the *Library Journal*, found its way onto
B&N shelves, and something of that must have been enough to
attract the attention of someone at the Seldon Public Library. I
learned, from the letter and then the phone call, that it was still in
the same place it had always been—an old bank building, across
the street from what used to be the drug store—kept alive thanks
to the efforts of the same civics committee that was on the letter-
head.

They were trying to save the Gorka Theatre and so were hosting
a local film festival for charity. Obviously not big enough to draw
in any *actual* celebrities, they had reached out to me and asked me
to host a few screenings, maybe even write a piece about it for the
Herald. Local boy makes good, that sort of thing.

So why did I say yes? Did I want out of the apartment, which
seemed too claustrophobic now, as I tried to navigate around the
not-quite-fight I seemed to be perpetually having with Kenzie,
who, bless her, just wanted to help me, but I didn't want to be
better just yet? Did I think it was finally time to confront Seldon,
maybe drive by the house where I grew up, or that other house, out
on the long dirt roads that criss-crossed each other like gridlines of
orange clay? Did I really care about saving the Gorka?

I remembered it from my boyhood. I had watched *Tremors* there
and the Tim Burton *Batman*. I remembered the big pickles that
they sold out of a jar on the counter, the Mountain Dews full
of crushed ice, a flavor that I still mentally associated with monster movies on the big screen, even though I hadn't had a Mountain Dew in probably fifteen years. According to the voice of the
lady on the phone, the one-screen theatre was no longer privately

owned, was instead kept limping along by the same civics committee that propped up the library, now dedicated to revival showings
of *The Wizard of Oz* and the like.

Did I think, as I told my therapist, as I intimated to Kenzie, that
maybe I could get another book out of this experience? If I was a
film writer, after all, then the Gorka was my ground zero, wasn't it?
I had memories of my parents dropping me off, the truck idling in
the grocery store parking lot across the street as my mom pressed a
few crumpled bills and pocket-warmed coins into my hands while
my dad wasn't looking.

The marquee was lit with neon pink, which spilled out onto
the sidewalk around it. I remembered the strange tingly feeling I
got when I saw older kids making out in the shadows of the alley
next to the theatre. I remembered the way that the guy behind the
counter—Sam Gorka, I know now, but didn't know or care then—
always knew my name, handing me my pickle or my Mountain
Dew and smiling at me beneath his paper cap.

There had to be a story here, right? About my going back to the
place where I learned to love movies, to love that tingle of expecta-
tion that crackled through the theatre like static electricity when
the house lights went down. About the long walks home through
the small town dark, hugging the middle of the side-streets rather
than the sidewalks, because the sidewalks were full of shadows that
suddenly loomed up tall. About sitting next to Stormy Willis in
those ratty theatre seats, letting my knee brush against hers. About
my own first kiss in that darkened alleyway, all hot and sudden and
confusing.

What had the Gorka been to me? A place to escape a home that I
remembered mostly as dark rooms and heavy silences, the furniture
and the walls and the dark curtains all blending into a fungal mé-
lange of lichenous drabness in my memory. Only one thing clear,
my father's voice, telling me how useless it all was. What was the
line, the one that Walter Matthau gets in *Hello, Dolly*? "You artists
produce nothing that nobody needs never." My father would have

agreed, even if he would have hated the movie, if he ever saw it, as he had seemed to hate most things.

That was the story that I had told even myself. That this trip back to Seldon would be good for me; good for my therapy, good for my nonexistent career. I dutifully ignored the voice in my head that knew better, that knew that if I was able to write about myself and my feelings at all then I wouldn't be writing about movies instead.

They've graveled the roads since I was here last. I listen to the tires make that satisfying crunch as they roll over the new gravel because I've exhausted all of the downloaded episodes of Werewolf Ambulance and Pure Cinema Podcast on my phone. I wasn't sure I would be able to find the house on my own, but here I am, rolling over the cattle guard and up to the place where the big gate used to hang. The sun is going down, it's turning the whole sky orange and red. The sun itself looks like a squashed tangerine and all the light is the color of that scene at the end of *Texas Chainsaw Massacre*, with Leatherface dancing in the middle of the road.

The house isn't where I grew up. When I was a kid it was my grandma's house. It had been my grandpa's farm once, but he died before I was born, and she hired young men from town to come take care of the cattle when it was time to sell them or brand them or do anything but milk and feed, which she handled herself until her dying day. I remember the house as a dark place—dim and faded, like an old sepia-toned photograph.

The sun doesn't help now, shining through the slats of the house, through the broken out windows, turning the whole place into a silhouette, a paper cut-out of a Halloween haunted house. My grandma died when I was in high school and my parents moved out here for my last summer. I spent three months in one of the upstairs bedrooms before I went to college, with a view out that window right there that took in the then-depopulated cattle pens, like something from a photograph of the Holocaust. But it was never home to me.

I park the car, shut off the engine. The fence is still here but the gate is missing. I walk up to the house, where all the windows are broken out, the paint stripped off by the merciless Kansas wind, the insides filled with broken wood and rat droppings. The house seems thin now, like a façade in a stage play or an old TV show. It seems like I could just reach out and push it over without much effort.

Why did I come here, rather than to the house where I spent most of my childhood, the house where now some other family lives? To my left are the cattle pens, and next to them the barn, which still seems solid and sturdy. Against the setting sun, it is a black block, a monolith. No light cuts through its walls or roof, but contrast also makes it impossible to pick out any details of the structure from this distance, and I don't walk any closer. Scared of it, as I always was when I was a kid, when it was still full of big, roiling walls of flesh, of animals with bland eyes that seemed to look through you, behind which I could detect no consciousness.

My room is in the Stardust Motel, next to the Pizza Hut on the edge of town that was there even when I was a kid and the Speedy Stop gas station up at the top of the hill. There's a Coke machine three doors down from my room that has ginger ale, and the bedspread is itchy, the shower missing its shower head so that the water just comes out in a gush, like from a tap. The water is pleasantly hot, at least, and the room only costs around $70 a night, so I don't complain to the scraggly-looking kid who sits behind the front desk, sporting a patchy beard and mustache that haven't yet completely grown in.

The town is different than I remember. Already when I was a kid the tides of prosperity that once buoyed up places like this were beginning to recede, and in the twenty short years since I was here last, they have drifted so far afield that they can no longer be seen, even on a clear day. More buildings stand empty than not, and those that have fallen have been replaced with characterless constructs of manufactured sheet metal, when they have been replaced at all.

Before checking in to my room, I drove down Main Street, looked in the empty storefronts. There's a Dollar General Store now that wasn't there before, and the lights from the grocery store were still on, though the place was closed for the night. I knew that the library wouldn't be open either, so I sat in the middle of the road on Osage Street and looked at the darkened marquee of the Gorka Theatre, the dark alleyway next door, before I drove back to the motel and picked up my room key.

No cards here, still keys with those big plastic keyrings that will ship the key back if you drop it in a mailbox somewhere. It reminds me of *The Shining*, but here the room numbers only go up to 23.

I should call Kenzie, but instead I just text her. Let her know that I made it okay. Then I do my usual hotel routine of turning on every light in the place, even if, in this case, that consists of a yellowy dome light populated by the bodies of a handful of dead bugs and a table lamp by the single queen bed. I take a scalding shower, then sit on the scratchy bedspread with my laptop open in front of me, pretending like I'm going to write up something worthwhile about my trip so far until I finally just put in a DVD and fall asleep to the sounds of big atomic ants eating people out in the desert.

The next day I meet the librarian for breakfast at the Main Street Café, where she just drinks coffee into which she dumps creamer after creamer. I tell her I don't drink coffee, and I order a Coke, even though if you asked me I'd tell you that I don't drink soda anymore, either.

She looks like someone who got shrunk in the wash. Her wrists are skinny, her hair and glasses both too big for her face. She wears a floral print dress underneath what looks like the jacket from a navy-colored pantsuit. She could have been the librarian when I was a kid; I don't remember that librarian looking any different than this.

She tells me how pleased she is that I was able to make it, how proud she is that someone from Seldon is a "famous writer." I don't bother to correct her. My eggs come out overcooked and rubbery on top of a pile of hashbrowns, so I chop up the whole concoction and dump some ketchup over it, wash it down with the forbidden taste of Coke.

Around breakfast, I answer the librarian's effusive if uninformed praise by letting bland platitudes fall out of my mouth, as I have trained myself to do. I tell her about how some of my first exposure to film writing came from the old orange Crestwood House monster movie books that they used to have in the library here, about my early memories of the Gorka. She beams, like she's supposed to, and I eat my food.

It's Saturday, and the film festival is supposed to start this afternoon. To my surprise, they're showing *Paper Moon* instead of *The Wizard of Oz*, and then they're following that up with some made-for-TV-type pioneer movie that I've never heard of that was apparently filmed nearby. "We also found an 8mm film that was shot by a local filmmaker back in the 1970s," the librarian says, "and the school had a projector that can play it, so we'll be ending the festival with that.

"We're so glad that you came back after all this time," she murmurs, pouring more creamer into her coffee, stirring and stirring it with a little metal spoon that clinks against the edge of the cup. "Everyone comes home sooner or later."

In the slaughterhouses, they used to kill cows with hammers, right? Until they replaced the hammers with those pressurized air guns, like in *No Country for Old Men*. I saw my dad do it once. Kill a cow. No, not a cow, a calf. Kill it with a maul, blood on blunt steel. My dad seemed huge then, leathery and creaking, like an automaton made of bone and sinew.

That's the memory I never tell to my therapist, to Kenzie, just like I never tell them that I was afraid of him, always afraid. Not of what he would do to me—the fear never got that specific—but of what he *was*. Something alien, something I could never understand, never get inside, while he was already inside of me from before I could form memories. My own voice in my head speaking his words, like a wooden puppet on the lap of a ventriloquist. Telling me how useless everything was, what a waste of time was everything into which I ever poured my energy.

In the end, he was the one who looked like a puppet, reduced and shrunken, hooked up to the marionette wires of the hospital machines, nothing like the leathery golem of my childhood memories, blood dripping from the hammer in his hands, the mindless squeal of that dying calf echoing in my ears as I crouched in the darkness of the barn, the smell of blood and brains and hide filling the air.

By then, the time to confront him was already past. My mother had died years before, and he and I had stood silently on either side of the casket, nothing more to say to one another, not even then. At the end, there was nothing left in that withered husk, nothing that burned out from behind those dark eyes. If I was going to stand up for myself, I had already missed my chance, so I just stood there silently once again, my eyes on the floor, while he stared at me, his eyes cold and hard and mindless, like the cows in their pens. I walked away without saying anything. He died sometime in the night, and I didn't drive back for the funeral.

Between *Paper Moon* and the other movie, *Frontier Song*, or whatever it's called, I walk out onto the street for some fresh air. The sun is sinking behind the grocery store, and someone has turned on the Gorka's marquee. Pink light paints the sidewalk under my feet, and I look up at the sign to see that about half of it is burnt out. Past it, I can see the stars just beginning to pepper the darkening sky.

The inside of the theatre looks almost exactly how I remember it—the ticket booth and the concession stand in the same place, the carpet still threadbare. The old movie poster frames have been taken down and replaced with painted reproductions of the posters for a couple of classic films, while the walls have been repainted and are already starting to peel again. The chairs inside the theatre are just as they always were—hard and narrow, smelling faintly like a thrift store—but I've got a couple of them roped off just for me, next to the librarian and a man who looks like a pastor and says that he's from the civics committee when he shakes my hand.

Normally I would never agree to host something like this without getting to see the films first, but there's not much that's required of me here. Most of the seats are empty, and those that are filled are all clearly occupied by locals. The majority are people who look like they just came in from church—old and flabby and attempting to look prosperous in suits that they obviously wear only for special occasions—while a few are local teenagers who are unlikely to appreciate anything that's on the day's docket.

Before *Paper Moon*, the librarian got up in front of the crowd—such as it is—and introduced me, talked about my book as though it was a *New York Times* best seller, and then I walked up in front to a scattering of compulsory applause. I talked a little bit about movies, about growing up in Seldon and coming to the Gorka, and then I sat back down and the projector sputtered to life, and that was it.

Before I left the hotel, I popped a pill from the case that I keep in my pocket at all times, and now, standing out in the growing dark in front of the theatre, I chase it with another one, dry-swallowing. The concession stand inside is open, staffed by a kid with greasy hair under the same kind of paper hat that Sam Gorka used to wear, and I decide to go in and see if they have any Mountain Dew, if they still have crushed ice.

Inside the lobby the librarian is talking to the guy from the civics committee. When they see me come in, they both smile big, beaming smiles at me. I smile back, like I've trained myself to do. I learned a long time ago that animals that behave themselves don't draw unwanted attention.

The pills make me drowsy, and during *Frontier Song* I mostly doze off, so that I'm half-surprised when the credits are rolling and the house lights are coming back up. The librarian shuffles to the front of the house and leads a round of undeserved applause for the movie that just finished screening. "While our volunteers get us set up for our third and final film," she says, "I want to say a few words about this theatre, and the movie that you're about to see. As most of you probably know, this theatre was started by Samuel Gorka way back in 1953, and it stayed in his family for two generations. What we're about to watch is a short film that Samuel shot right here in Seldon back in the 1970s, using all local cast and crew."

This time the applause is a little more heartfelt. Samuel Gorka had been the father of the Sam Gorka I knew; I remembered seeing him from time to time, a wizened man by the time I was a kid, who occasionally haunted the theatre like a ghost, mostly spending his time in the projection booth. A memory hit me then, sudden and hard, one that I had set aside and lost over the years, of Sam saying to me, "Dad treats those projectors like his babies. Nobody else knows how to run 'em like he does."

I look up at the window of the projection booth, but can't see anything behind it from this angle. My imagination conjures up an image of Samuel Gorka, little more than a mummified corpse by this time, shriveled up like those shrunken apple heads that Vincent Price used to peddle in the backs of comic books, still running the projectors that no one else knows how to operate. Before I can chase the weird fantasy too far, however, the librarian is sitting back down in the chair next to me, the house lights are going down, and the projector is sputtering to life once more.

The film is dark, which means that the house is kept dark, so that everything around me is murky and lost, save for the occasional glint off the librarian's glasses. My fingertips are resting on the cold, sweating surface of my Mountain Dew, the wax paper damp under my touch. The footage is amateur, handheld, like a home video. Something that I would expect to see in a modern found footage horror movie. The setting is dark, lit by the flickering orange glow of long torches stuck into the ground, of a fire that's somewhere off camera.

The cameraman is approaching a structure that I recognize, even past the darkness and the grain of the film. The door of the barn on my grandma's property is like the mouth of a cave. In the background are the cattle pens, newer than I have ever seen them looking, and within them dark shapes that are not cows shift and jostle.

There are people gathered around, lined up on either side of the dirt path which leads up to the barn door, like they are watching a parade. It takes me a moment to realize that they are naked, their skin decorated with crude daubs of paint or mud. The people in the crowd are a mix of genders and ages. Here sagging bellies hang over flaccid genitalia; there taut, firm breasts are decorated with circles around the nipples. One man strokes an erection, but the camera doesn't linger on the crowd.

From out of the barn door steps a minotaur, a sledgehammer cradled in its hands. No, not a minotaur, because the head isn't that of a bull. The figure is just a man, isn't it, in a rubber goat's head mask and yak-fur leggings? Like Satan on his rock in Hammer's *The Devil Rides Out*. But that doesn't look like a mask, even in the grainy 8mm footage. It looks like an actual goat's head, hollowed out for a man to stuff his own head inside. Yes, there's even something, black stuff that must be blood, dripping down from the stump of the neck, staining the man's torso in little smeared rivers, and all I can think is that he must be choking on the stuff inside there, his mouth and nose and eyes full of gore and filth. How could he stand it, even for the short duration that the camera will stay on him?

But the camera *does* stay on him, doesn't flinch away, as it would in a studio film, to preserve the illusion, that glimpse of something wrong that stays stuck in your brain because you can't fully process it, and so you fill it in, build it up. No, here it stays and stays, staring, transfixed. It draws slowly closer. Not a zoom, the cameraman actually approaching with shaky steps. Closer and closer to that bloody goat's head mounted atop that leathery, familiar body.

Up close, it's clear that the goat's head is real. There's nothing else it could be. And yet, and yet, how did they get the eyes to do that? To glow like that, yellow like that, with life behind them? Those slitted, sideways pupils slightly narrowed in the middle, like hourglasses turned on their sides, the yellow around them glowing like a Tiffany lamp.

The cameraman is kneeling in the dirt now, looking up at the figure towering above him. I'm six years old, crouched in the dark, watching my father bring the maul down on the head of the calf, watching how its eyes change when it dies, hearing that squeal that has never left my brain, the stench that I sometimes still think I can smell in my clothes. The goatman raises the hammer up above his head, and the film doesn't flinch as the blow falls.

I think that the camera is laying in the dirt now, still filming, but I can't be certain because the film is starting to run in front of me, to wobble and distort. I can feel the beads of sweat on the cup against my fingertips, and I try to stand up, but the theatre seems to spin. The librarian is asking me something, and there is laughter in her voice as I stumble against the seatbacks in front of me, pitch forward, and crumble into the darkness between the theatre seats, then into a deeper darkness yet.

I wake on my knees, with a bag over my head. Under my jeans, I can feel the dirt, and I smell the rank stench of old hay and animals. Through the bag, I can see the flicker of flames, and I know where I am, even before they pull the covering off.

I'm kneeling in front of the door of my grandma's barn, and all around me are the people from the theatre. They're dressed for an older kind of church now, their clothes shed, their naked bodies daubed with what I now know is not paint but blood mixed with earth.

I wish that I was thinking of Kenzie, regretting the distance that I have always kept between us, but mostly I'm thinking of myself, of the stench of that dying calf, and other memories that I thought time and distance and ritual had scrubbed away. The stone has stayed too long on the surface of the pond, and now those circling creatures below have started to rise.

The figure steps out of the darkness, and I know it immediately, even as I know that it is impossible. The severed goat head drips black blood down across that familiar chest, and the hammer rests in those familiar hands. Its steps are mechanical, like a puppet being pulled forward by invisible cables, like the figures in one of those mechanized dioramas in a penny arcade. It steps forward, one foot, then the next. The hammer rises in its hands; a spring being wound tighter and tighter.

I look up at the stars that seem like they're being blotted out by the goatman's shadow, and wait for the blow to fall.

Author's Notes: If "Baron von Werewolf Presents" traded in my pleasant childhood memories of watching monster movies on TV on Saturday mornings, this story makes use of my nostalgia for the local movie theatre in the little town where I grew up, albeit turned to somewhat darker ends. A lot of the rest is also culled from my actual childhood, from my grandma's old house and my own troubled relationship with my dad, though it's been repurposed and retrofitted to make the story work.

Originally written for a "goat worship" issue of Travis Neisler's *Ravenwood Quarterly* which sadly never came to pass, the title comes from the excellent 2014 film *Black Mountain Side*, which I saw at the H.P. Lovecraft Film Festival in Portland, though not the same year as the scene that kicked off the first story in this collection, lo those many pages ago.

This is its first time in print.

AFTERWORD &
ACKNOWLEDGMENTS

"Cruel" is not a word that I would normally associate with my own stories. After all, I'm the guy who wants to write "fun horror," right? And cruel stories are rarely fun.

I say "rarely," but the fact is that cruelty can sometimes be fun, can't it? Especially fictional cruelty. Someone like the Marquis de Sade would certainly have said so, and it's difficult to look at old-fashioned implements of torture and not see a certain macabre glee in their design. Then there is, of course, the Theatre du Grand Guignol, from which this collection and its title story take their name. The plays put on in that theatre were pretty much uniformly gruesome, grotesque, and, yes, cruel, yet I bet the audience had a hell of a time.

I took the subtitle of this book from the title of a collection by a French symbolist writer with the imposing moniker Jean-Marie-Mathias-Philippe-Auguste Villiers de l'Isle-Adam, or perhaps from a later collection of 150 stories by another French writer, Octave Mirbeau. Both collections were called "*Contes cruels*," though the former was more often translated as "Sardonic Tales" than cruel ones.

The so-called conte cruel gave its name to a whole school of fiction, though, of course, the fiction existed long before Villiers de l'Isle-Adam inadvertently christened it. Poe himself wrote no shortage of contes cruels, which H. P. Lovecraft describes in *Supernatural Horror in Literature* as "a class peculiar to itself," one in which "the wrenching of the emotions is accomplished through dramatic tantalizations, frustrations, and gruesome physical horrors."

Few enough of my stories—even the ones in this collection—would qualify for the appellation, and yet, as I was putting together the stories for this book, I found a streak running through them. Not quite cruelty, perhaps, but something akin to it. The protagonists of horror short stories rarely lead charmed existences, and their fates are seldom kind, even in my stories. But the sting in these particular tales was perhaps a bit fiercer than in my previous work. There was a little less light in the darkness, a little less hope, a little more acceptance of death and things worse than death.

How did Swinburne put it, in the stanzas that lent a title to yet another gathering of horror stories, this one by Manly Wade Wellman and possessed of possibly the best title any horror collection ever got? "At the door of life, by the gate of breath / There are worse things waiting for men than death," a sentiment that would be echoed by no less a personage of horror than Count Dracula himself, as embodied by Bela Lugosi in Tod Browning's 1931 classic.

It's a sentiment that the protagonists of most of these stories would probably find it difficult to disagree with, by the time their tale is told, though there is a kind of hope, often for the worst among us, in unexpected places. Sometimes monstrousness is a place to hide, after all, the only refuge we have left when we can find no succor and the world makes no room for us.

If my last collection was inadvertently about "death, and what comes after," as I said in my afterword for *Painted Monsters & Other Strange Beasts*, then this book is inadvertently a catalogue of the high cost that we pay for surviving trauma, and the ways in which the past never really leaves us nearly as far behind as we might like.

When I was assembling my last collection, my father had just died. As I was writing the stories in this one, I was working through therapy to deal with abuse and trauma, stemming from when I was extremely young. I'm not a big believer in "channeling my pain into writing," or what-have-you—if it works for other people, that's great, but it seldom does for me—but I can't deny that some of the pain I was trying to process found its way into these stories, regardless of my intentions.

So, while these stories may not be intentionally cruel, the worlds they depict often are. Yet, I hope at least, that they are not without their fun, too. These stories range farther afield than any I have collected before—to realms of sword-and-sorcery, to science fictional cities, to alien worlds as imagined through stop-motion animation, and to the Kansas City of the 1920s, when it was still the "Paris of the Plains"—even as their protagonists find themselves drawn, time and again, back to where they started from, to a place they tried so hard to leave behind.

***

Any book like this is a collaborative effort. While I may spend the time writing the stories and being way too picky about what order I put them in, plenty of other people are involved at every stage, from the earliest appearances of each of the stories on through actually making this book a reality.

This is the second collection I've done with Ross Lockhart at Word Horde, and I'm extremely happy that he chose to have me back, and grateful to him for helping to put together another great-looking collection. Not to mention Nick Gucker for the lovely (is that the right word in this situation?) cover art, and to Gemma Files for the introduction.

Whenever you write a few collections, you always run into the danger of repeating yourself in the acknowledgments, or of leaving people out. So I'll also just say that I'm grateful to everyone who gave one of these stories a home over the years, and to everyone who read this book. And, of course, to my wife, who has always been my first reader and best and most critical editor, and who was an enormous help with all of these stories, even though they are, in general, a lot more unpleasant than she would prefer.

"When I took *Tales from a Talking Board* out of the box,
my power went out."

—Anonymous Internet commenter

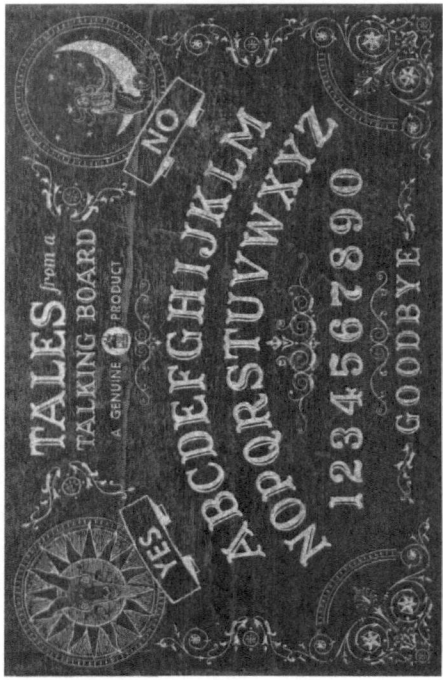

Can we speak with the spirits of the dead? Is it possible to know the future?
Are our dreams harbingers of things to come? Do auspicious omens and
cautionary portents affect our lives?

Edited by Ross E. Lockhart, *Tales from a Talking Board* examines these
questions–and more–with tales of auguries, divination, and fortune telling, through devices like Ouija boards, tarot cards, and stranger things.

So dim the lights, place your hands upon the planchette, and ask the
spirits to guide you as we present fourteen stories of the strange and su-
pernatural by Matthew M. Bartlett, Nadia Bulkin, Nathan Carson, Kristi
DeMeester, Orrin Grey, Scott R Jones, David James Keaton, Anya Martin,
J. M. McDermott, S.P. Miskowski, Amber-Rose Reed, Tiffany Scandal,
David Templeton, and Wendy N. Wagner.

Format: Trade Paperback, 228 pp, $15.99

ISBN-13: 978-1-939905-35-2

http://www.wordhorde.com

"these stories and characters are sewn together to create one hell of an exquisite monster."

—*This Is Horror*

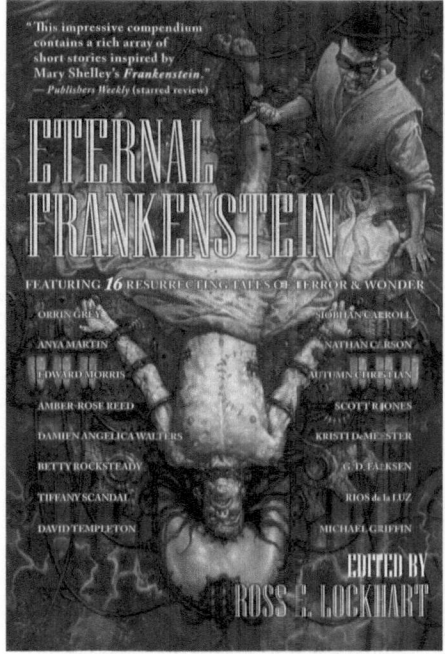

Two hundred years ago, a young woman staying in a chalet in Switzerland, after an evening of ghost stories shared with friends and lovers, had a frightening dream. That dream became the seed that inspired Mary Shelley to write *Frankenstein; or, The Modern Prometheus*, a tale of galvanism, philosophy, and the re-animated dead. Today, Frankenstein has become a modern myth without rival, influencing countless works of fiction, music, and film. We all know *Frankenstein*. But how much do we really know about Frankenstein?

Word Horde is proud to publish *Eternal Frankenstein*, an anthology edited by Ross E. Lockhart, paying tribute to Mary Shelley, her Monster, and their entwined legacy.

Featuring sixteen resurrecting tales of terror and wonder by Siobhan Carroll, Nathan Carson, Autumn Christian, Rios de la Luz, Kristi DeMeester, G. D. Falksen, Orrin Grey, Michael Griffin, Scott R. Jones, Anya Martin, Edward Morris, Amber-Rose Reed, Betty Rocksteady, Tiffany Scandal, David Templeton, and Damien Angelica Walters.

Format: Trade Paperback, 322 pp, $15.99

ISBN-13: 978-1-939905-37-6

http://www.wordhorde.com

"…a brilliant Cthonic horror fantasia full of creepy religion, grief, pain, sorrow and snakes." –Gemma Files, author of *Experimental Film*

When reporter Cora Mayburn is assigned to cover a story about a snake-handling cult in rural Appalachia, she is dismayed, for the world of cruel fundamentalist stricture, repression, glossolalia, and abuse is something she has long since put behind her in favor of a more tolerant urban existence.

As Cora begins to uncover the secrets concealed by a veneer of faith and tradition, something ancient and long concealed begins to awaken. What secrets do the townsfolk know? What might the handsome young pastor be hiding? What will happen when occulted horrors writhe to the surface, when pallid and forgotten things rise to reclaim the Earth?

Will Cora–and the earth–survive? The answers–and pure terror–can only be found in one place: *Beneath*.

Trade Paperback, 314 pp, $16.99

ISBN-13: 978-1-939905-29-1

http://www.wordhorde.com

"Bulkin serves up cerebral horror with plenty of bite."
—*Publishers Weekly* (starred review)

Word Horde presents the debut collection from critically-acclaimed Weird Fiction author Nadia Bulkin. Dreamlike, poignant, and unabashedly socio-political, *She Said Destroy* includes three stories nominated for the Shirley Jackson Award, four included in Year's Best anthologies, and one original tale.

"Weird fiction has been stuck in the era of new-fangled radio sets and fifteen-cent pulp magazines for ninety years. Finally, Nadia Bulkin has come to drag us kicking and screaming into the horrors of The Endless Now with a collection of hip, ultra-contemporary, politically astute, and chilling stories."
–Nick Mamatas, author of *I Am Providence*

Format: Trade Paperback, 258 pp, $16.99

ISBN-13: 978-1-939905-33-8

http://www.wordhorde.com

ABOUT THE AUTHOR

O rrin Grey is a skeleton who likes monsters, as well as a writer, editor, and amateur film scholar who was born on the night before Halloween. *Guignol* is his third collection of weird stories. You can find him online at orringrey.com.